ERICK S. GRAY

Solomon
Dark

WWW.BLACKODYSSEY.NET

Published by
BLACK ODYSSEY MEDIA

www.blackodyssey.net
Email: info@blackodyssey.net

Library of Congress Control Number: 2023919226

First Trade Paperback Printing: August 2024
ISBN: 978-1-957950-18-1
ISBN: 978-1-957950-19-8 (e-book)

Cover Design by Ashlee Nassar of Designs With Sass
To the extent that the image or images on the cover of this book depict a person or persons, such person or persons are merely models and are not intended to portray any character in the book.

All rights reserved. Black Odyssey Media, LLC | Dallas, TX.

10 9 8 7 6 5 4 3 2 1

Manufactured in the United States of America

Distributed by Kensington Publishing Corp.

Dear Reader,

I want to thank you immensely for supporting Black Odyssey Media authors, and our ongoing efforts to spotlight more minority storytellers. The scariest and most challenging task for many writers is getting the story, or characters, out of our heads and onto the page. Having admitted that, with every manuscript that Kreceda and I acquire, we believe that it took talent, discipline, and remarkable courage to construct that story, flesh out those characters, and prepare it for the world. Debut or seasoned, our authors are the real heroes and heroines in OUR story. And for them, we are eternally grateful.

Whether you are new to Erick S. Gray or Black Odyssey Media, we hope that you are here to stay. We also welcome your feedback and kindly ask that you leave a review. For upcoming releases, announcements, submission guidelines, etc., please be sure to visit our website at www.blackodyssey.net or scan the QR code below. We can also be found on social media using @iamblackodyssey. Until next time, take care and enjoy the journey!

Joyfully,

Shawanda Williams

Shawanda "N'Tyse" Williams
Founder/Publisher

Prologue

A full moon rose over the Atlantic Ocean, the second-largest of the world's oceans. The ocean moved like a conveyor belt driven by changes in temperature and salinity over large areas. Yet, there was nothingness for hundreds of miles in every direction. It was an oasis of silence in the middle of the sea. The beauty of the sea was rhythmic with chance calm. The sky above was dark, black, and beautiful. It was as if a black piece of velvet had been placed over the sky and sprinkled with shiny gems. It was a dark, serene night. The luminous moon gleamed like a beacon for ships crossing the sea, and the twinkling white stars gave harmony to the black-blue sky. The Atlantic Ocean exuded power and confidence yet became the connection between worlds. But for some, the center of the Atlantic felt like the edge of the world.

The sea was where people could lose themselves in the ocean's beauty, tranquility, and uncontrollable power—peace could be found in the middle of a chaotic world.

The slave ship, *Abigail*, cruised across the Atlantic toward the Americas. A breeze carried a salty aroma that swirled into the noses

1

of the crew, a far better smell than what was below. Unfortunately, a few unlucky sailors had to live and sleep without shelter on the open deck during the entirety of the Atlantic voyage. But they were the lucky ones, as slaves occupied the space belowdecks.

The sea and the saltwater smell were surpressed below, putrefied by appalling conditions. The conditions in the vessel's hold were overcrowded, smelly, dirty, and disease-ridden. Hundreds and hundreds of slaves were kept like cargo, squeezed into small spaces. They were chained together by iron legs, underfed, with barely any room to turn about. The men, women, and children were separated. The *Abigal* had become a floating prison for these souls.

The large wooden vessel, the sea, and the white men with dirty-blond hair and blue eyes that snatched them from their homes were foreign to the Africans. The enslaved were scared. There were ageless cries, suffering, praying in desperation, and pain below. Some Africans believed they would be eaten by these men or killed. The chains used on the enslaved Africans started to chafe and dig into their skins, making movement painful. The Europeans and the Americas had collided with their world. And this was the result of it—a hellish nightmare, being treated more like savage beasts than human beings and never seeing their homes again.

Before the enslaved Africans were taken aboard the vessel, they were vigorously stripped of their clothing, branded like animals, cattle, and had their heads completely shaved.

Amongst the enslaved below the deck was a man named Akasha. He was a strapping individual, tall and dark, possessing a powerful torso, and was an intense warrior like the blazing sun. But he'd been reduced to a prisoner of war—sold to the Europeans by other Africans, a rival tribe in Guinea. As a result, he'd become part of what they called a slave train. The men, women, and children on the slave train came from entirely different backgrounds, spoke different languages, and had probably never seen the ocean before.

Akasha came from a nation of dancers, musicians, and poets, and he was educated. His father was an elder and chief. His home, his land, was uncommonly rich and fruitful and produced all kinds of vegetables in great abundance. The women were beautiful goddesses; the men were warriors and scholars. His people believed that there was one creator of all things and that He lived in the sun, but his ancestors practiced African black magic. Akasha had a future with hope and dreams. Now, his fate was uncertain.

Akasha's breathing was faint as he sweated profusely, lying on his back naked, shackled, and bruised. He was sick, dying with wounds to his neck and chest. They appeared to be bite marks and deep scratches, and there was an unfathomable pain coursing inside of him.

Akasha lay there, restricted with sorrow and uncertainty. He thought about his wife and his children. He would give anything to kiss and touch his wife one last time, to hear his children's laughter and experience their playful banter. He loved them more than life itself. Now, it all was lost. Akasha mumbled a quiet prayer to himself, praying to the seven African powers and specific deities.

He feebly murmured in his African language, "Almighty Allah, the great Thumb we cannot evade to tie any knot; the roaring Thunder that splits mighty trees . . . the all-seeing Allah up on high who sees even the footprints of antelope on a rock mass here on earth. You . . . You are the one who does not hesitate to respond to our call. You . . . You are the cornerstone of peace and protection . . . protection for our children born or to be born to the great mother, Yemaya. And love, prosperity, and abundance to the queen Oshun so that it is never missing . . ."

Akasha reflected on his mortal life, knowing it would all be gone soon. A sudden chill went down his spine, and he saw a shadow fly over him. He could sense his soul drifting away from his body, ready to take him to a peaceful place, into the next world, protecting him. His eyes fluttered, sweat continued to drip from his skin, and before he closed his eyes for the final time, Akasha smiled and uttered, "Soon, my love. I'll come back to you."

He then took his last, jagged breath, closed his eyes slowly, and slipped away into his endless sleep, giving himself away to darkness.

Hours passed. The moon at midnight tried to break through the pall of the clouds, and the *Abigal* pitched and bucked in headwinds and seas, coasting in the black and calm night. All was well on the vessel. A few men were asleep, while some were on guard duty. The ship's captain, Sir Francis Hawkins, had taken comfort with one of the slave girls in his quarters. He was king on this vessel. Sir Francis Hawkins held absolute power over every individual on his ship. His responsibilities were extensive, and his friendships were few. He couldn't afford to appear vulnerable to his officers, crew, or the enslaved Africans. Mostly every night, Captain Hawkins had one of the youngest slave girls brought to his quarters, where he would rape them. He pleasured himself during the journey with slaves and food. At the same time, his crew was abused and mistreated.

Below the deck, the deterioration of Black men continued with despair and desperation in the cramped holds. There were a few dead, including Akasha. But then . . . his eyes opened abruptly, and the deceased had become awakened. His eyes were perfectly black with no whites at all. The purity of something changed, and evil was within them, lacking humanity. Instead, it was something demonic and possessed. Akasha pried open his restraints with tremendous strength and tossed the hampering neck and leg irons aside. He was hungry and hell-bent on revenge.

The door into the below-deck slave area opened, and two crew members descended into the room. Unfortunately, they were immediately hit with an ungodly stench and started to cough, gag, and cover their mouths.

"Damn, they all smell. I never smell anything like this in my life," uttered Johnathan, the youngest of the crew, fifteen years old.

"The captain wants us to check for the dead, remove them, and throw them overboard," said Henry, a seasoned sailor who was in his late twenties.

"How do they survive?" asked Johnathan.

"They're savages, Johnathan . . . like pigs in their own filth."

The men were unsympathetic to the moaning of the slaves below. The hundreds of Black souls were considered black gold and profits for the ship. They needed to be fed, forced to exercise, and kept alive until the ship reached its destination.

"Their own people gave them up," said Henry. "Wretched creatures if you ask me."

Johnathan was still green to the hellish environment on a slave ship. This was his first voyage, and he needed the money. He and Henry moved about the dark deck with a burning candle in a lamp. Unfortunately, it only illuminated a small area around them. Henry held the light slightly over his head, annoyed at the Africans' existence. He knew they were worth more to the captain than his meager life. The men inspected the cargo, poking at the slaves with a long stick to see if they were dead or alive. If a slave became ill, the crew would throw them overboard, and the slave would drown.

Below the deck was unnerving, unsanitary, and threatening enough for the crew. Still, there was something creepy and sinister in their presence for these two men checking for the dead below. Johnathan was shaky and worried. His eyes moved from slave to slave. All enslaved Africans were considered savages who would kill him in a heartbeat and easily tear him apart from limb to limb.

"Let's hurry this up, shall we?" uttered Johnathan nervously.

Henry chuckled. "A bit afraid, are we? There's nothing to be worried about, chap. They're shackled tightly."

The smell alone was getting to the young boy. But something made the hairs on the back of Johnathan's neck rise. The two continued to move through the rows of shackled slaves, inspecting and checking. But then, they came across something odd. There was a U-shaped shackle that had been damaged. The bolts across the opening seemed forced apart, and leg irons snapped into two pieces. There should have been a slave shackled and on his back. But it was an empty space.

Confused, Henry and Johnathan looked at each other.

"That's not possible," uttered Henry.

"Where did he go?" Johnathan asked with heavy breathing.

Henry shifted the light around the deck, searching for the anomaly . . . until the light from the lamp landed on a dark figure glaring at both men. Johnathan saw this creature and immediately froze with his eyes wide in horror. Its face was demonic, dark, with a look of rage and determination. Henry locked eyes with it, and though he appeared calm, he was nervous.

"How did you free yourself from your chains?" Henry growled at this figure, pulling out his knife.

With startling speed, Akasha, now the undead, lunged at Henry before he could react to defend himself with the knife. Akasha ripped into Henry's neck, teeth piercing the soft flesh as he clenched his jaws and ripped apart his neck. Henry howled, and his eyes bulged with sudden pain. Johnathan stood there in horror, realizing the rumors of Africans being able to tear a man apart were true. Akasha killed Henry like he was a mere bug. He spat out blood and chunks of flesh and growled. Johnathan trembled and begged, "Please. Please . . . I'm just doing what I was told to do. I want to go home."

Johnathan turned suddenly to run away. He screamed for help. Akasha chased him down before escaping from below and viciously killed him the same way he did Henry. There would be no mercy. However, the screams from the boy below alerted other sailors on the top deck. Three more men came barreling below armed with weapons but were quickly met with the same grizzly fate.

Akasha wanted revenge. *Burn it all down*, he thought. Then, and before other white men came charging below to suppress a slave revolt, Akasha, with tremendous strength, pried open the locks and chains that restrained his African brothers. Their hampering neck chains and leg irons were tossed aside. One by one, the other chains followed until, finally, nearly all the slaves stood free of their shackles.

A few enslaved Africans armed themselves with several sugarcane knives, terrifying weapons. The handles were square bars of steel an inch thick, and the blades were two feet long, razor-sharp, widening by regular gradation to a maximum width of three inches at the end. They were now in the hands of angered slaves, becoming deadly, hand-wielded guillotines.

Slaves poured from below with such ferocity they sounded like hundreds of lions roaring in the middle of the sea. Onboard were fifty-six crew members, and each man hurriedly took up arms to defend themselves or flee to safety from the ensuing bloody retribution. The captain was alerted. He sprang from the arms of a young slave girl and peered at what was his worst nightmare coming true.

Cannons and guns went off, killing a slew of Africans leading the charge, but it wasn't enough to end the retribution. The Africans wildly swung the sugarcane knives at their captors, slitting open their throats, cutting off their heads, and creating gaping wounds across their chests and faces. More cannons went off, and more bodies dropped. Burning candles and lamps fell over, setting the ship ablaze. Sailors fled aft, leaping from the taffrail and swimming in the middle of nowhere with the ship glowing with uncontrolled fire. Sailors that remained on the ship continued to fight for their lives, including Captain Sir Francis Hawkins. But it was becoming a fruitless task. The slaves, with machetes and other weapons, sprang onto the top deck and upon the remainder of the crew and the captain. Gunfire exploded, killing half a dozen Africans.

The captain scowled and removed his sword, and when three slaves rushed him, he evaded their attack and quickly ran the men through with his sword. The captain's first mate, Remy, grabbed an oar and screamed madly at the Africans, "Get back! Get back!" But the fear on his face was palpable. The slaves were beyond control, and the ship was burning, which was the end for him. His fate was inevitable. Remy dropped the oar and fell to his knees, surrendering to his doom. The Africans were quickly upon him; a machete rose and fell in one murderous stroke, and the first mate crumpled to the deck, his head split open.

However, the captain wasn't about to surrender so easily. The *Abigal* was his ship, his slaves, his profits. These men were animals to him. They were inferior, and he refused to die by their hands. The captain seethed with the sword still gripped tightly in his hand. He was ready to strike wildly with a murderous look upon each encroaching slave. He was trapped. Behind him was the dark, massive sea, and immediate death was before him. One slave charged, and the captain opened a long gash across his head.

"I'll kill you all!" shouted Captain Sir Francis Hawkins.

But it was an idle threat.

Then Akasha appeared before the captain with his dark, lifeless eyes and fangs showing. The captain was taken aback by this slave's demonic appearance. He uttered, "Oh God, the devil is upon us. God help me."

The captain lifted his sword, ready to defend himself, but was suddenly shaky. Akasha lunged at him quickly and sank his teeth into the captain's neck, rendering the man's sword useless. He tore out pieces of flesh like it was savory meat. Finally, Akasha released his full rage and tore this man apart like a branch snapping into two. He continued to feast while the ship sank into the Atlantic. Every man, woman, and child had succumbed to a watery grave.

Chapter One

The August heat was sweltering. It was one of the hottest days of the year, but it was the cotton-picking season. The cotton field was in full bloom, a visual purity, like an immaculate expanse of light, new-fallen snow. The cotton had grown from five to seven feet high, each stalk having many branches shooting out in all directions and lapping each other above the water furrow. Over two dozen slaves were working the field. There was a slave to each side of the row with their sacks around their necks that hung to the ground, the mouth of the sack about breast-high. And to make sure everyone was hard at work, an overseer on horseback patrolled, bullwhip in hand, eyeing the slaves at his mercy. Mercilessly, the overseer hurled his whip down at laboring slaves. The whip snapped like gunfire inches from the men, women, and children as they picked the cotton hastily.

Baskets were placed at the end of the furrows, and slaves dumped their cotton sacks into the baskets. Then they continued to pick until their sacks were again filled. Among the slaves feverishly working the cotton fields was Irene. She was a beautiful, fleshy slave wearing a headwrap. Irene moved through the rows at speed, expertly picking the cotton, her sack almost filled. The overseer, Colemon, stared at Irene momentarily, eyeing her every movement, and Irene did everything she could to avoid his unwanted attention. Everyone knew that Colemon had a penchant for slave girls and most nights took comfort with them, but Irene was a married woman. Her husband, Solomon, was the blacksmith on the plantation, and he was one of the best. And Irene was one of Master Walken's hardest workers.

Whenever Colemon's eyes lingered on her for too long, Irene quickly cast her attention away from him. She didn't want to create any trouble for herself. Even though she was one of the hardest workers in the field, she was still subjected to abuse and rape on the plantation. And so far, Colemon had left her alone. Mindy and Anna were his two comfort girls at night.

While Irene worked the cotton field, her husband, Solomon, was hard at work shoeing the horses by the barn. Solomon was a strapping Black man who stood six feet tall with nappy hair. He was one of the fortunate ones on the plantation. He was a blacksmith, one of the best. He started as an apprentice when he was ten years old. His daily routines would be cleaning out the forges, breaking up and hauling in charcoal for the day, nearly three bushels, along with sweeping and picking up tools and scraps of iron left on the floor from the previous day. Then he would start the fires in the forges, and before it would get warm, he would get breakfast from the big house.

While Solomon tended to one of Master Walken's horses, he looked across the cotton field, where he saw his wife working hard under the bright afternoon sun. And unfortunately, the overseer was breathing over her shoulder on horseback with a whip, threatening violence. Solomon paused for a moment and frowned.

He loathed Colemon, an evil rapist of Black women, knowing what the man was. Solomon wished his wife wasn't so close to the man every day. He wished Irene had a job doing master's laundry or caring for the livestock on the plantation. Irene was a great cook, but her abilities were wasted picking cotton from sunup to sundown.

When Colemon looked Solomon's way, he quickly averted his attention back to shoeing the horse. Solomon didn't want any trouble from the overseer. He knew Colemon would quickly land that whip across his flesh and chastise him for casting his eyes too long his way.

The Walken plantation was a wonder with an antebellum, ashen-colored Greek revival mansion centered on the plantation. The estate was grand with a center entrance, a deep wraparound porch, and several columns, two stories high with a piazza in front. A log kitchen, poultry house, corn cribs, and several slave cabins were in the rear.

Master Cornwell Walken and his wife, Cynthia, considered themselves good Christian folks. They were in their late thirties and had four children. Cornwell thought himself a God-fearing, righteous, and educated man who was quite articulate. And what he valued the most was protecting his position in a wealthy society. Cynthia was the doting wife. She would prance around the plantation in her cotton afternoon dresses and bonnets, ensuring she took care of the home well.

The couple was dressed immaculately for the summer weather. Master Cornwell Walken was a clean-shaven, handsome man. He stood on the porch in his gentlemanly appearance, clad in a riding coat, a cotton shirt, and neat trousers. Being the patriarch on his prized plantation, he took pride in his appearance.

Master Walken stood perched on his porch overlooking his slaves hard at work. It was the cotton-picking season, and this year, the fields were thriving with rows of cotton that stretched to the ends of the horizon, damn near eternity. This year's harvest was flourishing. There were dozens of baskets filled to the brim with cotton, ready to be processed and sold. But Master Walken was concerned about one thing: two of his slaves, Thomas and Malcolm, had taken off running a few days back, and he wanted them found. They were two hardworking niggers that he paid a hefty price for, and the loss of them would be dreadful.

Cynthia approached her husband, noticing his look of concern. "They'll find them, Cornwell. There's no need to stand there and fret. They couldn't go far."

Cornwell turned to his wife and replied, "I paid eleven hundred dollars respectively for them two niggers not even a year ago. We treat our niggers well, right? So why would they go and do something so stupid and run off? I won't stand for it, Cynthia. Our niggers running off in the night, making me lose stock."

"Eat some breakfast, dear. You'll feel better."

Cynthia looked over to where one of their slave girls, Nancy, was stretching wet cotton sheets across a long clothesline. She called out for her. "Nancy, please stop what you're doing and come here."

Nancy stopped her chores and did what she was told, approaching Cynthia and her master. "Ma'am?"

"I want you to fetch George for me and tell him to come here right away," said Cynthia.

Nancy nodded. "Yes, ma'am. Will do."

Nancy pivoted and marched away with a sense of urgency to look for George, one of the house slaves working in the big house and closely around the family. The Walkens had several house slaves who lived in the big house performing domestic labor like cooking, cleaning, serving meals, and caring for their children. George was their oldest servant. He'd been born and raised on the plantation and used to tend to Cornwell's father before he passed away.

"It's going to be a long, hot day, Cornwell. At least fetch you a glass of water for now."

But Cornwell was too riled up to eat or drink at the moment. He was a man about business and profits. There were many things on his mind, and having breakfast wasn't one of them. Immediately, George approached the couple from the rear of the house. In his early forties, he was a thin man dressed in livery attire.

"You call for me, ma'am?" George asked politely.

"Yes, George, bring my husband some toast and coffee," said Cynthia. "He hasn't eaten anything since sunrise."

"Yes, ma'am. Right away, ma'am," George uttered submissively.

"I said I'm fine, Cynthia," Master Walken protested.

"Nonsense. I will not hear of such a thing. You've hired good men to find them two niggers, so stop fretting over it, Cornwell. It's not the end of the world," Cynthia replied.

Cornwell turned to her as if she'd spoken blasphemy about their Lord and savior. But then, he blustered, "Not the end of the world, my dear lady? It might as well be if I allow these two niggers to run off after not a year's work on this plantation and spark ideas to others on my property. What kind of example am I setting on my farm, huh? I'll be the laughingstock of South Carolina not only to allow one but *two* of my niggers to escape. I will have no such thing. They *will* be found even if I have to go on horseback myself to look for them."

Cynthia sighed. "You're so worried about your reputation, Cornwell. It spoils you. Niggers run off all the time."

"Well, not *my* niggers!" Cornwell shouted. "I will have no such thing, Cynthia. I treat them well, don't I? I let them get married. I give them Sundays off, I allow them to visit their families on other plantations, and I teach them the gospel."

"And still, a dog will be a dog," she replied.

Cornwell stared at his wife for a moment. She was a pretty gal of petite stature. He loved his wife and family, but Cornwell felt she didn't understand the severity of the situation. Cornwell took himself to be an astute businessman. Growing up, he was considered the weak one of the family for not punishing his slaves accordingly and believing that treating them somewhat reasonably would keep them in line. Now, to have two slaves run off, Cornwell wouldn't hear the end of it from his older brother, Gideon.

As Cornwell continued to huff, George emerged from the big house carrying breakfast on a silver tray for his master. Cornwell looked irately at his servant and uttered, "I said I'm not hungry, George."

"Yes, suh," George replied meekly, pivoting away from his master.

Cynthia pouted. Her husband was as stubborn as a mule. Just then, something caught Cornwell's attention. A horse-covered wagon, flanked by several men on horseback, approached his plantation. Cornwell perked up, knowing these men were bringing him back his property. The horses' hooves pounded the dirt trail that led to the big house, and Cornwell eagerly removed himself from the porch. Every slave from the cotton fields to the big house and the barn gazed at the wagon and the "patty-rollers," or bounty hunters, riding smugly beside it, knowing that it meant they succeeded in capturing a runaway.

The wagon stopped, and Cornwell greeted the men with, "Gentlemen."

"Good day to you, Mr. Walken," Foxx replied atop his horse. "And a good day to you, ma'am."

Cynthia smiled his way.

Cornwell gestured to the wagon. Foxx grinned and said, "We caught him late last night."

"Just one?" Cornwell asked.

Foxx nodded. "Got him back some yonder from here, twenty-five miles north."

"Twenty-five miles, in two days," Cornwell repeated disbelievingly.

"These niggers are fast, sir," said Foxx. "They get to running, and they're like animals on four legs. Gotta sic the dogs on them."

Foxx dismounted from his horse and walked toward the rear of the wagon. He and another man roughly removed a chained slave from the wagon and threw him to the ground. They had beaten the man. He was shirtless with his pants in rags. His ankles and wrists were heavily restrained with leg irons, allowing him to walk but preventing him from running or kicking. Though he was captured and defeated, this Black slave carried a wild look in his eyes. He struggled with his restraints, but to no avail.

"He's one feisty nigger, I'll give him that," said Foxx.

Cornwell approached his property, or slave, with fire in his eyes. The slave was on his knees. Cornwell stood over him like a man ready to chastise his dog. But instead, he crouched eye level with his slave and scolded, "Malcolm, you're a hard worker, but you're stubborn too, boy. Why, huh? Why would you run away? I paid good money for you, boy. And don't I treat you well here on this plantation, clothe you, feed you? Don't I?"

Malcolm stayed silent.

"Where's Thomas?" Cornwell asked him.

Malcolm remained silent. Cornwell fumed. "I'm speaking to you, nigger. Where's Thomas?"

Malcolm frowned.

"If you want, sir, me and my men have ways to get these niggers to talk," Foxx interrupted.

Cornwell stood to his feet, upset. Malcolm remained stubborn, and Cornwell was done being nice. His overseer came riding over on horseback with the bullwhip in his hand as if on cue. Colemon grinned, seeing that they'd finally captured Malcolm.

"Colemon, take this nigger to the barn and string him up. And I want every slave on this plantation to stop what they're doing to witness this," said Cornwell.

Colemon nodded. Then he rode off to do what he was ordered. Cornwell approached Foxx and the other slave catchers and handed them their payment. Foxx smiled and uttered, "It's a pleasure doing business with you, Mr. Walken."

"There's still one more nigger out there, Foxx, and I want my property found and brought back to me," Cornwell proclaimed.

"And I promise you, we'll find him."

Foxx mounted his horse and rode off the plantation with his crew of slave catchers. Then Cornwell pivoted to see Cynthia staring at him.

"Now, will you enjoy breakfast before noon, dear?" she asked him.

Cornwell stared at her. Malcolm had him seething, and he wanted every slave—man, woman, and child, to bear witness to what happens when you escape from his plantation. Not even the hand of God would stop him from brutally punishing Malcolm for his transgressions.

Chapter Two

Like the other slaves in the cotton field, Irene stopped picking cotton, removed the sack from around her neck, and placed it on the ground. Colemon ordered them to, "Hurry up now. Get! Master Walken wants everyone near the barn."

Irene followed the others toward the barn nearby. She knew what was happening, but she kept quiet about it. It was a bittersweet break from the hot sun and backbreaking work of the never-ending cotton field. She'd heard it was Malcolm they had caught. She knew Malcolm well. Master Walken had bought him and Thomas from the auction eight months ago. Paid a pretty penny for them too. Malcolm was nineteen and built like a bull. He was powerful too. Master Walken would have Malcolm chopping lumber for most of the day, splitting upright logs on a stump, muscles rippling with each blow.

The slaves met in an open area by the barn. Over a dozen of them gathered around Malcolm, who was on his knees, naked and tied to a dead tree stump. Irene found Solomon, and she went to stand close to him. The two were happy to see each other but sad that it was under this circumstance.

"My love," Solomon uttered to her proudly.

Irene smiled, but her smile would be short-lived because their reality was about to strike like lightning. She grabbed Solomon's hand to find comfort during the cruelty they were about to witness. Each slave stood compliantly around the tree stump like children waiting for one of their own to be disciplined. No one dared say a word. The eyes upon poor Malcolm from his peers were filled with sorrow, uneasiness, and sympathy.

Master Walken and his wife were there to witness the punishment. Master Walken grimaced and gazed at the scene with an air of heartless satisfaction. His niggers needed to be taught a lesson. They needed to understand the consequences of believing in their freedom. It didn't exist. They were all his property, bought and paid. And he couldn't allow his property to just run off like the wind. Malcolm would become an example of what would happen if they ran off.

Colemon paced near Malcolm with the bullwhip in his hand. He unfurled the whip, stepped back, and took a few practice cracks. It was an intimidating sound like thunder in the sky. The snap of it made skin violently tear from its victim's flesh, and it made men, women, and even children holler like they were being consumed by hellfire. Colemon glanced at Master Walken, and Cornwell exclaimed, "Get on with it."

The overseer acquiesced. He stood over Malcolm with his whip, and he began to whip the poor slave. Lash after lash, Malcolm squirmed and hollered before it. His back started to welt, then more tears and screams in agony. Irene's eyes filled with tears too as she watched. She squeezed Solomon's hand tighter after each lash, becoming nearly too distraught to watch.

"This is your damn home, nigger . . . not north or south, but on Master Walken's plantation. You will work hard every day, live, and die here, nigger!" Colemon exclaimed as he continued to bring the bullwhip across Malcolm's bloody back.

After a full forty lashes, Colemon looked to Master Walken, who was not satisfied with the outcome.

"Did I tell you to stop? Go on," said Master Walken.

Colemon nodded, complying. He continued to strike Malcolm another fifteen times. Malcolm's back was now reduced to little more than torn meat and blood. The whip was wet with blood. Malcolm ceased struggling as his head sank listlessly to the side. His screams and prayers had gradually decreased into a low moan. He was dying.

"Enough!" Master Walken finally spoke. "Leave him there overnight."

The slaves were disbursed to go back to work while Malcolm was left tied to the dead tree stump, terribly lacerated and dying.

It was a warm night in the South. The humid summer days seemed to melt into even more humid summer nights, with the air so thick it pressed upon one's skin. The slaves were settled in their quarters, which were a direct contrast to the big house on the plantation. Irene and Solomon took shelter every night in a one-room log cabin that wasn't well built. Their conditions were appalling. They had a window but no glass and a shabby fireplace for the winter. Sometimes, when it rained, water leaked from the roof. The only furniture inside the cabin was a small wooden table and a rocking chair Solomon made himself. And the couple slept on a mean pallet at nights with the comfort of an old blanket to share.

Tonight's dinner consisted of cornmeal and salted fish. Master Walken's slaves would receive weekly food rations, usually cornmeal, lard, meat, molasses, peas, greens, and flour. It was distributed every Saturday to them. To supplement the basic provision provided by her master, Irene was permitted to grow her garden near her cabin. As a result, she had a vegetable patch for personal consumption or sale.

The night was young, but Solomon was restless. He couldn't stop thinking about Malcolm. He was still out there, tied to that dead tree stump, flogged, and dying.

"He's goin' to die out there, Irene," Solomon uttered.

"It's Masser's choice to release him, Solomon. What can we do?" she replied.

Solomon huffed, knowing Irene was right. Master Walken wanted Malcolm tied out there all night to make an example out of him. It was a warning to every slave on his plantation not to run away, or there would be dire consequences. But Solomon continued to fret. What he witnessed today wasn't different, but it was another reason why he wanted to run away. It was hard for him to sit by, knowing one day he might suffer the same fate as Malcolm—or worse—to idly watch his wife flogged by the overseer. And what could he do about it? Nothing. He was his master's property, to do with whatever his master pleased. He was no different than the hogs, chickens, and horses on the plantation.

"Sit and finish eating," said Irene.

"I'm not hungry."

"You need to eat."

"I said I'm not hungry right now," Solomon griped. "Let me be and think, woman!"

Irene pouted. "Don't sass at me, Solomon."

Solomon turned to her, immediately sorry for his reaction. "I'm sorry," he said.

He stared at his wife. The last thing Solomon wanted to do was upset her. She was everything to him, and he to her. Her dark skin shimmered in the dim light from the candles that lit up the small space. Irene stood in her headwrap and wool dress, a radiant beauty despite her shabby clothing. She worked hard picking cotton every day—from sunrise to sunset, then at night, she cooked and tended to her garden and sometimes appeased Solomon's needs as a man.

"I's just worried that one day, Masser will bring harm to you . . . Maybe he takes you from me, and I can't bear the thought," said Solomon. "That's why I want us to run."

Irene pouted again. "And go where?"

"North," replied Solomon.

"We's fine here, Solomon. We's safe. Masser treats us fair, long as we work hard and stay out of trouble. We stay married, we stay together. And he don't climb on top of me to do his business like other massers," she protested.

"We is nothin' here," Solomon argued.

"We is together here," Irene countered.

"But for how long?"

It was a daunting question. Master Walken made a promise to all of his slaves, that as long as they worked hard and did what they were told, then they wouldn't be sold off. He valued his property, and every last one of his slaves was as essential to him as the horses and animals on his land. So, he encouraged his slaves to get married, create children, and start a family. The bigger the family, the more his wealth grew. It was also believed that married slaves were less likely to be rebellious or run away.

"Masser Walken expects a child to bear my wound soon," said Irene. "How long we's disappoint him by being married but childless?"

Solomon grumbled. He had mixed feelings about starting a family. He wanted his children to be free. He wanted to become a free man. But like Irene, he also feared that if they didn't give Master Walken what he asked for, more slaves to add to his wealth, he would force Irene to lie with another male slave to become pregnant. Or maybe, he'll sell her off, believing she was infertile.

"My children d'serve to be free," said Solomon.

"'Nuff talk 'bout freedom, Solomon!" Irene exclaimed. "I should be 'nuff for you. We continue to make our home here. That kinda talk gon' get ya punished and sold off."

Irene was upset and worried about her husband. He preached about them fleeing to the North the entire summer, but she continued to be against it. It was too risky, and they had a lot to lose. And the chances of them succeeding were almost slim to none. But Solomon believed there was hope. Though Malcolm had been brought back, they hadn't captured Thomas yet, and it's been four days since he'd escaped.

"Come, lie with me tonight," Irene said, reaching for her husband, wanting to give him comfort and make him forget about escaping slavery.

Solomon stared at her for a moment. He couldn't resist the lures of his wife, so he moved closer to her, and she pulled him into her arms. Although they were properties of their master, their comfort on the plantation was satisfying and assuring. Each night, she got to lie with Solomon. And each night, there was the hope of them growing old together, though they were in bondage. Irene felt escaping wasn't worth the risk of losing her husband.

They hugged for a moment, and then the two shared a passionate kiss, one that showed how much they loved each other. Irene peeled away her dress and stood naked before her husband. She wanted sex, but she also wanted to get pregnant. They'd been married two months, and her wound was still absent of a seed.

Other slave women frolicked around the plantation with their big bellies. Some were young, and some were older. Pregnancy made them valuable to Master Walken. The more children they produced, the more privileges they were given. Irene was twenty-two years old and yet hadn't created children. Some of her peers whispered about her being infertile.

Irene and Solomon took comfort on the pallet, and though it wasn't a secure bed, it was enough for them to enjoy each other. They made the best with what they had or were given. Solomon was soon inside his wife in the missionary position. He grunted. After working hard all day, having the pleasure of home and solitude with Irene was nice. Irene moaned as pressure built in her stomach. Her muscles tightened around him, and she felt Solomon releasing himself inside her. Solomon then got up and smiled at her.

"I love you," he proclaimed.

"I love you too," Irene replied.

Solomon knew he could never lose her. He would die before allowing that to happen.

Chapter Three

With the sun yet again high in the sky, the slaves worked the field picking cotton. It was another hot day, and they started to sing a spiritual song. It was the only thing that distracted them from the tedium at hand. But there was no distraction from the heat. One of the slaves, Michael, started to falter before it, and eventually, he collapsed in the dirt. Though Irene and the other slaves took note, none moved to help him. None dared.

The overseer rode toward Michael and looked at him with no concern. Almost disgusted, aloofness dripped from his face. Then, with the bullwhip in his hand, he yelled, "Get up, boy!"

Michael had passed out and was unconscious. Nothing. Colemon frowned, and then he hurled his whip down at him. The whip snapped like gunfire inches from him, but still, Michael lay there from heat exhaustion. Colemon shot a look at a small boy nearby and said, "Get him some water."

"Yes, suh!" the boy uttered.

The boy ran off while Colemon, on horseback, towered over the collapsed slave as the others continued to pick cotton. While waiting for the boy to return with water, Colemon's attention swung to Irene. He watched her work feverishly, picking the cotton and filling her sack. Then, out of the blue, he said, "You're looking mighty fine there today, Irene."

Irene cringed. She kept her attention on her work, silently praying that Colemon's interest in her faded. However, Colemon's eyes continued upon her. Irene quickly sliced a finger while she plucked a fluffy boll of cotton from the top plant. Ouch! It hurt like a bee sting. A pulse of red floated into white, and Irene's blood ran onto that cotton. She brought her finger to her mouth to staunch the bleeding.

The small boy arrived with a bucket of water. He hurried over to Michael and tossed water on his listless face.

"C'mon now, get up!" the boy exclaimed, kicking Michael in his side. "Get up!"

Colemon glared at the two, then asked, "Is he dead?"

"No, suh," the small boy replied.

"Then if he's not up and working in five minutes, he'll have a punishment coming his way," Colemon uttered.

The boy tossed some more water on Michael's face and kicked him hard in his side. Michael suddenly came to and rose to his feet with Colemon glaring at him. And like nothing had happened, he picked up his cotton sack and returned to work.

The full moon was a mesmerizing celestial ball of light in the sky. It was a lovely, warm night, and the slaves had settled into their quarters for the night. But the activity from the big house could be heard down yonder. Master Walken was hosting a lavish dinner party inside the big house. Distinguished guests from every part of the county attended. Master Walken and his wife were known for their dinner parties and eventful gatherings. Cornwell Walken was an ambitious man who wanted to get into politics. So he wanted, or needed, to make friends in very high places, which meant hosting and entertaining regularly. And ambition in politics was costly.

Solomon emerged from his log cabin and stepped onto the dirt path. He stared at the big house up the hill. It was lit up like the moon in the sky, bright with activity and laughing white folks. Their horses and carriages with their slaves as chauffeurs were idling nearby until their return. Solomon huffed. He was alone for now. Irene was ordered to become one of the servers for their master's party. She had a pretty face and a certain allure that Master Walken felt his guests would like. Solomon hated to depart from his wife, knowing Irene was at their disposal. And she could be subjugated to any abuse, ridicule, or sexual cruelty by night's end. It was bad enough that she worked the cotton fields all day. Now, Irene was a servant until the master's party ended.

"Ya out here late, Solomon. Worryin' got ya up?" Marcus uttered.

"Masser Walken has Irene serving at his party. White folks up there actin' a fool. I can hear them from here."

"She be fine, Solomon. Irene know how to take care of herself now," said Marcus.

Solomon sighed heavily. He didn't question Irene's toughness. He worried about white folks' cruelty and the white man's desire. Irene was a sheep in the wolf's den, and the thought of being unable to protect his wife bothered him.

"No use to stand out here worryin'. Get you some sleep. Tomorrow 'nother long day," said Marcus.

"How is Malcolm doin'?" Solomon asked.

"He still alive, barely. Nancy and Patricia take care of him."

Solomon frowned. "Masser Walken an evil man."

"Masser Walken a reasonable man, Solomon. Malcolm should not have a run off. Masser says we work hard. We listen, we won't get sold off, and we won't get punished."

Solomon chuckled. "Fair man, you say . . ." Solomon uttered with distaste. "This not right. This not fair, Marcus. What Colemon do to Mindy and Anna every night, they comfort him wit' no choice, no say . . . Masser fair to *them*?"

"We do what needs to do to stay alive, Solomon . . . to keep our families t'gether; to keep from bein' sold away. I'm too old to leave for 'nother plantation, too old to be beaten and punished," Marcus proclaimed with pain and reflective familiarity.

Marcus was fifty-five years old, still healthy and strong but complacent. He'd been born and raised on the Walkens' plantation. He was around when Douglass Walken, Cornwell Walken's father, ran the plantation with an iron fist. Douglass raped his slave girls and fathered many children, and some were sold off for profit. Douglass Walken died from tuberculosis twenty years ago, leaving the reins to the plantation to his oldest son. Master Walken, his family, and the plantation were all Marcus knew. Marcus had a family once, a wife, children, and a slice of happiness on the plantation. Unfortunately, two of his children died from whooping cough when they were young, and his wife of ten years passed away from cholera. Diseases took his family away.

"Irene tells me what ya been discussing wit' her while you two lie t'gether," said Marcus. "It's a foolish plan, Solomon. It's risky, and ya gon get y'self punished and sold off. Where Irene be then?"

"In a better place. Thomas is north, found freedom. I's knows it."

"Thomas is a fool too!" replied Marcus.

"You's a fool for believing this is it," Solomon argued.

"You's be a nigger wit' dreams, and you be a nigger that dies," Marcus proclaimed. "Fifty years, Solomon, and not once have I seen any niggers escape this place. They's come back beaten, broken, and sold off to a worse plantation. You's have it good here wit' Irene. Don't make trouble for ya'self, yuh hear?"

Solomon huffed. He wasn't looking for trouble but knew it would come to him soon.

The Big house was a ball of joy tonight. It was a lively affair, a dinner party thrown in a fairly splendid house. Cornwell Walken's guests were all dressed in their most acceptable attire, the men in their jackets and trousers, the women in their flowing evening dresses, being people of means. In attendance were ten couples, all white and some reasonably young in their twenties. The furniture had been set aside in the living room, and the couples danced. Three Black fiddlers provided the music, playing with light determination and servitude. They were garishly dressed for the affair.

The slaves, men and women, stood by with vacant stares. The women were dressed in long, stark white cotton dresses, and the male slaves wore neat shirts buttoned to the neck. They all stood perfectly rowed, holding silver trays of hors d'oeuvres, waiting for any orders given to them. With them, Irene. When called, the slaves served the guests with a faint, seemingly forced smile and not so much of a whisper as instructed.

Cornwell held court with several men in the living room, a drink in his hand, a cigar in the other, and a grin on his face like a young schoolboy. Before him stood General Mathews, commander of the state militia, Statesman Julius Turner, Reverend Randall Mason, and John Meyers, a wealthy businessman and landowner. Cornwell admired these men. When his father passed, these respected figures took him under his wing and continued to shape and mold him as his father did before them.

"I hear you're interested in politics, Cornwell, like your daddy was," General Mathews said.

"I've given it some thought," Cornwell replied.

"I think you'd fit well as a politician, Cornwell. You have the look of one," said Julius.

Cornwell nodded and smiled, appreciative of the compliment.

"Well, in my opinion, politicians are too serious of a matter to be left to the politicians," Reverend Randall uttered.

The men laughed.

"Reverend, I do believe there's a thing called separation of the church and state for a reason," General Mathews replied.

"God shouldn't be left out of politics," Reverend Randall proclaimed.

"I never said He should. But there should be certain limitations. And suppose it was left up to you, Reverend. In that case, you'd probably allow niggers and our lovely wives to vote too," General Mathews replied.

Reverend Randall grinned and replied, "Romans 13:1–7 says, 'Let everyone be subject to the governing authorities, for there is no authority except that which God has established. The authorities that exist have been established by God . . .'"

"Consequently, whoever rebels against the authority is rebelling against what God has instituted, and those who do so will bring judgment on themselves," General Mathews chimed. "I'm familiar with the good book too, Reverend. Everyone and everything has its place, including niggers. We're the authority, and niggers have no right to rebel against us, for God has made us the authority."

"Gentlemen, tonight is a night of laughter, drinks, and union. Let's leave talk of politics and niggers where they belong, outside," John Meyers chimed.

"I agree," Cornwell expressed.

Cornwell looked at his servants and called over Cherry. She moved toward the men with her smile, ready to comply.

"Yes, Masser Walken?"

"More drinks, gentlemen?" Cornwell asked.

"I do require a refill," said General Mathews.

"Yes, suh," Cherry uttered.

As she poured for the general, he eyed her closely, with an acquainted gaze of lust crawling onto his face. Cherry was seventeen years old. She was thin, dark, and pretty. Her ebony skin shined, and she kept her hair in two long braids. Done serving, Cherry moved back into the line with the other servants, but General Mathews focused on her.

"I heard President Tyler signed the bill authorizing the United States to annex the Republic of Texas," Julius said before puffing on his cigar.

"Oh, enough talk of presidents and bills and religion. It's starting to weary me," General Mathews exclaimed. "Let's make things interesting tonight."

"What do you have in mind, General?" the reverend inquired.

General Mathews glanced back at Cherry standing with the other slaves. Another grin appeared on his face. He turned back to Cornwell and said, "Cornwell, I must say, you do have some mighty attractive Black wenches in your possession. Have you ever partaken in any special delight with them?"

"I'm a reasonable man to my niggers, General. They work hard, stay loyal, and I treat them with dignity, privileges, and assurance of family."

General Mathews laughed. "Niggers and privileges are like giving pigs amnesty for being a filthy animal. They are there for us to care for and do what we please with them. Nothing more, nothing less. But there are some, I do find, sweet and tasty."

General Mathews glanced back at Cherry.

"You've become sweet on Cherry, I see," said Cornwell.

"I have. She has become quite a sight for my sore eyes. Black is always tasty."

"General, you contradict yourself. For nearly a moment ago, you've called them filthy animals. Now you wish to lie with one," John Meyers stated.

"Lying with Black wenches is exciting. Like any white-blooded American in this room, I enjoy a nice piece of dark meat. Juicy. And to watch them mate is a thing to see. I *revel* in it," said General Mathews.

"You are a peculiar fellow, General," Reverend Randall said. "But fornication, especially with Blacks . . . Frankly, I find it uncivilized."

The general chuckled. "I'm an honest man, Reverend. We should partake in my odd desires this evening and have some fun. Cornwell, I wish to see your nigger Cherry lie with one of your male niggers."

Cornwell was taken aback by his request. "General, there are ladies present. Have you forgotten?"

"No. They shall retire for the night," he replied. "And to make it worth your while, Cornwell, I will back your political ambition with a healthy donation. They're just niggers. Surely, you have no attachment to any one of them."

Cornwell thought about it. It was an odd request, but he needed the money. So he looked at Cherry and said to her and his slaves, "Cherry, Andrew, Kimberly, Nathaniel, Irene, follow me."

Chapter Four

"Go on now, Cherry, Andrew; undress," Cornwell ordered them as he sat in his French Louis Philippe Period walnut desk chair.

Cherry and Andrew stood in the center of the room, baffled by their master's demand. Cherry was frightened and hesitant. She didn't want to take off her clothes. She didn't want to be subjugated to whatever twisted perversion they had planned for her. The look on their pale faces was palpable. She was nothing but entertainment for them.

Cherry stared at Master Walken and meekly uttered, "Masser, please—"

General Mathews angrily marched toward Cherry and growled, "Didn't your master tell you to do something, you Black wench? Do it!"

Then the general grabbed her dress and violently ripped it open, exposing her breasts. Cherry's face crumbled. Tears started to well up in her eyes, and they threatened to fall. She was helpless. Andrew removed his clothing, becoming utterly naked in front of everyone. The men in the room gawked at his member like a prized specimen in the zoo.

"I must say, the nigger is well-endowed, just like a horse," Julius mocked.

"Animalistic creatures that deserve castration," said John Meyers.

"Jealous, John?" the general replied.

The party had wound down, and the women had retired, leaving the group of inebriated men to their perverted desires. While Cherry and Andrew were forced to undress for the pleasure of drunken men, the other slaves stood by silently, knowing the worst was yet to come. Irene watched as Cherry peeled away her torn dress, it falling to her feet and her nakedness becoming the center of attention for everyone.

"I must say, I do enjoy the sight of a naked Black nigger," the general uttered.

"I can't have no part of this uncouthness," the reverend uttered before pivoting and marching out of the room.

The general and others grinned at his departure, with the general uttering, "Excuse the reverend. The man has no stomach for such delights."

The men laughed.

Things were becoming interesting. Cherry and Andrew stood naked and quietly like specimens on display. Cherry shivered and cried faintly in front of the men. She tried to cover her breasts and privates, at least trying to savor some dignity, but it was ineffective. And for a moment, they were gawked at like they were on an auction block.

"For God's sake, Cornwell, they're not statues. Have them get on with it," the general uttered.

Cornwell stared at Cherry as she cowered in her nakedness, her eyes still filled with tears. Andrew stood next to her with a deadpan gaze. If he was feeling any emotions about his predicament, he didn't show it. Cornwell sat in his desk chair, a glass of brandy in his hand, legs crossed, and said to Cherry and Andrew, "Go on now, you two. Lie with each other, as the general said. Do it before you're punished."

Cherry remained adamant, quivering, crying. Finally, Andrew had to take charge. He grabbed Cherry by her arms and forced her to the floor. She was on her back underneath him. Cherry moaned and cried until Andrew whispered, "Hush, girl. Close ya eyes. I'm not gon get whipped cuz of ya foolishness."

Cherry closed her eyes tightly, giving in as Andrew parted her legs. Her muscles tensed, her legs trembled, and she soon felt Andrew at her opening. Then he was inside of her, thrusting and groaning. The two started having forced sex while everyone watched, including their peers.

The general laughed and hooted, "There, finally. And look at that nigger go! That's a strong nigger you have there, Cornwell."

The other slaves watched in dreadfulness, knowing they might be next. Irene tried to hold back her tears too as she watched Cherry on her back, becoming a spectacle for drunken white men. She thought about Solomon and wished her husband somehow could come and rescue her from such madness, but it was impossible. So she silently prayed and hoped they didn't make her participate in their iniquity.

Cornwell covertly signaled Nathaniel, who stepped forward with a tray of cigars. Nathaniel grabbed the general's attention, and he said, "Yes, another strong young buck. How old are you, boy?"

Nathaniel was nervous, answering, "I-I believe nineteen, suh."

"Nineteen, huh?" The general stepped closer to Nathaniel, his eyes fixed on the young man's features. He then took Nathaniel's chin into his grip, inspected him quickly, and said, "You're a handsome nigger, Nathaniel. I do say so myself."

Nathaniel stood there silently, allowing the general to touch him, groping him in uncomfortable places. The general stroked Nathaniel's cheek up and down with the back of his fingers. He touched his ears and rubbed his chin. It was a combination of nervous excitement and preening and touching.

The general stared at Nathaniel and said, "Undress, nigger."

Nathaniel nodded obediently and did what he was told. He slowly unbuttoned his shirt, removing it. Then he unbuttoned his trousers. Finally, he was naked in front of the general, waiting for further directions. The general turned and cast his immoral gaze upon the two slave women standing in the room, Irene and Kimberly. Irene tried not to tremble from fright. It haunted her that she'd rather have Kimberly subjected to the sexual horror happening. And though they both were the same age, Irene was a married woman; Kimberly wasn't.

It seemed like an eternity in purgatory with the general's eyes upon them, ready to pick one of them for his sadistic pleasures. Andrew was still having sex with Cherry on the floor. They remained in the missionary position with Cherry's eyes closed.

"You, come over here." The general pointed to Kimberly. "What's your name, girl?"

"Kimberly," she replied.

Irene thinly exhaled with relief but wasn't out of the frying pan yet. Kimberly stepped forward in horror, knowing what was expected. She glanced back at Irene, her eyes pleading for her help. But there wasn't anything Irene could do. She was expected to partake in the same debauchery.

"Come on, now, Kimberly. Get over here," the general said.

Kimberly approached the general, and like with Cherry, he grabbed her roughly and tore open her dress to reveal her breasts and womanhood. Kimberly cringed and gasped. The general shoved her toward Nathaniel and said, "Get on with it, you two."

Like Cherry and Andrew, Nathaniel took control of Kimberly, and the two lay down naked near where the first couple was having sex. Cornwell and his guests sat and watched as Nathaniel penetrated Kimberly. The general stared gleefully at the vile activity. He then raised his glass and announced, "Now, we have ourselves a party, gentlemen."

It was sickening. And Irene was the last one standing. When Cornwell stood from his chair and looked her way, Irene's heart sank into the pit of her stomach. She expected to be next. Instead, but surprisingly, Cornwell said to her, "Go on home, Irene. You're done for the night."

Relief hit Irene like an unexpected thunderstorm. She concealed her glee and hurried to the door. But before she departed from the room, she noticed the general unbuttoning his shirt, and he had Nathaniel and Kimberly in his sight.

Irene hurried from the big house and ran toward the slave quarters, grief-stricken as if she'd participated in the orgy in Master's study. She heard plantation owners entertaining their friends by forcing the enslaved Blacks to have paired sex and orgies. The white men often would participate in the debauchery. What she witnessed was unthinkable, and she cried for her fellow slaves.

When Irene arrived home, Solomon was outside, waiting for her. She quickly rushed into his arms, overwhelmed with tears. She didn't want to let him go.

"What they do to you, Irene?" Solomon asked, fearing the worst.

Irene didn't answer him. She continued to cry in her husband's arms. She didn't want to speak of it. Not yet. Solomon ushered his wife into the cabin and closed the door.

Before the two lay together that night, Irene opened up and told Solomon what had happened inside the big house. He sat there quietly, but he was upset. Solomon's eyes watered from his emotions. The thought of his wife being raped or forced to have sex with another man while others watched had him seething. Irene took Solomon's hand into hers and gazed into his eyes. She knew what he was thinking.

"Promise me, Solomon, you won't do anything. Masser Walken, he sent me home," she said.

Solomon wiped away the few tears from his face and frowned. "Masser Walken not a good man, Irene."

"Lay with me, Solomon. Don't let me go tonight," said Irene expressively.

Irene pulled her husband closer to be with him in comfort. Solomon held her tightly with a frown. His anger was boiling, but he had to swallow that anger and let that steam of rage dissipate. Solomon knew if he acted on it, there would be severe consequences, and he might lose Irene. So he held her and looked compassionately at her, knowing he would give his life to protect hers.

They fell asleep holding each other.

Solomon was hard at work in his shop forging a few farming tools the following day. His clothes were covered in soot, and his hand was filled with blisters. It was another hot summer day. Heavy sweat percolated from Solomon's skin, and it was hard for him to concentrate on his work. What Irene told him last night stuck with him. It bothered him deeply. Earlier this morning, he'd passed Cherry and Kimberly while he walked to his shop. They were mute, disturbed, and raped. Yet, they were expected to carry on with another hard workday. They couldn't look at Solomon. Both girls were preoccupied with shame and guilt.

The sun was at its peak in the sky. The enslaved people were hard at work on the plantation, and Irene was filling her sack with cotton, trying to meet her daily quota. The heat inside the barn became intense, so Solomon stopped working for a moment to gather a breeze for himself. Then, clutching his hammer, he stepped out of the barn and soon noticed a wagon approaching the plantation. He recognized it as the same wagon from last week. They were slave patrollers, or patty-rollers. They were the same men who brought back Malcolm.

The wagon approached the big house, and Solomon watched from a short distance. Master Walken greeted Foxx and his men by the porch. The sight of Master Walken and Foxx made Solomon grip his hammer tightly as if he were ready to strike someone with it. Instead, he glared at the white men, wondering what business brought them back to the plantation.

"We found ya second nigger, Mr. Walken. Unfortunately, he resisted and put up a fight. We had to put him down," said Foxx.

Foxx dismounted from his horse to show Mr. Walken the body of Thomas. He was sprawled in the back of the wagon, shot multiple times, and killed.

"Got the nigga near North Carolina, hiding in some barn."

Cornwell Walken looked at his dead slave and frowned. "Damn it!"

Cornwell seethed, hoping they brought Thomas back alive. He couldn't discipline a dead nigger or profit from one.

"I s'pose catchin' one nigger alive is better than 'em both dead," said Foxx. "We did the best we could, sir."

Cornwell frowned and scolded. "If you did your best, I wouldn't have a dead nigger in front of me, Foxx."

Cornwell pivoted and marched away, leaving Foxx and his men to deal with Thomas's body.

Solomon continued to watch Master Walken and Foxx. He saw that Master Walken was suddenly upset and had a hunch why. Later, it was confirmed by George, the house nigger.

"George, what got Masser upset?" Solomon asked him.

"They found and killed Thomas," George answered.

The news was crushing. Solomon felt deflated and stumped. He hoped and prayed Thomas was finally gone from this place and had found freedom up north. But he came back dead. Solomon thought back to what Marcus had told him earlier. *"You's be a nigger wit' dreams, and you be a nigger that dies."*

And for once, Solomon felt skeptical about escaping.

Chapter Five

Ellison's Cave was near Walker County, on Pigeon Mountain in the Appalachian Plateaus of northwest Georgia. It was over twelve miles long and 1,063 feet deep. It was isolated. The blackness was thick as velvet and seemed to engulf the world, hiding everything like a heavy curtain. The absence of light seemed so complete that not even shadows survived. The cave was dark with jagged edges, had a bad smell, and something malevolent hidden within.

Suddenly, deep inside the cave, the still dirt shifted, becoming aggressively disturbed. Someone or something was fighting its way to the surface covered by darkness. Whatever it was, it twisted, wriggled, and turned underneath the rocks and soil. A figure protruded from the ground ... an arm, a face, a man. He was naked and unbalanced for a moment, registering his surroundings, and this figure was undaunted by the eeriness of Ellison's Cave. This evil presence welcomed the darkness, the smell, and the isolation of the deep cave. It had awoken from its long slumber. Now, he was hungry ... and vengeful.

Though the cave was pitch black, it was familiar with it. It moved through the splits of the cave without light or guidance, reaching an opening that stretched 300 feet to the surface. After that, it started to climb the rocky walls effortlessly, like a spider ascending its web. And then he loomed from one of the cave's crevices into a full moon night and the vast timberland.

With remnants of dirt from his long slumber of seventy years, Akasha started to make his way east.

It was midnight on the Cullens' plantation, twenty miles east of Ellison's Cave. The cotton field was in full bloom underneath the full moon night, a visual purity, like an immaculate expanse of light, new-fallen snow shooting out in all directions. The estate was large, and the big house was a splendor serving as a symbol of wealth and prosperity for the plantation. The Cullens were one of the wealthiest families in the county and maybe in Georgia. They owned nearly three dozen enslaved people, and Mr. Caesar Cullen was a good businessman, buying and selling crops and enslaved people at the best price. He poured profits back into his plantation while spending at least some of his earnings on luxurious consumer goods.

Commodity prices for crops such as indigo, rice, and tobacco had fallen. But cotton was king. The deep south made large-scale cotton production profitable, and the number of bales of cotton produced in the American South grew tremendously in twenty years.

Caesar Cullen and his wife, Victoria, were asleep in the main bedroom, and their four children were also sleeping comfortably. Their oldest boy, Michael, was lying naked with a fourteen-year-old slave girl in his bedroom. A few of the house slaves were slumbering in small cabins near the big house, and a slave girl slept in the kitchen.

The many other enslaved people were asleep in small cabins in slave quarters far from the master's house but under the watchful eye of an overseer. It was quiet; nothing moved or stirred inside . . . until a floorboard creaked on the second floor of the big house. The sound awakened Victoria. She sat up and looked at the doorway. It was dark, and she grew nervous. Finally, Victoria decided to wake her husband by repeatedly nudging his side and saying, "Caesar, wake up. I heard something in the house."

Her husband grumbled. He barely opened his eyes and replied, "It's probably Nancy sneaking food again, dear. I'll punish her in the morning."

Nancy was one of their house slaves. But Victoria was sure it wasn't her she heard. Before she got comfortable in bed again, she heard another sound. This time, it seemed closer and louder. Victoria glanced at her husband, who was asleep again. She was alone. Victoria removed herself from the mahogany four-poster bed and lit a candle. Then she cautiously walked into the hallway with the candle dancing in a dark room. She moved farther down the hallway, passing the children's bedroom and seeing they were all asleep.

Eventually, she descended the stairs into the main room with the candle still dancing in the dark.

"Nancy, that better not be y'all sneaking food from our kitchen," Victoria uttered nervously.

Their house was large, with many rooms to cover. There were expansive living areas for entertaining, charming nooks, sunrooms for relaxing afternoons, and extra bedrooms for a growing family. With the sun percolating through every room in the day, the place was a charm. Still, Victoria felt she was roaming in unfamiliar territory in the middle of the night.

Victoria covered two rooms with the candle. Then . . . She saw it. A shadowed figure crouched in the darkness, and Victoria suddenly froze. She squinted into the dark, her eyes adjusted, and she saw the shape of a man. She believed it was one of their niggers intruding into their home, and she feared the worse—a slave rebellion happening on her plantation.

"What do you want? Get out!" Victoria hollered.

Akasha took a half step into a shard of moonlight. He was still naked and threatening. Victoria gasped, then she screeched at the sight of him. Quickly, Akasha crossed to her with unmatched speed and attacked her. Victoria felt her feet fly out from under her as her entire body became suspended. Akasha had lifted Victoria by her throat, and the fear on her face was palpable. Her eyes were wide with fear. Akasha didn't give her a reason. Instead, his fangs fiercely tore into her throat as he ripped pieces from her flesh and began to spew blood.

Mr. Cullen snapped awake from hearing his wife's screaming. He pushed off the covers and immediately leaped from the bed. He eyed the military sword mounted on the wall near the bed. He reached for it and ran out into the hallway, where he found his children coming from their bedrooms.

"Papa, what's going on?" his daughter Mary asked.

"Go back into your rooms. Now!" Mr. Cullen shouted at them.

Mr. Cullen ran downstairs to where he heard his wife's screams and quickly found the threat inside his home. He stood shocked at what he saw. Akasha stood over Victoria's body. She had been brutally murdered. Her crimson blood pooled underneath her. Mr. Cullen gripped the military sword tightly while glaring at Akasha with profound rage.

"You fucking nigger! You dare put your dirty black hands on my wife!" he screamed madly. "I'll kill you!"

He charged at Akasha, raising the sword. Akasha stood there undaunted by the man's advance with a weapon. And when Mr. Cullen swung to strike him, Akasha swiftly moved out of its way, and the sword clashed with air and nothingness. Now, it was his turn to attack. Immediately, Akasha thrust Mr. Cullen forward and flung his body to the ground. Mr. Cullen had the wind knocked out of him. He shook with fear as Akasha stood over him, crowding him. His eyes were deep and dark. He didn't talk. Instead, effortlessly, he picked up Mr. Cullen and wrapped his hands around his neck, digging his sharp fingernails into his flesh.

"Please, don't kill me . . ." Mr. Cullen pleaded.

Akasha felt no remorse. His sharp fangs ripped into Mr. Cullen's artery, shooting blood into his mouth. The pain became blinding for the husband, and his eyes started to dilate. His vocal cords were paralyzed. Quickly, the man was dead, and his children were next.

The piercing screams from the big house had awakened everyone in the slave quarters, including the overseer, Kessinger. He and his son hurried from their cabin with shotguns and raced to the big house, knowing there was trouble.

The oldest son, Michael, staggered out of the big house when they reached the porch, shirtless, bleeding, and badly injured. He made it to the foot of the steps and dropped. Then he crawled along his stomach, blood seeping from his mouth. Akasha emerged from the big house coated in the family's blood. Naked, he walked behind Michael and brutally snapped his neck. Kessinger and his son witnessed the horror and immediately raised their shotguns at him.

"Boy, you're a dead nigger!" Kessinger shouted.

Kessinger fired the shotgun at Akasha, and the impact sent him flying backward onto his back. They assumed he was dead. Both men cautiously ascended onto the porch to inspect the body, but he was gone when they reached the doorway. The son was immediately spooked.

"You shot him, right?" the son exclaimed. "I know you did."

"I couldn't have missed him," Kessinger said in exasperation.

"Then where did he go?"

Before Kessinger could utter a response, the glint of a figure sprinted through the dark. It then burst from out of nowhere and attacked him. It was Akasha, ripping the father apart right in front of his son. Kessinger screamed like a banshee as his body was viciously torn. His son stood by cowardly, clutching the shotgun, trembling. He had never seen anything like it before—a nigger demon, he believed.

When Akasha finished with Kessinger, he stepped forward, crowding the son.

"Get back!" the son hollered. "I'll shoot you, I swear!" The shotgun trembled in his grasp.

Akasha grinned diabolically at the frightened boy, who was only sixteen. He could sense the boy's blood roasting with fear. It was fresh; it was alluring. Akasha continued to crowd the boy.

"I's warn you, get back! I'll shoot you!" the boy screamed.

The commotion had brought the plantation slaves closer to the big house. Crowds started to form near the horrifying site. They saw their overseer and their master's son dead on the porch, and the floor was soaked with their blood. The son looked at the enslaved people nearby and hollered, "Somebody, help me! Please. One of ya!"

But there would be no help for the overseer's son. The son fired the shotgun, to no avail. His eyes widened with terror. Somehow, he'd missed, and he tried to run. Akasha hurled toward the boy as he stumbled over his own feet and fell face forward.

"I'm sorry," the boy cried out, panting, tears running down his cheeks in blankets.

But there would be no mercy. Akasha's fangs pierced deeply into his throat, and his blood spewed everywhere as he screamed out in pain. Then he rammed his hand into the boy's chest and ripped out his heart. Blood fell from Akasha's mouth when he stood up, and he squeezed every drop of blood out of the heart. The enslaved people stood shocked at what they saw. They too were terrified. The entire area was splattered in blood, and Akasha's brutality created eight mangled corpses.

Akasha descended from the porch and slowly approached the enslaved people gathered nearby. Though they were many, they stood there horrified by one man. He'd slaughtered the entire Cullen family in one night.

"Please, we's don't want no trouble," a man uttered.

Akasha glared at them in silence, not attacking them. He then spoke, saying, "Let it begin."

Then he took off into the woods.

Chapter Six

Walken's slaves populated the wooden benches in the open area on the plantation. The ground represented a church, and a Black preacher stood before two dozen brown faces listening to the Christian gospel. However, there was sadness amongst the Blacks. The news of Thomas's death spread, and they were heartbroken. Master Walken had Thomas's body burned until there was nothing left of him but a pile of ashes. Then Master Walken scolded his slaves, warning them of harsher treatment and crueler punishment if any of them ran off like Thomas and Malcolm.

"I will sell your children and work every last one of you until there's no more breath in you left, even on Sundays, if any of you run off," Master Walken exclaimed. "Do you understand me?"

His slaves nodded. They were meek and afraid. Thomas and Malcolm's actions had cast resentment and offense into their master. He was afraid to lose money and property and didn't want to look weak to his family and peers.

Solomon and Irene sat together on the bench, holding hands and listening to the preacher's words. His name was Paul, and he was anointed to preach God's word to the enslaved people from a redacted version of the Bible.

"Ephesians 6:5 . . . Slaves, obey your earthly masters with deep respect and fear. Serve them sincerely in your heart, as you would serve Christ," Paul preached.

Master Walken wanted every enslaved individual on his plantation to attend church every Sunday morning and to take in God's word from the good book, the Bible. He wanted to condition them with the spiritual justification of slavery because, sometimes, physical oppression didn't work. And Paul read from a Bible that had been significantly changed. It was called the Slave Bible. It was like a regular Bible except that it had redacted almost 90 percent of the Old Testament, and only half of the New Testament remained. The contents, or rather *lack* of contents, of the Slave Bible didn't mention anything that could remotely inspire a rebellion. It only reinforced institutionalized slavery and obedience.

Sunday mornings were Solomon and Irene's day together without chores or work. Although enslaved, it was a slice of freedom given to them by their master. So it was when Irene cultivated her food on a small plot. After church, the two walked hand in hand toward the slave quarters. It was a beautiful day, and Irene was all smiles with Solomon, but he seemed bothered by something. Nevertheless, they enjoyed each other's company with limited conversation.

"It's a beautiful day t'day, Solomon," said Irene.

"It is," Solomon replied matter-of-factly.

"Sumthin' wrong, Solomon?"

Solomon sighed. He and Irene stopped walking, and he looked at her and uttered, "I can't get Thomas out of my mind. I was shol' he found freedom."

"Solomon, ya heard Masser. One of us run off again, he gon' punish us all. Please don't think about Thomas. Think 'bout me.

Let us walk and be wit' each other t'day. And how 'bout I's make us some smoke meat and cornmeal at the cabin?" Irene proclaimed to him wholeheartedly.

Solomon smiled. It was fine by him.

They continued to walk home, but unfortunately, Overseer Colemon approached them on foot. Seeing him coming their way, Irene and Solomon averted their attention from his. Their eyes were cast to the ground, showing helplessness while they walked. But Colemon's attention was heavily on the couple, especially Irene. His look showed dominance. Colemon smiled at Irene and said, "You look mighty fine today, Irene. Happy Sunday to you."

"Good day to you too, suh," Irene replied meekly.

Colemon grinned. "And how 'bout you fetch me a pitcher of water, Irene, and we see each other later on?"

Solomon looked angrily at Colemon as he held the overseer's gaze for a moment, seemingly unafraid. Seeing this, Colemon scowled. It was a sign of disrespect to eyeball him, and Colemon was ready to make an example out of Solomon.

He stomped toward Solomon and scolded, "You have a problem with your eyes, boy? You don't like me staring at your nigger wife? She a mighty nice-lookin' girl for you to keep to yourself. How's 'bout I have her come to my cabin tonight, boy? Keep her 'til morning."

Solomon clenched his fists. He knew he could easily beat this white man to a bloody pulp. And though Solomon was seething from the remark, he had to keep his composure. If he were to sass back at the overseer, it surely meant punishment. Irene stared nervously at them and was immediately afraid for her husband.

"I's have no problem fetchin' you that pitcher, suh," Irene chimed.

Colemon ignored her. He continued to glare at Solomon and remarked, "Nigger, she may be your wife, but don't forget she's Mr. Walken's property on this plantation, like the hogs and chickens.

And if I say so, she does what I tell her to do. So don't forget ya place, boy."

The tension was thick between the two men. But the friction was quickly altered when two white men on horseback came galloping onto the plantation toward the big house, catching everyone's attention. This scene pulled Colemon away from Solomon, as he was curious about the sudden arrival of these men. So he hurried toward the big house to see what news these two men had brought today.

Mr. Walken and his wife emerged from the big house to greet the men arriving unexpectedly on horseback with urgent news.

"Gentlemen," Mr. Walken greeted. "And what is the nature of your presence on my land?"

"Mr. Walken, have you seen a group of niggers around here stirring up trouble?" a man named Benjamin asked.

"Can't say I have, gentlemen," Mr. Walken replied. "Why do you ask?"

The look on the men's faces was severe. But then, Benjamin said, "We believe there's a rebellion happening. A family in Walker County, Georgia, was brutally murdered a few days ago, killing even their youngest child of five. And we reckon a group of armed niggers are targeting families on plantations."

Cynthia gasped. She was taken aback by the news. "Oh my God."

"Walker County is some good miles from here, gentlemen, in Georgia," Mr. Walken mentioned. "I'm sure if there is a rebellion, it will be suppressed immediately."

"Mr. Walken, don't underestimate the distance of this tragedy. Two families miles apart have been murdered within days of each other. We're riding around to different farms, putting everyone on alert," Benjamin declared.

"How many slaves do you believe are participating in this uprising?" Mr. Walken asked.

"We have no idea, but it's happening during the night. We urge you to keep vigilance over your land and slaves until this revolt is crushed, and every nigger responsible is hung from the gallows."

"Will do," Mr. Walken replied.

Benjamin looked at Cynthia, who was worried, and said to her, "No need to worry, ma'am. I can guarantee you that we will find these niggers and give them the swift justice that God Himself would be proud of."

"I believe you will," she replied.

The two men nodded. "Good day." They turned on their horses and left the plantation to warn other white men and women of the potential danger. Although the messengers of the rebellion promised them a swift suppression and the tragedy happened nearly a hundred miles from their land, Cynthia looked at her husband with worried eyes. Mr. Walken huffed. News of rebellious enslaved people was horrifying. It wasn't too long ago when Nat Turner's rebellion slaughtered sixty-five people within two days.

Colemon walked toward the couple, wondering what news they'd heard. He noticed the troubled look on Cynthia's face and asked Mr. Walken, "Sir, is there trouble brewing?"

Mr. Walken relayed the news to his overseer. The information of a white family, including children, killed by enslaved people made Colemon furious.

"I don't want any trouble on my plantation, Colemon. I don't want the news of a nigger rebellion spreading. Do you understand me?" Mr. Walken said to him.

Colemon nodded. "Yes, sir. There won't be any trouble comin' from ya niggers, sir. I can assure you that."

"Good. I'll be in my study reading the good word, and I don't want to be disturbed at all," said Mr. Walken.

"Yes, sir."

Mr. Walken turned and went back into the big house. But his wife lingered on the porch, still worried about the news she'd heard.

"Is there anything else, ma'am?" asked Colemon.

Cynthia groaned, then said, "It's just plain awful, niggers killing families and children. Savages. What is this world coming to?"

"No need to worry about a nigger rebellion here, ma'am. I'm skilled at keeping niggers behaved. Niggers are like cattle. They don't think but react. And they need a shepherd to guide 'em and lead the way. And the crack of a whip keeps a nigger obedient, ma'am," Colemon proclaimed.

"Well, you make sure they stay obedient, Colemon."

"It's my job, ma'am."

With that, Cynthia pivoted and walked back into the big house. Colemon frowned. The thought of good Christian white folks killed made him ready to take out his anger on the enslaved people on the plantation.

The night was young, humid, and quiet. Solomon and Irene took comfort in their one-room cabin. Tomorrow was another workday, and they needed their rest. Still, most importantly, they wanted to spend quality time together and attend to a few things before resting. Solomon was working on his rocking chair, and Irene was busy with her clothing. She was expected to cut and sew her clothing. Master Walken allowed the enslaved people on his plantation an annual allotment. The men were given eight yards of cotton cloth to make shirts, five and one-half yards of osnaburg for two pairs of summer pants, and two and three-quarters yards of jeans for winter pants. Plus, a coat made from blanket cloth and two pairs of shoes. The girls received thirteen yards of shirting for three shirts and a gown, two and one-half yards of osnaburg for a petticoat, and five yards of linsey for a winter coat. And because Irene was a field worker, a blanket coat and two pairs of shoes.

The couple was busy with their work . . . until an unexpected loud knock at the cabin door startled them. They looked at each other, concerned. The knocking was followed by, "Now, y'all open up this damn door, you hear? This is Colemon, and I won't knock again."

Apprehension registered on their faces. This wasn't good. Solomon and Irene knew Colemon being at their cabin this time of night wasn't pleasant or beneficial. Irene's dreaded look at her husband said it all. He was there for her, to rape her.

"I'm bein' nice by knocking first," Colemon exclaimed.

"It will be okay," Solomon told her.

Solomon reluctantly walked to the cabin door and swung it open to reveal Colemon staring at him, holding a bottle of whiskey. Colemon drank it like it was water, and he was drunk.

"Sumthin' wrong, suh?" asked Solomon.

"Yes, something's wrong," Colemon remarked, then he pushed his way into the cabin, intruding on their privacy.

"Irene, I need you to come wit' me now, no fuss," Colemon said.

"Suh, me and Irene, we were gettin' ready fo' t'morrow workday, suh, and Irene needs her rest," said Solomon, trying to intervene carefully.

Colemon didn't want to hear any excuses. He made up his mind; he wanted to be with Irene tonight. He'd put it off far too long now, and she was too pretty to ignore. He wanted to fuck her tonight.

Irene stood away from Colemon, scared and hesitant to go with him. Fear showed on her face when she looked at Solomon, her eyes screaming at him. *Please, do something.*

"I said come with me now, you Black wench! I'm not gon' tell you again," Colemon shouted.

Once more, Solomon came in between Colemon and his wife, uttering, "Suh, please, Masser Walken gon' need her healthy fo' t'morrow's work. Irene his best worker."

"Solomon, you get in the way of Irene and me one mo' time, I swear ya be lynched by morning," Colemon warned him through clenched teeth.

Colemon didn't care what excuses Solomon gave him. He was filled with lust and a desire to comfort himself tonight with Irene. He pushed Solomon out of his way and marched toward Irene. Colemon grabbed her by the forearm and tried to remove her from the shack. Irene resisted by pulling away from him, screaming.

"No! No! Please, don't do this!" she hollered.

Solomon couldn't stand by and watch his wife being dragged away to be raped. And before Colemon could get Irene out of the cabin, Solomon rushed forward and forcefully removed the overseer from his wife. He angrily pushed Colemon off Irene while shouting, "Get off her!"

Colemon stumbled backward, losing his balance, and fell to the ground. Solomon knew he messed up. He'd reached the point of no return. He put his hands on a white man—overseer at that, and he knew the punishment would be dire.

"Boy, you just caused some serious hell for ya'self," Colemon exclaimed.

He stood up and charged at Solomon, ready to kill him. But Solomon fought back. He swung his right fist and slammed it into Colemon's jaw. It was a staggering blow. Solomon struck Colemon again, and then his nose began to spew blood. They wrestled inside the cabin, but Solomon was stronger and fiercer. He lifted Colemon from his feet and slammed him onto the floor. Solomon was now on top of Colemon and punched him repeatedly. Memories flooded Solomon's mind like waves of destruction, and he had nothing but resentment for Colemon, Master Walken, and every white man who enslaved him and his people. He thought about Thomas's death and Malcolm's brutal whipping.

"I'm gon' kill you!" Solomon screamed madly.

Solomon slammed his elbow down with crushing force against Colemon's skull.

"Solomon, stop it!" Irene screamed.

Finally, Solomon came back to his senses and stopped beating Colemon. He stood up, and a whimper of exhaustion escaped his lips. Colemon had been badly beaten, but he was still alive . . . barely. Irene was horrified, Solomon too. They both knew this meant certain death for him. For sure, Master Walken would have him lynched.

Irene's eyes showed absolute fear.

"Solomon, run. Please, go! Now!" she said to him.

"No. I's can't leave you, Irene. Come wit' me," he replied, reluctant to leave her behind.

"I can't!"

"Please, Irene, come wit' me."

"No. My sister, mama, what masser do to them on the Jenkin's plantation? I's can't leave them behind," Irene sadly replied.

Solomon's eyes were teary. Irene had made up her mind. She was staying behind. Solomon knew he had no choice but to leave without her. But it was hard. He hugged Irene, who was choked back with tears.

"I's comin' back fo' you," he promised her.

And with that, he ran from the cabin and into the woods. Watching him go, Irene became overwhelmed with feelings. She dropped to her knees and cried, "Oh God, please watch over him to safety."

Chapter Seven

Mr. Walken and several other white men interrogated Irene inside the cabin. Mr. Walken was furious. They had attacked his overseer. He was barely alive, and another one of his slaves had escaped. This event provoked outrage throughout the county, and an angry mob wanted to lynch Solomon.

"Why would your husband do something so foolish, Irene?" Mr. Walken yelled at Irene. "Where is Solomon?"

"I's don't know, Masser!"

"She's lying," Foxx uttered. "Don't go easy on this wench, Mr. Walken. A white man nearly lost his life tonight. You know, like I know, what that means."

Mr. Walken huffed. He glared down at Irene, who was on her knees in front of her master in full-blown tears. She was at his mercy, although she did nothing wrong. Four white men towered over her with sinister stares. They were ready to torture her, rip her apart like they were a pack of wild dogs.

Seething that her husband had beaten a white man, Foxx stormed closer to Irene and kicked her in the chest, and she fell onto her back. Then he screamed, "Where is your nigger husband, you bitch?"

"I don't know!" Irene hollered.

Foxx turned to Mr. Walken and said, "We'll get a posse rounded up. Do a thorough search of the property, and then go into the woods. This nigger couldn't get far. We'll catch him. I promise you that."

"I want him alive, Foxx. Do you understand me," said Mr. Walken. "And any harm done to my niggers on my property will be taken up with the sheriff."

Foxx frowned. To ask to bring Solomon back alive after what he did to Colemon was unwise. But Mr. Walken had the final say-so. It was his nigger.

Foxx nodded. "We'll bring that nigger back alive." *But maybe not in one piece.*

Foxx and his men pivoted and marched out of the cabin, leaving Mr. Walken with Irene. He was disappointed with her.

"You and Solomon, y'all were my best workers," Mr. Walken uttered. "But for what he's done, both of you will be punished."

Irene continued to cry and whimper. She knew there was a possibility that she would never see her husband alive again.

Solomon ran for his life. He pushed through the woods, plowing through thickets of trees, with branches slapping his face and arms. He stayed away from the main road. But he had no idea where he was or in which direction he was going. It was dark, and he was ill-prepared. He continued to run but tripped and lost his footing, crashing to the ground. His escape seemed pointless with the odds against him. Then he noticed that he was by a stream. The stream glittered in the moonlight. Solomon ran to it to quench his thirst. He took in gulps of water while keeping his head on a swivel. Then he sat by the stream momentarily, catching his breath and bearings. He lifted his head and gazed up at the stars. He saw the Big Dipper above the trees. Beyond it, the North Star.

Solomon was exhausted. It felt like he'd been running forever. He had no idea how far he had traveled. But he knew he wasn't safe. As he gazed up at the stars, he remembered something his mother once told him when he was young.

"Always keep the river to your left and the North Star ahead. Then, if there are no stars, keep following the river," said his mother years ago.

Solomon exhaled. She died when he was twelve. She was a good woman, and he hated how his mother lived a life of servitude. Now he had a wife, and he wanted his own family, but what good was having a family in bondage? The thought of leaving Irene behind was painful and disheartening. He knew that someday he had to go back for her. Solomon couldn't have absolute freedom without his wife by his side—because a life without Irene was bondage itself.

Solomon collected himself, and he continued to run, running fast over tree roots and fallen limbs. *North, keep heading north*, he told himself. It was dark, a bit cold, and he was growing tired. The night was his cover, but dawn was approaching. Fatigue hit him quickly. Solomon wanted to rest. He needed to rest, but there was nowhere safe for him to lie and close his eyes. He feared if he stopped to sleep, he would wake up captured. And everywhere he looked, there was vast wilderness and silence. The silence was a good thing for him. It meant he was alone . . . for now.

Running for hours, Solomon could no longer escape fatigue and sleep. He had to stop and rest. Finally, he found some comfort on a bed of pine needles hidden against a ridge.

Abruptly, the woods came alive with sounds, and Solomon was jarred awake by a tidal wave in his soul. He heard the faint sounds of dogs barking in the distance. They were tracking his scent. Solomon jumped to his feet and took off running. They were close. Panic hit him like the bullwhip from the overseer. He tripped over the carcass of a dead animal, stumbled, and hit the ground. But he quickly got back on his feet and ran like a panicked animal because his life depended on it.

The sound of the dogs barking was looming. Behind him, the darkness became illuminated by torches carried by slave catchers. Solomon knew he was in trouble and couldn't outrun the hounds. But he was going to try. His legs moved like an engine underneath him, with men on horseback thundering toward him. If surrounded by the slave catchers like a trapped stag, Solomon was willing to fight every last one of them to his death. He continued to push through the trees, coming into a large clearing.

Solomon paused for a moment. There was no hiding in the clearing, but he couldn't turn back. Then, in the distance, he heard the dogs barking. He had no choice and ran like the wind was underneath his feet. His goal was to make the clearing before they spotted him. But halfway through the clearing, the dogs spurted from the tree line and charged at him. Solomon quickened his pace, believing he could outrun these mutts, but to no avail. The dogs lunged at him from behind as they were trained to do, and soon, several slave catchers on horseback were charging his way to aid the dogs.

Solomon hollered and wildly fought off the dogs as they brought him to the ground. He kicked and screamed with teeth ripping into him. Foxx hurriedly dismounted his horse with a devil's gaze and moved toward Solomon, clutching a billy club. He wanted to lynch Solomon. But unfortunately, Mr. Walken wanted his nigger brought back alive.

"What have we here? A nigger that likes to beat white men," Foxx growled. "I'll teach you, nigger."

He stormed toward Solomon and struck him repeatedly with the billy club. Solomon tried to resist and fight back, but he was outnumbered, and with the dogs gnawing at his legs, he became immobile. Foxx and his men beat Solomon until there was nothing left to beat. When they were done, Solomon lay there bloody, nearly unconscious. Foxx removed his knife from its sheathing and crouched near Solomon. He placed the sharp blade against Solomon's face, yearning to cut out a piece of him. He wanted the nigger to scream like he was on fire.

"I should cut out yo' eyes, nigger, for what you did to Colemon," said Foxx.

Solomon couldn't move. The only thing he could do was wait for his fate, believing that he was a dead man.

"Lucky for you, Mr. Walken wants you alive and in one piece," Foxx uttered, disappointed. "Chain him up and put him in the wagon," he told his men.

They placed shackles, restraints, and an iron collar around Solomon's neck. He was thrown into the back of the wagon to be carried back into slavery. As Foxx mounted his horse, he glared at Solomon and uttered, "One day, you'll be all mine, nigger, and I'ma pick you apart piece by piece."

Foxx then spurred his horse and rode off with the wagon following behind him. Solomon sat in the back of the wagon, defeated but angry. He figured his fate was sealed. But his biggest worry was Irene. What would happen to her?

Chapter Eight

The full moon was shining down on the sprawling Ellison plantation as a cool, light wind was blowing, sending leaves dancing on the forest floor. The Ellison plantation in the Blue Ridge County of Georgia was a marvel of engineering with vast lands and copious crops. The big house was regarded as one of the finest examples of Greek Revival residential architecture in the United States. The white pillars stretched to the heavens, and the place looked more like a palace than a home. John Ellison was the patriarch of the plantation. He was married to Louise, and they had six children, four of them grown, and nearly five dozen enslaved people. He was wealthy, and the plantation was a machine with production and agriculture.

However, things were eerie quietly on the plantation. It was after 10:00 p.m., and activity inside the big house was still. The place was dark, and the enslaved people had settled into their quarters for the night.

Suddenly, a young, partially dressed white female came bursting from the front door to the big house, screaming in horror.

Barefoot, she ran toward the slave quarters beyond yonder with her face awash with tears and horror. Her name was Mary, one of the oldest daughters of John and Louise. She looked like she had seen the devil himself. She had been attacked but somehow could escape.

She reached the slave quarters, screaming and panicking, and began banging on the cabin doors, awakening everyone.

"Help me! Someone, please, help me. Help me!" Mary cried out.

Men, women, and children came out of their shabby homes to find Mary beside herself with grief and absolute fear. Then, finally, Brenda, one of the older ladies, cautiously approached Mary to aid her.

"What's wrong, Ms. Mary?" Brenda asked.

Mary started to scream. She was in shock. Something terrible had happened to her family. Her heart hammered in her chest as fear tormented her.

"Ms. Mary, please, calm down. We's want to help you," said Brenda.

"What happened, Ms. Mary?" a younger man asked, stepping closer.

Mary was so afraid that the slaves she'd known for years suddenly became a threat to her. First, her eyes widened as she started to sweat with fear, then she hollered, "Get away from me!"

"Ms. Mary, please. We just wanta help," Brenda said.

"No! No! You are all animals. You killed my family!" Mary shouted.

Anger soon stirred within her. She saw their black faces, all crowding around her, and instead of sympathy, she saw evil—a threat to her.

"Get away from me!" Mary screamed.

Brenda and everyone else knew this meant trouble for them. They did nothing wrong, but immediately, they were targeted. Mary desperately backed away slowly from them, repeatedly looking over her shoulders. She found herself surrounded by her slaves. Then she screamed again, "Get away from me!"

Mary spun around and dashed for the woods, disappearing from the plantation. Her fear boggled the enslaved people. They had no idea what had happened to her family. The big house was quite a way from the slave quarters. The enslaved people wondered what happened to Master Ellison and his family. They worried that repercussions could fall back on them.

After 2:00 a.m., several armed white men came thundering onto the Ellison plantation on horseback. Mary had made it to town, and she spilled horrors to the locals about her entire family being killed by a nigger. Everyone was up in arms, ready to implement revenge. News of another white family slaughtered made rage pulse through their veins. When they reached the big house, they smelled death in the air.

Thirteen men descended from their horses to approach the big house. They carried shotguns and pistols and uneasily walked toward the building. The floorboards creaked when they entered the residence. Other than a whisper of the wind, a deathly silence reigned. They traveled farther inside, cautious, with their attention rotating from room to room. Soon, they were shocked with dreadfulness. Their lanterns illuminated the dark space before them, and the thin light came across Ellison's oldest, Julius. He was sprawled across the floor in a pool of blood. Someone or something had ripped out his entire throat.

A man named Donald gasped at the sight. "What in the hell …"

They continued to move about the house only to find the mutilated bodies of the entire family. It was a massacre. The men froze suddenly, their eyes wide with sadness, followed by molten anger rolling through them when they saw the children's bodies.

"No one nigger did this," uttered a man named Conner.

Everyone agreed.

They were deducing that the enslaved people on the plantation were responsible for the Ellisons' demise—a revolt of some kind. So the men stormed from the big house with their anger spiked. They mounted their horses and hurried toward the slave quarters to demand answers or mete out justice by force and brutality.

Grasping their rifles and pistols, with revenge stamped inside of them like a heartbeat, the men began charging into the homes of the enslaved people with cruel intentions. Gunfire erupted, screams echoed, and the slaves were brutalized and beaten as the posse set fire to their cabins. Men, women, and children were being slaughtered. The Ellisons were good folks. The angry posse believed their deaths were going to be avenged like the hand of God slamming down on evil itself.

An enslaved man in his forties dropped to his knees in front of the posse. He was bleeding and scared. He clasped his hands together and begged, "Please, suh, we's had nothing to do with what Ms. Mary had told ya—"

Bang!

He was shot between the eyes, and his body dropped at their feet. They continued to hunt down everyone in the area, killing and maiming. Then, noticing a young girl fleeing the chaos, one of the posse members took off after her on horseback. The frightened girl hurried toward the barn across a clearing to escape and hide. She was in tears. Her pursuer, Billy, followed her and watched her enter the barn. He dismounted from his horse with the pistol in his hand and grinned. This was the opportunity to comfort himself with the young girl when he got his hold on her. *Might as well have me some fun tonight*, Billy thought as he neared the barn.

He slowly walked into the barn. It was windowless, two-story, dark, large, and quiet. But Billy knew the girl was hiding somewhere inside.

"Where are you?" Billy exclaimed. "There's nowhere to run."

He searched for her, listening closely for any sound from her. Then he heard the faint sound of the girl whimpering. Billy pivoted to his right, sneering, knowing she was close.

"I'll make it quick," said Billy mockingly.

He found her hiding behind a large log pile—a glimpse of a tormented face and tears in the dark. Billy grinned. "There you are, you Black wench."

The girl was so frightened she couldn't move, and she couldn't scream. Billy crowded her with his height and wicked gaze. She was pretty, so he unbuckled his pants as he moved closer to her. The girl quivered and cowered on her knees. There was no escape from him.

"You be still now, yuh hear?" said Billy.

Before he could attack her, he heard a sudden sound inside the barn. It startled Billy. He wasn't alone. He pivoted quickly with his grip tightening around the pistol.

"Who's there?" Billy hollered.

There was no response, nothing but darkness and silence. Billy scanned the area for signs of a threat. He moved away from the girl, poised with his pistol to kill any wandering nigger.

"It's best you show yourself now," he shouted.

He slowly examined his surroundings and immediately saw a face cloaked in shadows. Billy quickly raised the pistol at what he'd seen, but it disappeared. He heard another strange sound behind him and sharply pivoted in its direction, seeing nothing at all. Whatever it was, it moved fast. The hairs on Billy's skin stood up, and the noises scared him even further. He found himself suddenly going from pursuer to being pursued. Something was stalking him.

"I said show yourself right now!" Billy shouted, trying to sound more intimidating than afraid.

Something was hidden from Billy for the moment, but then Akasha loomed from the darkness. The sight of him was terrifying. He was tall and black with dark, soulless eyes, and his fangs glistened in the darkness. His presence shook Billy's spine and froze his heart.

"What are you?" Billy asked.

"Death," Akasha replied.

Billy quickly raised the pistol to kill him, but Akasha hurtled toward him with fearsome speed. Billy shot at the figure, only to gasp as the gun was torn from his hand and tossed away, lost in the darkness.

"Oh God!" Billy screamed.

Akasha ripped open Billy's face. Then Billy felt his shin bone snap into two. He dropped to the ground, hissing in pain and blinded by the darkness. He clutched his right leg. The leg was broken. Helpless and in deep distress, Billy tried to crawl away from the threat. He dragged himself toward the exit, crying in pain, but to no avail. He looked at the girl still cowering by the log pile. She was too scared to move. Her fear matched his.

"Help me," he cried out.

But it was too late for him. Billy's fate was sealed. Akasha attacked him again. Billy tried to hang on to something to keep from being dragged to his death. He fought like a banshee against this dark figure. Still, it was fruitless as he was quickly pulled away into obscurity, vanishing in the dark, screaming.

Hearing his scream, the young girl whimpered. She feared she might be next.

Once again, Akasha appeared from the darkness to stare at the girl. She was mute, paralyzed with terror, and shivering uncontrollably. He could smell her fear. The image of Akasha in his demonic form and sharp fangs was terrifying.

"Weakness and fear is the true curse," he told her.

The young girl remained cowering and crouching by the log pile as Akasha slowly approached her, her terror mounting with every step.

"I can make you whole and vengeful. I can make them fear you," he added.

"Please, I don't wanna die," she cried out.

"No. No death. No bondage. No more power to our enslavers," he proclaimed calmly.

Akasha towered over the frightened girl as her fear spiked. He crouched at eye level with her and stared at her intently. He inhaled her scent and then extended his hand to her as a sign of solidarity.

"Don't be afraid. Be excited," he said.

The frightened young girl locked eyes with Akasha. Suddenly, she went from fearing him to becoming enamored by him.

"You will now become their pursuer, *their* nightmare in the dark . . . unstoppable. What they've taken from you, you will slaughter them for it. You will become a force unlike anything they've ever seen," Akasha promised her.

She nodded and faintly smiled.

He continued to stare at the young girl and ready his fangs to prepare her for a different life consisting of vengeance and power. Then, finally, he quickly sank his teeth into the side of her neck. The girl twitched and shuddered from the violent penetration of her flesh, feeling her blood draining and her soul vanishing. At first, her eyes were wide from the attack, but then they gradually faded closed as she died.

Akasha walked toward the barn's exit. The moonlight was like a spectral-silver halo in the sky. From Akasha's view, he saw the slave quarters burning and heard the screams of many enslaved people being tortured or killed. It was a captivating scene.

Instead of intervening, his gaze remained deadpan. Finally, he turned to leave the area and ventured forward into the night—the fading sounds of many dying.

Chapter Nine

When Irene saw the wagon arriving with Foxx and his henchmen, she immediately knew they had found her husband. She looked heavenward with waterworks shimmering in her eyes. She squeezed her eyes shut as tears ran down her cheeks. Her nightmare had come true. Foxx rode proudly on his horse like a victorious general in the war. The wagon pulled behind him, moving toward the big house. Irene couldn't take her eyes away from the wagon. She was so afraid that a fellow slave girl took Irene's hand into hers and squeezed.

She whispered to Irene, "Be easy, Irene. Solomon is strong."

"They might kill him," said Irene.

Irene was powerless to help her husband. The only thing she could do was stand by and witness his fate.

The wagon stopped at the porch of the big house, and immediately, Mr. Walken and his wife came trotting out of the place. Mr. Walken hurried toward the wagon, eager to see the runaway. At the same time, his wife remained on the porch, looking eloquent in a visiting dress.

"This nigger didn't get too far, Mr. Walken. Caught him twenty miles west of here," said Foxx, climbing down from his horse.

Foxx's men removed a shackled Solomon from the back of the wagon and tossed him facedown onto the dirt. Mr. Walken stormed toward Solomon and glared down at him. He then kicked Solomon in his side with anger and frustration.

"Boy, I'ma put a hurting on you so bad, your mama going to cringe from the grave," said Mr. Walken.

Foxx and his men laughed.

"Everything you ever loved on this plantation is lost to you, you stubborn, ignorant nigger!" Mr. Walken continued. "Including Irene."

Knowing he was going to lose Irene hurt Solomon more than anything.

"I wanted them to find you first before I sold her off for you to watch," said Mr. Walken.

Solomon wanted to spring from the ground and kill his master, but the restraints kept him immobile. And he was too weak to move. The only thing he could do was cry out and clench his fists tightly against the dirt.

Mr. Walken looked at Foxx and uttered, "I want him punished now."

Foxx grinned, ready to oblige. "Will do, Mr. Walken . . . We'll teach this nigger."

They dragged Solomon away, with Irene watching in horror from a distance. She knew what they had planned for her husband for nearly beating a white man to death and then becoming a runaway would be sinister. But when Master Walken looked her way with a livid gaze that hooked onto her, Irene froze.

Irene and the other enslaved people were gathered in the courtyard, where Solomon was strapped to a wooden post, ready for the worst to come. It was centered in the middle of the square. A man named Samuel was now in charge of everything. He'd become the new overseer while Colemon was healing. And Samuel was determined to set a cruel example of Solomon. He paced behind Solomon, dragging a ten-foot bullwhip. Foxx stepped to Solomon and ripped off his shirt, then he said to him, "Don't die on me, nigger. I still want my piece of you."

He laughed and walked away while Solomon was prepped for a whipping. Solomon's eyes locked onto Irene's. She was in tears and afraid. But Solomon focused on his wife, trying to remain strong and calm for her. She was angelic and deserved so much better. Then suddenly, Solomon recognized three white men aiming toward Irene. He immediately knew what they were going to do. They grabbed her arm, but Irene pulled away from them and resisted.

"No! No!" she hollered.

"Don't make it worse for yourself," one of the men shouted.

"Get away!" Irene continued to shout and resist.

She knew what they were there for—to take her away from everything she'd known and loved. Irene looked her master's way for mercy or forgiveness. Instead, Mr. Walken stared back impassively. It was their punishment—separation.

"Masser, don't do this! Please!" Irene hollered.

Solomon pulled at his restraints, his eyes watered with anger and malice. He was desperate to free himself as he watched them attack Irene. It was happening. Their master had sold her to God knows where.

"You did this!" Mr. Walken exclaimed. "She's gone, Solomon, and I will make sure you'll *never* see her again."

Irene continued to resist, swinging at her attackers while the others watched on in shock and horror. Then, in a flash, another white man carrying a shotgun approached Irene and smashed the weapon's hilt into her face with a crack. She hit the ground, stunned, blood spilling.

Solomon smoldered with resentment as raw anger shot through him when he yelled, "Get away from her! No! Irene! Irene!"

They dragged Irene away toward the wagon, bruising her arm. And as Solomon watched the love of his life being carried away, Samuel struck him with the whip. But the pain of losing his wife was much worse than the crack of a whip.

Crack! Crack! Crack! Crack!

Solomon winced in pain while Irene was placed into the back of the wagon.

Crack! Crack! Crack! Crack!

Tears itched Solomon's cheek, and his chin trembled as he watched the wagon pull off from the property with the woman he loved fading from his view. Solomon started chewing on his lower lip as his eyes continued to well up with tears. Finally, he looked away, defeated.

Hours passed. The day had transitioned into the night, with the stars blanketing the sky. Solomon remained tied to the wooden post. He was alone, cold, and mutilated. His eyes were nearly lifeless and slowly drifting close. Solomon wanted to die. All he could think about was Irene. She was gone, and there wasn't anything he could do about it.

Solomon dreamed about her that night. They were in a sprawling, green field, holding hands and laughing. Irene was in a flowing white dress, and he was clad in a handsome white suit. They were together in happiness and harmony. The bright sun and heavenly blue skies above matched their joy. They owned farmland and had several beautiful children. Their children came running their way with the purest smiles. He was a father, and Irene was a mother. It was the life Solomon wanted for them, what he dreamed about. It was freedom, family, and togetherness. But then, everything started to change. The green field had altered into mud and dirt, the sky went black, and Irene began to sink into the ground. Solomon leaped to help her, but she sank quickly into the ground. It was becoming harder to hold onto her, and soon, she was gone . . . The ground had taken her. And Solomon was overcome with grief.

Morning came, and Solomon remained slumped against the wooden pole. He'd survived the night with infected puss bubbles protruding from his back. His face was gaunt, his body wracked with abuse . . . but his heart was devastated. Solomon squinted his eyes at two figures silhouetted against the sun. Samuel and another enslaved person arrived to find Solomon alive and fully alert. Samuel was taken aback. He leaned closer to Solomon and grinned.

"The nigger lives. You learned your lesson, boy?" asked Samuel.

Solomon's wild eyes shot up at Samuel. He remained silent, defiant still. Samuel's grin altered into a frown. He glared at Solomon and growled, "I asked you a question, boy."

"Oh, yes, suh. I've learned," uttered Solomon. But something was unnerving about his subservience.

Solomon lay facedown on a cot. His back was covered with streaming strips of cotton. A woman named Sally sat at his side, trying to nurse him back to health. The wounds were familiar to her, and she became a master at healing them. Then another woman named Beth arrived with a thin blade and a bottle of brown liquid. Sally slowly peeled back a cotton strip to reveal an infected wound. Then she took the blade and began cutting a shallow incision into the bubbled flesh.

"You harness something special, Solomon," said Sally. "You's a fighter. Don't let 'em break you. But God almighty, I know Irene will come back to you. She will. She's a fighter too, yuh hear me, child?"

Solomon remained quiet as Sally applied pressure to the wounds, sending blood and puss oozing from his flesh. The brown liquid steamed as she poured it across his injuries. Beth stood quietly, watching her mother work her magic to heal Solomon.

At that moment, Samuel appeared in the doorway, and both ladies acted as if they did not see him but grew nervous of his sudden presence. They dared not to look his way.

"Mr. Walken wants this nigger in the cotton field by week's end, yuh hear?" said Samuel. "You make sure he's healthy by then, Sally."

Sally nodded obediently. "Yes, suh."

Samuel glared at Solomon being treated and exclaimed, "You hear that, boy . . . ? Your privileges are gone. And I'm gon' ride you like hogs on slop."

Samuel then turned and left.

The horse-drawn wagon arrived at a small farmhouse in Franklin County, North Carolina, seventy-five miles from the Walken plantation. The wagon stopped in front of the main house on a modest piece of land. It wasn't a sprawling plantation with dozens of enslaved people tending to it, but only a dozen. It belonged to a man named Randall McHenry. His farm grew and harvested tobacco.

Randall emerged from the house, smiling. He was an overweight, heavy-bodied man with light hair, high cheekbones, and blue eyes. He stood a total of six feet tall and wasn't the most attractive man. His manners were repulsive and coarse, and he never enjoyed the advantages of an education.

Randall continued to smile as he descended from the porch and said to the wagon driver, "What yuh got for me?"

The wagon driver climbed from his horse, scrambled to the back of the wagon, and pulled back the flap to reveal Irene, who was chained. Randall lit up like daylight upon seeing her. "She's a pretty one; paid good money for her."

Randall reached for her, but Irene recoiled.

"It's all right, girl. Ya home now . . . in North Carolina," said Randall politely. "There's no need to fret or be afraid. I'ma take good care of you."

Irene stared at him with fire blazing in her eyes. She continued to recoil from him, becoming stubborn. Randall immediately showed he had no patience for her shrinking away and stubbornness.

"Come on out of that wagon now, yuh hear, girl? Before you make it worse for yourself," Randall warned.

But Irene continued to resist.

"She's stubborn as a damn mule," said the wagon driver.

"She's gon' need fixin' all right. And I'm fittin' to do that before day's end," Randall replied.

They both climbed onto the wagon and forcefully removed Irene from it. She fought by kicking and screaming, but she was quickly overpowered and backhanded by Randall. Irene fell facedown into the dirt with Randall crowding over her, frowning.

"I will not tolerate any defiance on my farm, nigger!" he exclaimed.

Irene whimpered from the ground. She was afraid to get back up and accept this new horror she was thrust into.

The few slaves that Randall had silently looked on, minding their business. Then Randall was joined by a man named Hawk with a German shepherd. Right away, the dog raced toward Irene, full tilt, barking. Irene scurried backward just as the dog lunged for her, his canines peeled. But Hawk yanked him back. The dog fought against the weight of a choke chain inches from Irene, who retreated, pinned against the wagon wheel. Hawk displayed a toothless grin, enjoying the moment. He was a man in his thirties with a wad of chew wedged between his rotten teeth. A bullwhip rested on one side of his hip, and a pistol stowed against his other.

"Once he gets a taste of nigger blood, he ain't gon' stop," said Hawk to Irene. "Best for you to do what Mr. Randall says and make it easy for ya'self."

Irene cowered against the wagon wheel. Randall smirked and uttered, "You ready to behave now, nigger? Either I get a piece of you, or good 'ol Tobias here will."

He referred to the dog.

Irene nodded reluctantly. Randall then called over one of his female slaves, Penny, a girl a few years older than Irene. She hurried his way with, "Yes, Mr. Randall."

"Penny, take our new guest here to the shack. Make her feel at home and get her ready for tonight," Randall instructed.

"Will do, Mr. Randall," said Penny.

Penny helped pull Irene to her feet and shepherded her to the shack nearby. The wooden hut was no bigger than where she came from with dirt floors. There was an old bed and a table. It was bleak and unpleasant. Irene looked around, but there wasn't much to inspect. Penny turned to leave, but Irene stopped her by asking, "What is he goin' to do with me?"

Penny turned to catch her eyes with Irene. She sighed and replied from her own experience, "Just close ya eyes and let him finish. That's the only advice I can give you."

With that, Penny left, closing the door behind her. Alone, Irene started to shed tears.

Hours passed, and night had fallen. Irene lay on her side on the bed when the door to the shack opened, and Randall entered with a bright gaze.

"Yuh definitely a pretty one," he said, marching closer to Irene, unfastening his pants. "It's gonna be real nice 'round here now. Yuh see."

Irene tensed up. Randall became naked from the waist down and joined her on the bed. Irene tried to resist. Randall ripped her dress, forcefully grabbed her by her forearms, and slammed her against the bed. Quickly, he was inside her, and Irene wailed and fidgeted underneath him.

"Stop ya fussin' now, girl, before I sick Tobias back on ya," Randall exclaimed.

Irene whimpered. "I'm a married woman."

Randall laughed at her comment. "Married? You's a nigger, and niggers ain't got no rights to be married. Here on my farm, you do what I say when I say . . . that includes fucking. You make nice, I make nice. Now, girl, I'm tryna be nice. You stop me again, and I won't continue to be nice."

He continued inside of her while Irene clenched her fists, tensed up, whimpering, her eyes constantly watering, and allowed him to finish.

Chapter Ten

It was a cool fall day, the beginning of October. The weather was gorgeous and bright but raw and bleak, with the wind rustling dry leaves and shedding leaves from deciduous trees. The fall air smelled crisp and cold on some days and damp and earthy on others, depending on the weather. The duration of daylight was becoming noticeably shorter. And the night was becoming unpleasant with vengeance and bloodshed.

The South was becoming a scary place, not just for the enslaved people but for the privileged white people and plantation owners. News of a violent and brutal slave rebellion spread throughout Georgia, South Carolina, North Carolina, and Virginia like a raging wildfire. In one month, five families have been brutally slaughtered during the night. Women, children, and men had their throats ripped open or were murdered so viciously that their bodies were unrecognizable. These attacks were creating violent backlash against the enslaved people, free Blacks, and even abolitionists. No one was safe. The South wanted justice for these murders, and they were determined to implement it by any means necessary.

In Jeffersonville County, Georgia, an army of armed militiamen and angry white men began roaming the countryside to end this believed slave revolt and lynch those responsible. Unfortunately, it was where the most recent attack happened. On the Van-Point plantation, twenty miles outside of Jeffersonville, eight people were killed, even an infant boy. Their niggers screamed for mercy, but their pleas for mercy fell on deaf ears. There would be no mercy until the culprits of this slave revolt were all found, tried, and lynched.

Men wearing flour sacks with holes cut out for eyes and mouths carried torches, rifles, and shotguns. They encroached on the slave quarters on horseback, burning for justice. It didn't matter how old these enslaved people were. These white men wanted every last nigger swinging from a rope or tied to a tree and burning slowly.

Four Black men sat beaten, stripped naked, and tied to a tree or stake. Their fates are sealed.

"Please, suh . . . We's innocent!" a slave named Monty cried out. "We's had nothin' to do with them killings. I swear to you, suh!"

A man named Rip dismounted from his horse and approached the enslaved people still alive. He was a beastly-looking man who stood six-one, was dark, and bearded. The dead were all around him and his knight riders. Black bodies were paraded across the ground, either shot, stabbed, or beaten to death. Some men and women were lynched right there, and a few Blacks were able to escape the horrors . . . for now . . . fleeing into the woods, terrified.

Rip crouched closer to Monty, scowling. His hatred for Monty was palpable . . . a savage beneath him with Christian blood on his hands. Rip spit his discarded chewed tobacco in Monty's face. Monty was terrified of him, trembling, his eyes wide with fear. He knew what this man and his cronies were capable of doing. The tied slaves too were scared.

"Listen here, nigger. I'm gonna ask you some questions, and it will behoove you to be truthful, you hear me, nigger?" Rip growled.

Monty nodded. *Yes.*

"Who's leading this slave revolt?" Rip asked him. "Give me a name."

"I's . . . I's don't know," Monty uttered.

"Don't lie to me, nigger."

"It's no lie, suh!"

"Lots of good white folks dead, children too," said Rip. "You can end this, boy. Just give me their names and location."

Rip slapped him several times.

"Tell us something, boy! Talk, nigger!" Rip shouted.

Monty's eyes watered as he frightfully stared at Rip. He couldn't tell him what he didn't know. The only thing Monty could do was plead for mercy with his eyes and tremble.

"Let's just end these niggers and be done with it, Rip," uttered Trevous. "We'll find these niggers eventually. Stop this horseplay."

Rip glanced at Trevous; the man was impatient. But Rip figured he was right. He stood up and glared at the four Black bodies either bound to a tree or tied to a stake. He huffed, and then he gave his men the order. "Burn 'em."

Trevous grinned. "Yes, sir!"

Trevous lit a match and didn't hesitate to set Monty and the others on fire. A mighty roar of absolute agony followed as the flames spiraled upward. Each man tried to flail from the fire, but they were attached to their grizzly fate. Rip and the others stood by silently, watching flesh becoming charred skin. The burning flesh replaced the smell of gunfire and tasted bitter on their tongues. And finally, their screams became muted.

"Niggers know how to burn fast, huh?" Trevous laughed.

Rip had seen enough. He mounted his horse again and said to the others, "Let's go. There are others out there that we need to find. This uprising will end soon."

Trevous and the other men nodded, agreeing. They climbed on their horses and rode away from the unrecognizable object of fused flesh and wood. Each one was scorched almost into a new state of existence by the searing heat.

Akasha's action had set off a massacre of up to one hundred Black people in the region. These incidents had put fear in the hearts of Southerners, resulting in harsher punishments and laws against enslaved people, deepening the schism between slaveholders and Free-Soilers. The violence unleashed on whites was so shocking that severe measures were put into place to protect plantations and families. It made it more difficult for enslaved workers to travel beyond their homes. Nearly every white man, woman, and child took up arms to protect their lives, homes, and property. Thirty Black people had been accused of participating in this rebellion equivalent to Nat Turner's over twenty years ago. They were executed while angry mobs or white militias were beating others.

The South was tearing itself apart with madness. Militia companies were riding to different counties, delivering supplies of arms and ammunition. Whatever was happening, it was happening like a spreading plague—fear, violence, revenge. No one was safe.

It was nearing dawn when enslaved people began pouring from the woods, running for the river toward the rapid waters. Over a dozen enslaved people, some carrying their children and meager belongings on their backs, started splashing through churning water toward the other side of the stream. They were scared and desperate, seeking safety and freedom.

Chasing behind them was Rip and his men on horseback. Seeing men on horseback hunting them, the enslaved people desperately tried to cross. Some would rather drown than go back into slavery or die at the hands of an angry mob.

Rip and his men climbed off their horses at the river's edge, clutching their rifles and Colt revolvers. They glared at men, women, and children wading through the churning waters, screaming and panicking.

"Niggers trying to swim," Trevous uttered, smirking.

"What do you want us to do?" another man asked Rip. "Go in after them?"

They weren't there to return enslaved people to their enslavers on the plantation. It wasn't that kind of party. He knew Mr. and Mrs. Van-Point personally, and for Rip, the Van-Points were a good, Christian family. And to see them brutally murdered, along with their children, he took it hard, personal. So, when he came across their mutilated bodies, the sight of the carnage nearly took the wind out of him.

Rip stared angrily at these people wading through the river. It didn't matter if they were part of an uprising or not. A message needed to be sent. And he was willing to send it.

"Open fire on them. Kill every last one of them niggers," Rip instructed his men.

Every last man standing by the river raised their rifles and Colt revolvers, and they took heated aim, obliging to Rip's demands. Multiple shots rang out, and the first to fall was a young woman and her child. Quickly, their bodies were washed away by the river. More rapidly fell to the gunfire. It didn't matter their age. Another woman slumped backward, shot in the back, and fell into the river. It wasn't justice. It was absolute murder; it was a public execution—an atrocity of unspeakable cruelty.

The river became a watery grave, and when the smoke finally cleared, eighteen people were killed. Only three survivors made it across the other side: a young boy, his sister, and a middle-aged male. They would continue to run, and Rip and his men would continue to hunt them down.

Chapter Eleven

I t was a cool evening, and Solomon staggered into his shack from an intense day of hard work. Sweat and dried blood crusted from his shirt to his back. He grimaced as he peeled off his shirt, revealing several lines of fresh stitches. He was exhausted. Overseer Samuel wanted to work Solomon to death. Solomon was no longer a blacksmith. He couldn't be trusted, especially with complex and sharpened tools. Therefore, Mr. Walken tossed him into the cotton fields for hours or had Solomon do hard labor throughout the plantation. Blisters filled Solomon's hands, and they ached.

Solomon rinsed his hands and face in a nearby pot of water. Suddenly, he stopped and frowned. He looked at the chair where Irene used to sit in the evenings with a needle and thread, stitching either a dress or pants for him. It had been weeks since she'd been sold off. Only God knows where. Then suddenly, Solomon started to swell with grief, and he became choked with tears. He missed his wife, and he wanted her back. The shack and the plantation became a nightmare without her.

Solomon fell to his knees, his fists clenched, and his tear-stained face became puffy. There was no way he was going to survive. He wanted to escape from the wave of sadness, but it was impossible. He never felt so alone or afraid in his life. The thought of Irene being raped, whipped, abused, and alone somewhere was terrifying. Solomon planned on escaping again, but it was too soon. With a simple twist lock, the solid leg irons around his feet prohibited him from going anywhere. It allowed walking but prevented running or kicking.

Sally and Beth did a tremendous job healing Solomon back to health in a short period after his whooping. He owed the mother and daughter his life.

Solomon remained on the floor in silence for a moment. The air felt stale inside the small cabin. He seethed in contradiction of the perpetual nightmare of captivity before him. Slavery was routinized and mind-numbing, a repetition of the same tasks or movements day in and day out. Not only did Master Walken want to break him physically, but he also wanted to break Solomon spiritually and destroy or alter his mind-set. Master Walken and Samuel's goals were to break the will of their enslaved. The enslavers believed they were gods. Therefore, they felt it was necessary to darken Solomon's moral and mental vision and, as far as possible, to crush his power of reason.

Solomon didn't want to remain mentally and emotionally locked up in the chains of slavery. He wanted God to transform him physically and spiritually. He didn't want to die a broken, enslaved, and lonely man. For so many, slavery was their normality. It had been ingrained into the fiber of their being since birth, with the enslaved seeing their own value through their master's eyes. No. Not for Solomon.

"I can't die here," Solomon uttered to himself.

He continued to think about Irene and knew he needed to continue fighting for her. Solomon angrily gripped the leg irons around his feet and wished he could break free from them. But instead, he clattered the chains and hollered. This went on for ten minutes until Solomon fell slumped on his side against the floor in tears and agony. His thoughts clouded with memories of his wife and, soon, her fate—their fate.

While Solomon lay on his side, nearly looking lifeless, the cabin door opened. Solomon didn't turn to see who it was entering. Instead, he began to hear his footsteps approaching, the sound of boots threading and stomping his way, and feeling the presence of evil.

"Turn around and look at me, boy," Samuel barked.

Solomon huffed. Instead, he would stare at where Irene used to sit, her beauty smiling at him, sewing and laughing. He didn't want to look away from her chair and break that memory of her.

"You hear me talkin' to you, boy?" Samuel shouted, then kicked Solomon in his back. "I said turn around now and look at me."

Solomon cringed. His wounds were still fresh and painful. Reluctantly, Solomon turned over to stare up at Samuel, towering over him. They locked eyes, with Solomon aching for revenge.

"I bet you want to know where she is. She's gone, nigger, and you will never see that wench again. And I wish I could see you stretched at the end of a rope, but Mr. Walken still sees some use in you," Samuel proclaimed.

Solomon remained on his back, glaring up at the overseer. Samuel placed the heel of his boot against Solomon's chest, applying pressure.

"You're one feisty nigger, but I'm going to change that. I'm going to break any fight inside of you like I do the dogs and horses on this property," Samuel uttered. "I'm goin' to remind you that you're nothing but property, nigger. Do you know what 'buck breaking' is, nigger? Of course, you don't. It's something mostly practiced in the Caribbeans, and I've wanted to carry it out here."

When he mentioned "buck breaking," Samuel started grinning like a kid on Christmas Day.

"I'm going to fuck you, nigger," Samuel continued. "I fancy strong bucks like yourself. I love seeing that fight diminished from a strong, aggressive buck when I'm inside of them like a woman bent over a tree stump, your buttocks propped up into the air. And I'm going to flog you first, so you'll be too weak to fight back. Too bad Irene won't be around to watch it, to see her husband raped with his pants down, humiliated."

Solomon couldn't fathom what Samuel was telling him. Rape?! He scowled up at Samuel, his fists clenched as he trembled with rage.

"Maybe I should start now," Samuel uttered, unbuttoning his pants.

Solomon saw the perversion in Samuel's eyes. Samuel looked at Solomon like Colemon did Irene that night—with lust and superiority. This wasn't what his life was supposed to be. Solomon couldn't accept harmful circumstances to himself as the natural order of things. The thought of being abused and raped infuriated him, and enough was enough. He would rather die than be subjugated to flogging and rape. And hopefully, after death, he would be reunited with Irene.

"You hear me nigger?" Samuel continued to taunt him. "I'm going to break you."

With Samuel's pants unbuttoned, Solomon's fury sprang to life. They took everything from him. And he knew once it began, there was no turning back. They, for sure, would kill him now. So, with rage nearly consuming him, Solomon, though chained by his ankles, managed to spring to his feet and attack Samuel, lunging forward and tackling him backward. The sudden attack had caught Samuel off guard. He collided with the floor, Solomon on top of him, punching him wildly.

"I'm gon' kill you!" Solomon screamed.

Samuel saw the rage in Solomon's face, and fear quickly devoured him. He desperately tried to fend off Solomon. He reached for the knife in its sheath while fighting off Solomon with his right arm. But Solomon smashed his elbow into the side of Samuel's skull. Then he banged Samuel's nose with his forehead, spewing blood from it. Samuel's vision went fuzzy, and his body went limp.

"I'm gon' kill you!" Solomon screamed again. "I hate you. I hate you!"

Solomon wrapped his strong hands around Samuel's throat while he huffed and puffed with animosity. Then he heard a voice inside his head, "*It is for freedom that Christ has set us free. Stand firm, then, and do not let yourselves be burdened again by a yoke of slavery . . .*"

Solomon knew he would rather die than remain a slave.

"No! No! Please!" Samuel began begging for his life, knowing he couldn't defeat Solomon physically.

But Solomon was determined to take this man's life, and there would be no one around to stop him as Irene did with Colemon. Every pain, hatred, and loss that Solomon experienced surged through his hands, and he squeezed firmly around Samuel's neck. Samuel clawed at his fingers and tried to pry Solomon's hands away, but Solomon's grip was too strong to wiggle out of. Finally, Samuel's hands started grasping at Solomon's throat. He was slowly losing consciousness. His face began to turn into a sickening color as he gasped for air. Then Solomon took the man's life with one final motion, snapping his neck.

Samuel's body lay dead, and Solomon tried to catch his breath. Now, there was a dead overseer inside his shack. It was time for him to flee. But he had one problem. He couldn't run with the leg irons. Solomon desperately searched Samuel's body for the key to the chains, and fortunately for him, they were on him. Quickly, he fumbled with the lock, and the chains became unlocked. Solomon stood, finally unshackled.

Cautiously, Solomon emerged from his cabin and looked around. He was expecting more trouble to come his way, but there wasn't any. Samuel had come alone. Solomon looked back inside the cabin again, glaring at the dead white man on the floor. His eyes went from death to the spherical light in the sky. It was a full moon, a sign to him.

"Solomon." Someone called out his name.

Solomon turned to see Marcus coming his way. For some reason, an uneasiness grew between them. Marcus glanced down at Solomon's feet and noticed the absence of his leg irons.

"You causing more trouble for ya'self, Solomon?" Marcus asked him.

Solomon remained quiet, frowning. Marcus then peered into the cabin and saw Samuel's body. A fear cultivated on Marcus's face. He uttered, "Boy, what have you done?"

"What needed to be done," Solomon replied.

"They gon' for sure kill you now, Solomon."

"Let 'em come," Solomon growled. "They took everything from me."

Marcus saw something unfamiliar in Solomon's eyes, something terrifying to a humble and passive man like himself. He saw resistance and a purpose. Marcus was a man nearing his sixties. He never knew the feeling of fighting back or dying for the love of something . . . freedom, a spouse, human rights, rather than living in captivity. Marcus remained mentally and emotionally locked up in the chains of slavery. But Solomon had had enough. He had enough of being told what to think, what to do, how to act, how to dress, how to perceive himself and his place in the world.

Marcus grinned oddly at Solomon. "I wish I had your fight and courage, Solomon. I'm becomin' an old man who will one day die on this plantation, but you, you's finally free. Go. Run!"

Solomon nodded, pivoted and took off running into the woods. Marcus continued to grin, exhaled, and prayed, "Lord, please protect that boy, for he's a warrior, not a slave."

Chapter Twelve

ornwell Walken poured himself, John Meyers, and General Mathews each a shot of whisky, then sat by his desk and tossed back the drink. It was a quiet fall night, and all was still on the farm. The three men sat in Cornwell's den, where they could converse privately. News of a slave revolt and a farmer's family brutally killed fifty miles in Georgia had reached them. Cornwell and John sat across from the general in cushy-armed chairs with concerns on their faces.

"Believe me, gentlemen, there's nothing to worry about," General Mathews stated. "These are just a few savage niggers not knowing their place in society. Like a sickness, this too will be suppressed."

"I'm having a hard enough time already on my farm, General. My takings are down because of caterpillars dining on my cotton throughout the harvest and nearly destroying all my crops. My field was nearly ruined. So now, the last thing I need is for this nigger revolt to become a problem for me and create difficulty with my niggers," John Myers griped.

Cornwell nodded in agreement.

"It won't," the general replied.

"And how can you be so sure, General?" Cornwell asked him. "These killings of white men and their families have been happening for over a month. It's moving north, and yet, the culprits haven't been identified or found."

The general removed himself from his chair and walked to where Cornwell kept his whisky. He poured himself another glass. Then he turned around with a self-righteous look and replied, "You know both horse and nigger are no good to the economy in the wild or natural state. Both must be broken and tied together for orderly production."

Cornwell and John glanced at each other, wondering where the general was going with his statement.

"Pardon me, General," Cornwell uttered. "Do you care to elaborate?"

The general smiled as he knew about a secret that no one else did. Then he proclaimed, "A nigger uprising is as common as bees to honey. Even a loyal dog will eventually snap at its master to test him. And it's our job to place these niggers back into the place where they belong and dimmish the light of any troubled niggers."

"My God, are you drunk, General?" John asked.

The general laughed. "Far from it. I'm inspired. Psychological and physical containment must be implemented on our farms, gentlemen. These few bad apples roaming the countryside causing an uproar will be contained, niggers will be lynched, and our quality of life will continue. It is God's will."

The general downed his whisky. Then he grinned and added, "But I must say, this talk of niggers and uprising has made me quite excited. And I do feel the need of some nigger company. Where is my sweet Cherry tonight, Cornwell?"

Before Cornwell could answer the general, there was an urgent knock at the door.

"Cornwell, open this door. I need to see you right away," Cynthia announced from the other side.

Cornwell stood from his chair to answer the door. Cynthia entered the room, and immediately, both men stood to greet the lady of the house with respect.

"Ma'am," they uttered respectfully.

Cynthia looked at her husband with uneasiness. Their house nigger, George, stood at the threshold of the room docilely, waiting for Ms. Cynthia's instructions.

"What is it, Cynthia?" Cornwell asked his wife.

Cynthia looked at George and demanded, "Tell him, George."

George took a few steps inside the den and nervously glanced at Mr. Walken. He carried some news that he was too afraid to share.

"Tell him, George, right now," Cynthia said.

"There's a problem, suh, down at the slave quarters," said George.

John and the general were listening intently.

"For God's sake, come out with it, George. I don't have all night," Mr. Walken exclaimed impatiently.

"It's Solomon, suh. He done run off again."

Cornwell was shocked. "How? He was chained by the ankles!"

"There's another problem, suh," George added.

"What now?"

"It's overseer, Samuel . . ."

Cornwell, John, and the general stared at Samuel's body on the floor, the leg irons next to him. Cornwell Walken was beside himself with anger.

"How did this happen? How did he get away?" Mr. Walken exclaimed.

"Seems like you have more urgent matters to deal with, Cornwell," the general said. "This the second time this nigger done ran off. I must say, are you losing control over your farm?"

Cornwell frowned. He felt not only embarrassed but also belittled by his peers. First, Colemon had been badly beaten. Now, Samuel had been murdered. Solomon had become a threat to his dignity and livelihood.

"I want him found! You hear me?!" Cornwell shouted.

"And then what, Cornwell? This nigger, Solomon, apparently he's like a rabid dog that needs to be put down. If not, then he'll infect your other niggers. Then you'll have the origin of an uprising here on your farm. And soon, they'll kill you and your family in your sleep," the general stated, antagonizing the incident.

Cornwell knew the general was right. He had to cut out the damaged root. Solomon was becoming more of a threat than a benefit. He marched out of the cabin, knowing something needed doing right away.

"It's time to tighten the reins on your niggers," John Meyers said to Cornwell.

Slaves were quietly peeking out of their cabins. With word spreading from the South of an uprising and now a dead overseer and an escaped slave, Cornwell couldn't control his anger. He glared at George and another enslaved person named Julius and shouted, "I want every nigger out of their homes now! *Now*, George!"

"Yes, suh!" George replied, and then he hot-footed to execute the master's wishes.

George and Julius knocked on every cabin door, ordering everyone out of their homes. Cornwell, the general, and John Meyers stood in the center of the slave quarters, watching the procedure like gods from above.

"I'm intrigued to see what penance you're going to implement on your niggers," the general stated.

Cornwell didn't respond to him. He was too upset. The men watched as every enslaved person came pouring out of their cabins and hurtled like they were cattle into the center of the slave quarters. The enslaved people stood grouped outside their homes with their heads lowered, each man, woman, and child docile and scared.

. Cornwell glared at what he considered his property and yelled, "Who knew about this?"

No one answered.

"Someone better say something to me now! A man is dead, and one of my niggers has escaped again. I will not tolerate this imprudent behavior on my farm! I want answers!" Mr. Walken shouted.

He stepped intimidatingly before the group of slaves. They continued to keep their heads down and avert their eyes from their master. Mr. Walken angrily grabbed a woman from the group. He shoved her into the dirt. Then he forcefully grabbed a young boy, slapped him repeatedly, and pushed him into the dirt alongside the woman.

"I will severely punish every last one of you," he yelled.

Mr. Walken angrily clutched another enslaved person. He was an older man in his forties. He began assaulting the man with a stick until blood and bruises covered his face. The man howled in pain, but Mr. Walken became unhinged with anger and irritation.

He then looked at everyone else and shouted, "I will not allow any other problems on my farm. This ends tonight."

An hour later, every man, woman, and child was butt naked, standing in neat rows in the fields. Mr. Walken made them lift heavy logs over their heads; if one group dropped that log, they would all be flogged. He needed to teach them that if one man escaped, he would punish them all for that man's sins against the plantation. While Mr. Walken watched them being punished, several men on horseback came galloping onto the farm. It was Foxx and his men.

Through his gritted teeth, Foxx said to Mr. Walken, "This nigger kills a white man and escapes again. He's an abomination that needs to be put down, Mr. Walken."

Mr. Walken nodded, agreeing. "You find him, and you do what needs doing, but I want him to suffer first."

Foxx grinned. Finally. "Oh, he'll suffer all right. We'll see to that."

Foxx then turned his horse around, and he and his men galloped off the farm to hunt for Solomon with sadistic pleasure.

Chapter Thirteen

The darkness of the woods pressed in on Solomon from all sides. His body screamed for him to keep running. The trees seemed to close in on him, choking out the moonlight. Solomon began to breathe the cool air more rapidly. Everything from the twigs, the black and brown thorns, to the roots wrapped around the woods, almost like teeth, waited to tear him apart. It felt like unseen creatures moved branches, even trees. In the distance, he heard the dogs barking. Solomon's heart hammered in his chest as he sweated with panic, adrenaline coursing through his veins.

Solomon felt his entire body working, his leg muscles running warm. He pushed harder and faster away from hell on earth. But thrusting forward, his legs soon became tired. He had no idea how long he'd been running, but it felt like forever. It was still dark, and Solomon had no idea where he was. The faint sound of dogs meant men on horseback weren't too far behind them, racing his way. He was determined not to be captured so quickly, even if he had to die fighting. Solomon wasn't going back. He remembered his last harrowing experience with the dogs. He picked up a large wooden stick this time, and when the dogs came sprinting at him, he wildly swung the stick at them, fighting back. He became just as vicious as the canines. It was life or death, but as he fought off the dogs, he saw Foxx and his men approaching, and absolute terror devoured him. Solomon knew this time they would kill him, maybe torture him first. When he locked eyes with Foxx, the sneering look on the man's pale face was diabolical.

"It's time for me to start skinning away pieces of you, boy!" Foxx exclaimed, galloping toward Solomon. "And I'm going to take my sweet time doing it."

Solomon screamed. The dogs were still attacking, and he continued to fight them off with the large stick gripped in his hand. Foxx's men aimed their rifles at Solomon, but Foxx didn't want to kill him right away.

"No!" Foxx shouted. "I want this nigger alive for now."

He wanted the gratification of seeing Solomon suffer. The dogs were temporarily called off. Solomon was trapped. There was nowhere for him to go. Foxx climbed off his horse and cautiously approached him.

"Now, Solomon, there's nowhere for you to run. You're surrounded, boy. Drop the stick, nigger!" Foxx demanded, scowling.

"I'll kill you all!" Solomon shouted madly.

Foxx chuckled. "Oh, you've killed enough white men, nigger. And today, you're going to pay for it. I assure you, boy, you *will* pay."

Solomon was outnumbered five to one. They had guns; he had a simple stick. Yet, the ferocity in Solomon's eyes had them worried. He was a man with nothing to lose. They ominously surrounded Solomon with their weapons and cruel intentions. Solomon gripped the stick so tightly that splinters dug into his fingertips, drawing blood. He swung their way wildly but connected with nothing but air as he heatedly looked at five threatening faces, his attention on a ceaseless swivel. The dogs continued to snarl and bark, ready for the attack order. Solomon's breathing became ragged; he was tired—but fuck it. He was prepared to die. However, he wanted to kill as many of them as possible before they killed him.

"Nigger, you're only making it worse for yourself," Foxx shouted.

Solomon and Foxx glared at each other with mutual hatred. For Solomon, it became unbearable when they took away Irene. Foxx grew impatient toying with him, so he ordered, "Take this nigger down!"

William, one of Foxx's men, charged toward Solomon, but he was violently met with a mighty blow to the face, and he went down. While Solomon was distracted, another man named Grant attacked him from behind. He slammed the hilt of his rifle into Solomon's head and knocked him out cold.

Solomon opened his eyes slowly. It was still dark, and he found himself tightly tied to a tree. He couldn't move. A campfire was burning nearby. Foxx and his men had taken refuge in the woods until dawn. They were cooking, keeping warm, and talking by the campfire, unaware Solomon had become conscious again. Solomon struggled to move, but he felt like a root underneath the tree. He wondered why they hadn't killed him yet. What were they going to do with him?

Foxx noticed Solomon was conscious; he grinned. "The nigger is awake."

He made his way over to Solomon, crouched close to him with a taunting gaze, and uttered, "Look at you, nigger! Bet you are wondering why we haven't lynched yo' black ass to a tree yet. But you see, that be too easy to do. What you did to Samuel, you see, he was rather a beloved figure 'round here, and you off and murdered him. There's a mob of white men ready to rip you apart, boy."

Foxx removed a bowie knife from its sheath, and he placed the tip of the blade near Solomon's genitals. Solomon squirmed and frowned.

"Yeah, I could cut away your boy parts bit by bit; make it hurt really bad," Foxx expressed. "Now, when it comes to making a nigger regret the error of his ways, believe me when I tell you, I know every goddamn trick in the book. And I gotta ax to grind with you, boy."

Foxx pressed the razor-sharp blade harder against Solomon's nut sack. Solomon cringed; he was helpless. He glared at Foxx with absolute hatred, and Foxx returned the disgusted gaze.

"How's that blade of the bowie feel against you nut sack, nigger? I can cut it off cleanly with one stroke without breaking a sweat. You know what happens to a nigger when their nuts are cut off? The blood never stops. Seen it happen plenty of times," Foxx scoffed. "Yep, nigger, I do wanna snip yo' nuts. But I wanna get creative with you first."

Foxx stood up and turned to his men near the campfire. Then he shouted, "What you think we need to do with this nigger, fellows? He's a handful."

"Just give him to the dogs. They'll make do with him," Williams hollered.

Foxx grinned at the idea. A man named Joseph shouted, "Just let the nigger hang from a tree, Foxx. No time to toy with ideas."

"Nah, Samuel and Colemon were friends of mines. I want this nigger to suffer," Foxx replied.

"Well, whatever ya decide to do, hurry it up. I need to go and drain the swamp," said Grant.

While Foxx and the others discussed different ideas on torturing and killing Solomon, Grant wandered away from the campfire to a secluded area to pee. He took a position against a tree, unbuttoned his trousers, and started to release himself. He needed to do this badly. While peeing, the sudden rustling of leaves behind him startled him. Grant quickly pivoted toward the rustling to see nothing but woods and darkness.

"Who's there?" he hollered.

Of course, there wasn't a response. Grant figured it was probably an animal rushing by. So, he went on to finish his business. But soon after, the rustling of leaves continued from a different direction. And it seemed closer. Grant pivoted abruptly, removing the Colt revolver from its holster and aiming it at the sound.

"I said, who's there?" Grant shouted.

He had wandered far off from his men, but he could still see the brightness of the campfire in the dark. Maybe it was nothing, but his nerves were getting the best of him. He heard about the nigger uprising happening in Georgia counties. But that was happening nearly a hundred miles away. Grant felt a sudden gust of wind followed by the loud rustling of leaves and the pitter-patter of something moving fast. Something was out there. He outstretched his arm with the revolver at the end, ready to shoot whatever came his way. A man's silhouette quickly moved past him. Grant spun and fired at it.

Boom!

Whatever it was, he missed. Instead, the gunfire caught the attention of the others.

"Grant! What's going on out there?" Foxx hollered.

But Grant was too occupied with jitteriness to respond. So, instead, he wheeled back and forth. It felt like some entity surrounded him that he couldn't directly see. And this wasn't just any creature. It was *stalking* him. Then he saw a man—a nigger—nearby. He was shirtless, muscular, and demonic. Grant couldn't comprehend what he was looking at, but his face was filled with fear. This man was feral with weird eyes, like mesmerizing black orbs, and he had fangs and sharp claws for fingernails.

Grant fired another shot at this being as it ran at him full speed. There was no stopping it, and it viciously attacked him.

Foxx and the others heard Grant's screams. They hurried to where he was, but he was gone. There was nothing left of him besides his hat.

"Where did he go?" William exclaimed.

Each man had their weapons drawn, rifles, and pistols. Something terrible had happened to their friend. They knew it. They inspected the area where Grant once stood and found blood on the leaves.

"What is this?" Joseph uttered, looking closer. "Is this blood?"

Before anyone could respond, something hit the tree nearby fast with a loud thump and fell to the ground. It sounded like a bird flying blindly into something. All four men swung in the same direction, and shots went off, but nothing was there. Foxx was the first to vigilantly move toward whatever it was that hit the tree like a bullet. When he finally got a good look at it, he gasped in horror.

"What is it, Foxx?" Laundry asked.

Foxx was speechless. Grant's severed hand was lying on the ground. His Colt revolver was still attached to it.

"What is this shit?!" William cried out.

The heebie-jeebies hit them like lightning striking.

"What kind of animal would do this?" asked Joseph, shocked.

The men then heard leaves crunching underneath someone's foot. Next, something darted past them, and it seemed to vanish quickly. Then the sound all but disappeared. Nevertheless, there was a disturbing odor about.

"I don't like this. Let's get out of here," Laundry said.

Then, right away, it happened in a flash. Something snatched Laundry with frightening speed and dragged him into the night. He screamed. Foxx and the others tried to chase after it, desperate to help their friend while wildly firing shots to stop it, whatever "it" was. But he too was gone. Now, only three men were left, and full-blown panic started to set in. Whatever it was, it was unnatural.

"No! This isn't happening!" Foxx yelled. "Come out now and face me like a man!"

"Do you *really* want that?" a voice roared from the dark.

Foxx and his men tried to see where it came from but couldn't pinpoint the location. Foxx tried to remain calm and firm, but the other two men were terrified and had panic written all over them.

"Whatever you are, I'm not afraid of you," Foxx proclaimed heatedly with his gun raised.

Akasha was no longer in hiding. He appeared with his dark silhouette gradually materializing before the men, with the leaves crunching underneath his bare feet. His face was covered with white men's gore. He patiently stood under the moonlight, allowing the men left alive to get a full glimpse of him. His fangs were on display with his claws drawn, wet with crimson. He was no nigger like they've seen before. He was terrifying.

"What kind of nigger are you?" Foxx growled.

"I was once a man, but now, I just want my vengeance," Akasha proclaimed.

Joseph and William didn't hesitate to open fire, but Akasha's skin was like armor. With a snarling roar, he lunged at them with his claws drawn, fangs extended, and angrily crashed into both men. They were no match for him as his claws slammed into their jaws. Then his fangs plunged into their flesh with a loud, bone-crunching sound. Blood spewed everywhere. The men's screams were filled with agony.

Helplessly, Foxx witnessed this horror wide-eyed, knowing his demise was near. Instead of fighting this creature, he took off running for his horse. Solomon, who remained tied to the tree, observed the horror on Foxx's face as he leaped onto his horse to ride off. Solomon had heard the white men's screams, and he became scared himself.

Foxx rode his horse with intensity. When he glanced behind him, it looked like the devil himself was chasing him. Akasha moved with a speed that matched the galloping horse. Foxx leaned forward with his body slightly raised from the saddle. He used the pressure of his legs to urge his horse to move through the woods like lightning. He held the reins in both hands in the bridge configuration.

Akasha was coming for him, and Foxx moved with his horse because his life depended on it. He maneuvered through the trees proficiently, riding as if Beelzebub were on the horse's heels. When he looked back again, it appeared he'd absconded from the threat. Foxx breathed a sigh of relief and continued to ride frantically for help. But suddenly, he was struck by a blurred figure that came out of nowhere and knocked him off his horse. Foxx tumbled to the ground. Whatever hit him created immense pain. He stumbled to his feet and desperately reached for his gun, but to his horror, it wasn't in its holster. Immediately, Foxx shrank at the sight of Akasha in his demonic form. Defenseless, he tried to run but couldn't outrun this being. Akasha's claws ripped into his back, tearing his flesh apart like it were paper-thin. Foxx collapsed in pain and terror against the dirt.

"Please! Please! Don't kill me!" Foxx begged.

Akasha looked fiercely down at a man who believed he was superior to Blacks and had done unthinkable horrors to enslaved men and women.

"You dare to beg me for mercy when you see my kind as inferior. And your kind keeps us in bondage with fear and cruelty," Akasha growled.

His appearance was contorted into a demonic form. His eyes were black and soulless. His skin was so black it rivaled the night and stretched tightly across his physique. Akasha's sharp fangs that could tear anything apart were hanging half an inch from the skin. He could rip off Foxx's entire arm directly with a powerful bite. And his breath reeked of decay and blood.

Foxx cowered in the dirt. He once took pride in implementing brutality and mercilessness while hunting runaway slaves. Now, he was on the other end of the spectrum, scared and begging for mercy when he never offered leniency to the enslaved.

"I'll give you whatever you want—money?" Foxx beseeched.

"I don't want your money," Akasha snarled.

"What do you want then?"

"Your life!" Akasha uttered.

There was no bargaining with him. Foxx would soon become his prey. Knowing that he couldn't bargain with this creature, Foxx attempted to run. But the sharpness of Akasha's nails ripped into his flesh from behind. Foxx's neck, face, and arms all received the wrath of his vicious attack. Akasha heatedly clawed and dug into him as Foxx painfully tried to pry himself away. His screams seemed to go on forever. Then Akasha tore out his vocal cords as his sharp nails drew blood. He violently fed while ripping the man apart, and when he finished, there was nothing but a heap of crumpled and knotted flesh at his feet.

Chapter Fourteen

Solomon heard the bone-chilling screams of a man being brutally killed. It was accompanied by a feeling of dread that penetrated him like a cold chill. He knew it was Foxx. He felt no sympathy for the man. However, he feared he might be next. Solomon remained tied to the tree. His ragged breath moved in and out of his mouth at regular, gasping intervals. He struggled with his restraints, yearning to jerk himself free and continue to run. But he was still a root to the environment. It was dark and cold, and this area of the woods felt like a very frightening place.

Solomon could smell the trees in the chilly air around him. He could also hear the silence. The screaming had stopped, and now it was quiet, maybe *too* quiet. Whatever killed Foxx was probably coming back his way now, and Solomon braced himself for whatever was to come. If it was his fate to die, then so be it.

He knew there was danger lurking in the dark shadows of the foliage, a powerful entity that killed five armed white men with a single blow. His mother used to speak of deities when he was young . . . supernatural beings considered divine or sacred.

She used to believe that specific deities were upset with Africans accepting Christianity in America. Africans had their own form of worship and religion before the Europeans discovered the continent and felt it necessary to introduce Christianity, through which they claimed to show Africans the "one true God."

Therefore, certain deities were angry and vengeful about this and cursed those who accepted this Christian belief. So Solomon lowered his head into his chest and closed his eyes. If he were going to die, he would die thinking about Irene. Suddenly, with his eyes closed, he heard the crunching of leaves and earth underneath someone's feet. It sounded thunderous to Solomon. Whatever it was, it moved closer to him while he remained paralyzed. This menacing aura held him in a tightened grip. Solomon could sense its presence directly in front of him. His heart pounded in his ears. But he fought this fear by thinking about his wife and how much he loved her. Solomon sat there calmly, awaiting his fate like everyone else, with his eyes closed.

"Look at me," a voice spoke to him.

Solomon opened his eyes to see Akasha standing before him. Solomon was surprised. He didn't see a monster, but a man, a Black man. Akasha was no longer in his demonic form, but his presence was still frightening. His face and hands were coated with blood, and his eyes remained soulless. Nevertheless, Solomon remained watchful and quiet. He was in chains while Akasha stood free and threatening. Finally, Solomon looked up at him and held his stare, becoming undaunted.

"I can smell your blood, feel your beating heart, and the sense that you're ready to die tonight. But not out of fear, but for something else . . ." Akasha said.

"Who are you?" Solomon asked. "Are you death?"

"I can be. But I also can be your salvation," Akasha replied wholeheartedly. "I can sense anger and longing for revenge with you. They took something special away from you."

Solomon didn't respond.

"Do you want it back? They believe you and I are inferior and subhuman," Akasha continued. "And that they're justified in killing, abusing, and enslaving us because they believe we're lesser than them. I watched you try to fight them off. It was impressive. You're a warrior at heart."

Akasha moved closer to him with inquiry.

"Do you like being in chains and enslaved by them . . . excluded from society?" asked Akasha.

Solomon continued to hold his soulless stare. Akasha's eyes were dead, without expression, and the strong smell of death was upon him.

"They've taken something special from me too, something I can't get back," said Akasha.

Akasha then crouched closer and cocked his head to the side to study Solomon with a hungry glint in his eyes.

"Could you become a companion of death and walk with me through the world, through the dark?" Akasha asked him. "I can teach you all I know. And you can achieve what you fully desire . . . revenge. I can turn you into a god, and together, we can destroy this wretched country that sees us as unequal and tortures us with enslavement and rape."

"How?" Solomon asked.

"Through death," Akasha said with conviction. "Death isn't the end; it will be the beginning of life as you know it. They won't be able to stop you—stop us."

Hearing about death was daunting. Akasha moved closely to Solomon and reached for the iron restraints that kept him fused to the tree. He broke the iron collar around Solomon's neck and effortlessly released him from his chains. It was like snapping a twig. Solomon was amazed by his strength. He was free.

Akasha awaited his answer to a life of limitlessness, power, and revenge.

"And if I says no?" Solomon said.

Akasha's reaction didn't change. He stared at Solomon expressionlessly and replied, "Then you'll die. Not by my hands but by those who continue to enslave you and your kind. Those who feel entitled to trample our humanity, rip us from our countries and families, and seed our women with their offspring. But I can promise you there'll be no more pain, suffering, or fear. I can give you the power to prevent annihilation. I can give you the power to have them fear *you* absolutely."

Solomon had been enslaved since the day he was born. Now, this man was promising him a life he couldn't imagine, something godlike. He only wanted to run away with Irene, head north to freedom, and live a life of comfort and peace. Solomon thought about all the horrors bestowed against him by white men. He remembered when he was ten years old, and his master used to rape his mother right in front of him. He remembered the whippings, the torture, the brutal overseers, the exhausting hard labor from sunup to sundown, and the constant fear of losing Irene. Slavery was hell on earth, and Solomon wondered if there was a god, then why did His people have to suffer?

"I's just want to be free and find Irene," Solomon said.

"And they won't be able to stop you," Akasha assured him.

Solomon knew he had to decide and trust what this man, or this being, was telling him. For him to live fully, he would have to die. He nodded, wanting everything that Akasha had promised him. It was the only time Akasha grinned, but it was slightly deceptive.

"Don't be afraid, for everything shall end in your favor," Akasha added.

Akasha's breath was hot against Solomon's neck, making him writhe in discomfort. Then, Akasha opened his mouth to reveal his sharp fangs. Solomon gasped as Akasha gripped his hair and pulled his head back, exposing his neck. Soon, that discomfort was replaced by the sharpness of Akasha's fangs burying themselves into Solomon's veins, draining his life. The shock of unbearable pain in his neck sent Solomon into shock. It felt like fire was streaming through him. The burning that filled him became warm and numbing, with an intense heat forming in the pit of his stomach. Solomon's surroundings became blurry . . . and then everything went black.

The darkness felt heavy, oppressive, and almost supernatural. Solomon tried to open his eyes and failed before realizing they were open. There was no sun, no moon, and no stars. It felt like someone had shut everything off, and he'd been swallowed up by nothingness and could not see his two hands in front of his face. The absolute absence of light deprived him of his senses. *Where am I?* he thought. Then Solomon realized he had been buried alive. He tried not to panic. Suddenly, he understood the essence of darkness. It was a breathing terror delighting itself at devouring every last particle of brightness. And he found full strength to dig himself from whatever grave he was buried in.

Solomon emerged from the ground and found himself in an unfamiliar atmosphere. It was still night but quiet. Covered in remnants of dirt, Solomon looked around to deduce that he was in a barn somewhere on farmland. It was empty, spacious, windowless, and dilapidated. There was no livestock. It was filled with the smell of rotting, musty hay. A chill ran through the cracks in the barn, rustling the hay and kicking up dust. Surprisingly, Solomon wasn't cold. He was something new.

He had become reborn to the undead. A wave of awkwardness hit Solomon quickly. His physical state was altered entirely. His muscles, bones, organs, blood, everything had changed with his awakening. He started to hear and see things with precision, and there was a sudden increase in strength.

"You must feed, or you'll die," Akasha stated.

Solomon pivoted quickly to find Akasha sitting in the corner of the barn. His darkened silhouette became brightened by Solomon's new abilities. It was as if he were seeing Akasha in the day. It freaked him out.

"What am I?" Solomon asked nervously.

"You are their worst nightmare coming true," Akasha replied. "Now, you must feed off me soon or die."

Akasha bit his wrist, drawing blood. He then presented it to Solomon to feed.

"Drink," he uttered.

Solomon stared at the bleeding wound apprehensively.

"You must willingly drink the mixed blood to become a real vampire, or else, the thirst will destroy you," Akasha added.

Solomon stepped closer to him, gawking at the blood. He could feel his thirst increasing along with his heavy breathing intensifying. He had never before felt anything like it, the urge to consume blood.

"Do it now!" Akasha ordered him.

Solomon relented and grabbed Akasha's wrist with necessity, and he began to drink. What he tasted was indescribably sweet, like heavenly nectar beyond anything a human could comprehend. He growled while he fed, and then, Akasha pulled the bleeding wound from Solomon's fangs, exclaiming, "Enough!"

But Solomon wanted more, and Akasha was pleased.

"Their blood is much tastier," said Akasha.

The sudden strength Solomon felt was captivating. He felt like he could take on anyone—the world. There was no fear, no cold, no weakness that he knew of right away. He didn't need a horse to move fast. Solomon felt like he was a one-person army.

"I must teach you, brother," Akasha said. "And together, we will destroy everything they've built from our harsh labor, brick by brick. They took something from me, from us—now, together, we will take everything from them."

Akasha and Solomon locked eyes, forming a brotherhood between them, a bond that couldn't break.

"You are me; I am you," Akasha added.

Akasha believed they shared similar interests, ideals, and experiences. They wanted revenge against the wealthy plantations and to free their people from slavery by any means necessary. Akasha wanted war.

Chapter Fifteen

The narrow, impressive clipper ship was about to arrive in Norfolk, Virginia. It was a windy but bright afternoon and a nearly sixty-five-day journey across the Atlantic. The vessel had limited bulk freight and a large total sail area. It carried goods and people from as far away as China, Europe, and Africa. But this particular ship was arriving from England and New York, bringing a man named Kaiser Adelberg, who was from Germany.

The ship's bow was wide and raked forward, allowing increased speed on the open ocean. It moved at one hundred miles per hour and was designed to carry a small, highly profitable cargo over long distances at great speeds. Kaiser Adelberg stood at the ship's bow, gazing at a looming America. Kaiser was in his late forties. He was distinguished, highly cultured, and knowledgeable. Kaiser stood six feet, and he was a handsome man with a Van Dyke beard. He wore a broad-brimmed hat, a dark coat, breeches, and a deep red waistcoat. His black cravat was fastened with a stick pin, and he wore heeled boots.

Kaiser came from a wealthy family in Düsseldorf, Germany. He was a mysterious man, quiet but observant. He moved with a walking cane containing a hidden sword, but he wasn't crippled or weak. Kaiser was skilled in combat, weaponry, and, most importantly, supernatural vampires. He came from a bloodline of bounty hunters. He was a vampire hunter adamant about permanently destroying them. He and his family were part of a brotherhood called The Holy Command. These were men and women who pledged to protect humanity from evil entities. They kept themselves physically and mentally strong to seek out and face their powerful opponents.

Kaiser Adelberg had extensive knowledge of vampires and other monstrous or undead creatures, including their powers and weaknesses. He used this knowledge to combat them effectively. Word had gotten to the Holy Command about the brutal killings of wealthy families on southern plantations, and unrest had stirred throughout the South. Everyone believed it was a slave uprising. Many enslaved Black men and women had been killed, yet the culprits haven't been caught yet. Kaiser knew these murders were the doings of a vampire. Though vampires had become prevalent in Europe and Africa, America had been unaffected so far by the supernatural. But the Holy Command believed it was inevitable for a nest of the undead to begin, especially with the Atlantic Slave Trade bringing enslaved people to the Americas, and maybe some were infected. There was a case nearly a hundred years ago, the sinking of the *Abigail*. The ship went down in the middle of the Atlantic. It was presumed everyone was killed on the vessel due to an uprising with their cargo. A year after the ship's sinking, an agent was sent to America in the 1700s to investigate strange events happening on southern farms, but he was never heard from again.

The vessel was busy with activity. As it sailed, enslaved men were seated and huddled on the deck. These were captured runaways being brought back to the South from the North. Sailing from New York to Virginia, the captain and his first mate had moved among them, looking them over for prospects to do labor. Kaiser was against slavery. He believed it was a barbaric and primitive practice, and he detested America's chattel slavery. It was immoral. Europe and England were far ahead of America with their abolishment laws toward slavery. In 1838, the British abolished slavery with legal emancipation granted, bringing the British Empire into a new era. Kaiser believed there was an evil entity for America to worry about far worse than a slave rebellion.

The clipper ship docked at the Virginia port. It was one of the busiest in the young nation, with vessels of every shape and size flying various flags. The docks were bustling as goods were loaded and unloaded from ships. It was a bit of controlled chaos, with multiple languages spoken and shouted.

Kaiser stepped off the vessel onto American soil, clutching his walking cane and satchel. It was his first time in America. He had heard so much about it . . . the people, the culture, the wealth, and the brutality of slavery. It was an astonishing place of opportunity and growth, but it came with blinding prejudice with the institution of slavery. His attention was captured as men, women, and children in chains were carted back and forth like cargo. It was disheartening to see. Kaiser heaved and went on his way.

Sun-kissed light poured from the sky, and the streets were animated. Finally, Kaiser approached a portly-looking man atop a horse-drawn carriage. He held his eyes as he came to the carriage, then asked in his German accent, "Good day, my good friend."

"Good day to you too, sir. Do you require transportation?" asked the carriage driver.

"Yes. I do. I need to travel to the train station," said Kaiser. "I'm on my way to Georgia."

"Get on board, and I can get you there before the next train leaves the station, sir."

Kaiser smiled and climbed into the carriage. Georgia was where they believed a slave uprising was happening. So far, an estimated seven families had been murdered. Men and women were scared, mobs were lashing out, southern plantations were under attack, and enslaved Blacks were massacred by the dozens. Word had gotten back to the Holy Command, and they felt it was urgent to send a representative to the South immediately.

The steam train chugged through the farmlands of South Carolina. Kaiser sat by a window in a passenger railcar near the engine room as the train headed south. He clutched his satchel and seemed distanced for a moment. As he continued to travel further south, the more he witnessed the horrors of slavery and the inhumane treatment of Blacks by white people who felt superior. At the Virginia train station, Kaiser saw a group of recently captured runaway slaves in shackles. He stared at these men of different ages, observing the fear on their faces as they were being returned to the plantations and their masters. One enslaved man pulled on his chains toward the train tracks, nearly pulling the other enslaved people with him. He would rather commit suicide than be thrust back into slavery.

Kaiser witnessed free Blacks heading north harassed by the marshals, wanting to see their papers of freedom. He watched a middle-aged Black man dressed in a boldly checked waistcoat, a patterned cravat with fly-front trousers, and a dark frock coat treated like he was subhuman despite his formal attire. This man trembled in front of the marshals and presented them his papers—the fear of being identified as a fugitive lurked.

South Carolina's landscape was picturesque with its endless cotton, tobacco, vegetables, fruit, and livestock fields. And the plantations in South Carolina were massive. But harvesting these fields were dozens and dozens of enslaved Blacks, along with their overseers, menacingly breathing down their necks with bullwhips and shotguns. Sometimes, Kaiser wondered what was worse, humanity with its ominous caste system or the creatures in the night.

Kaiser sighed, diverted his eyes from the sprawling landscape, and removed an art pad from his satchel. He started to sketch. Along with being a vampire hunter, he was also a skilled artist, and sketching helped him relax and think. Finally, his creation started to come to life. It was a creature of the night, a demonic-looking vampire with fangs as sharp as razors, claws, and bloodlust eyes. It was a mystery why he sketched something he believed to be an abomination.

Inside his satchel were other drawings of various creatures he encountered over the years while with the Holy Command. Kaiser nearly lost his life during some of these intense encounters. But these sketches of monsters and vampires reminded him never to underestimate anything and not take life for granted.

"What are you drawing?" a ten-year-old boy asked who was sitting across from him with his mother, who was asleep.

Kaiser looked at him, smiled, showed him his detailed sketch of a vampire, and replied, "A monster."

"A monster?" the boy laughed. "Monsters don't exist."

Kaiser grinned. "Oh, they do exist, my young friend. And this is a vampire. It's a very dangerous creature."

The boy looked intrigued. "What is a vampire?"

Kaiser didn't mind enlightening him about such a creature. He sat erect and looked at the young boy. "Vampires are evil beings who roam the world at night searching for people whose blood they feed upon. They can come in all shapes, sizes, and faces. They're the undead, nocturnal creatures that subsist on blood."

The boy stared at Kaiser in awe with wide eyes. "Are vampires monsters like Frankenstein?"

Kaiser chuckled. "So, you know about Frankenstein."

The boy nodded. Yes. Then he asked, "Is Frankenstein real?"

It was an odd question to reply to. Kaiser thought for a moment, then replied, "Frankenstein is a character, a being created in a novel for entertainment. But I suppose he can be real too."

"But how do you kill a vampire?" asked the boy.

"Good question, my young friend. Vampires are strong. Some of them can have the strength of a hundred men. They are fast and deadly, and they are fully able to turn a person. But vampires cannot come out during the day."

"Why not?"

"Because the sunlight will kill them. Vampires are allergic to sunlight."

"Why?"

"Because they're dark creatures. The sunlight represents good and light, and vampires are not good," said Kaiser. "Also, they don't like silver and maybe fire."

"Have you killed a vampire?"

"I have, a few over the years. They can be hard to kill, though. It would be best if you were trained in fighting a vampire," he proclaimed.

"Can I kill a vampire?" asked the boy.

Kaiser chuckled. "I think you should stick to something safer, my young friend. Hunting and fighting vampires can be troublesome and dangerous. They'll kill you in a heartbeat. And if you ever come across one, run."

"But I want to be brave, like you."

Kaiser felt flattered, and he continued to grin.

"What nonsense are you telling my son?" his mother interrupted.

"Oh, pardon me, ma'am. Your son was just curious about monsters," Kaiser responded.

"Well, I don't want him learning nothing about monsters. They're not real, and the only thing he needs to know is the good Lord," she proclaimed.

"I understand, ma'am. I do apologize for any inconvenience."

Kaiser winked at the boy, who grinned at him, and he went back to sketching his creature.

Hours later, the train pulled into the Georgia station of Blue Ridge County. Kaiser exited from the train behind the boy and his mother. People bustled about, primarily white, and engaged in various activities. One activity was of a lawman passing leaflets of a fugitive slave on the run. The area was chaotic with activity and noise of quick-pacing travelers boarding or departing from the train. Young porters helped passengers with their luggage.

Kaiser took in his surroundings with a keen eye, observing the great white pillars that guarded the entrance to the railway, which held handcrafted iron gates. And a few beggar boys were being whisked from sight. He was officially in the Deep South.

Now, it was time for him to hunt.

Chapter Sixteen

Blue Ridge was a charming town tucked away in the countryside. It was a Southern small-town gem that boasted some pretty stunning scenery, including the magnificent River Falls nearby, a significant mark on the area. The school, church, hotel, and several taverns were the centers of the social life in the community. The place was bustling with movement. Men, women, and children enjoyed the warm fall day. It was a thriving place. Everyone was privileged and free, like a bird.

Kaiser took in the town and its citizens as he rode in the back of a one-horse carriage. There was a certain beauty to the area, but there was a blemish to their way of life: slavery. He rode past an active slave auction and frowned. About one hundred buyers were present, white men looking to purchase free labor. The enslaved people were kept in the horse barn stalls, soon ready to be displayed on the raised block.

"Can you halt for a moment?" Kaiser said to the carriage driver.

The man nodded and brought the carriage to a stop near the auction. Though Kaiser despised the practice of slavery, he was curious about its inner workings.

"Are you interested in buying a nigger?" asked the carriage driver.

"Excuse me?" Kaiser questioned.

"You might get a good price for a nigger. This auction results from the breakup of an old family estate that included two plantations. Unfortunately, the families were killed in that slave revolt a few weeks back. The majority of these niggers had never been sold before. Most had spent their entire lives on one of the two plantations," the carriage driver proclaimed.

Kaiser was surprised at his openness. He talked about the enslaved as if they were cattle.

The carriage driver added, "The auction rules stipulate that the niggers be sold as 'families.' But there's no guarantee of that. Maybe you can get yourself a nice wench for tonight. She'll keep you in good company."

He laughed. Kaiser remained stoic.

The buyers clustered around the platform while the Negroes were gathered into sad groups in the background to watch the progress of their selling, which they were so sorrowfully interested in. The buyers lit their fresh cigars and got ready their catalogs and pencils. The first lot of human chattel was led onto the platform by a sleek mulatto, himself an enslaved person, who seemed to regard the selling of his brethren lightly. The expression on the slaves' faces who stepped on the block to be sold was all the same: anguish, fear, worries—with blighted homes, crushed hopes, and broken hearts. Some enslaved people were skilled in their crafts, like cooks, blacksmithing, carpentry, and shoemaking, and some slaves were taught to use machinery. These skilled enslaved people were sold for more and were sought by the buyers during the auction.

However, the majority of those sold were rice and cotton field workers.

Kaiser continued to watch the auction take place from the carriage. It saddened him to see some enslaved men and women regarded with perfect indifference. Every enslaved person being sold would turn from one side to the other at the auctioneer's word so the crowd might reasonably observe their proportions. Then, when the sale was made, the enslaved person would step down from the block without caring to cast a look at the buyer.

The mulatto brought a young, pregnant woman with her child of four onto the platform. It was most likely she was pregnant with her former master's child. She and her young daughter were barely clothed. She clutched her daughter closely with her eyes cast down in shame and distress. Buyers started to bid simultaneously. The expression on these men's faces was of joy and desire. She was a fertile woman. The child she carried was considered property, and she would bear her master more children in the future.

A burly man in a top hat and frock coat won the bid. He'd paid $2,500 for the entire lot. One of his slaves approached the pregnant mother and child and indifferently seized them. He secured his property while the mother looked in hopeless despair.

Kaiser had seen enough. "Take me to the hotel," he said to the driver.

The man nodded and yanked the horse's reins for them to move forward. Kaiser sat back and looked ahead. They traveled down Main Street toward the hotel. Kaiser continued to observe the town, taking in the general stores and daily activities. There were a few glances his way from the locals. It must have been apparent to them that he was an out-of-towner.

The driver brought the carriage to a stop in front of the hotel. It was called "The Royal." It was three stories tall. It was a fine-looking place made of brick and hosted twenty-five rooms. The driver helped Kaiser exit the carriage.

"Good day to you, sir," said the carriage driver.

Kaiser nodded and carried his luggage inside the lobby, including a steamer trunk. It was a fancy place with a fireplace and large front windows decorated with rare Bavarian-etched ruby glass panes and tin ceilings. He walked to the front desk, where a well-dressed man with a beautiful woman of color was dressed in a beautiful white lace dress, complete with white lace gloves, a fancy ladies' hat, and a white parasol. To see a white man with a Black woman contrasted with what he'd witnessed earlier at the auction. The man signed his name on the registry. The hotel clerk checked a box on the registry book indicating he had a dark female companion. Kaiser watched the two walk away to their room.

"Good afternoon to you, sir," the hotel clerk said brightly.

Kaiser smiled at the clerk and replied, "Good day to you, sir."

"How can we help you today? Are you here on holiday?" asked the clerk.

"Business," Kaiser replied.

"Well, welcome to Blue Ridge, Georgia."

Kaiser had to ask. "I'm surprised you allow Black people to stay here."

The clerk smiled, then replied, "Blue Ridge is a doting community, sir. But that was Mr. Randall with his pretty pony."

Kaiser was clueless about what he meant.

The clerk continued. "White masters love to take their pretty ponies here for a treat of romantic excursions. Seeing how bad the other slaves have it always makes the pampered pony appreciate their privileged position. You know, just in case they forget."

It was news to Kaiser.

"Will that be a problem for you, sir?" the clerk asked.

"No. It won't."

"And how long will you be staying with us?"

"Until my business concludes here in Georgia," Kaiser replied.

Unbeknownst to Kaiser, a silver society ran through Blue Ridge at night that catered to white masters infected with the condition generally referred to as *Nigger Lover*. And at night, the streets, the bars, taverns, bistros, and buggy riders were ruled by wealthy white masters showing off their pretty ponies.

Kaiser entered his room, which was decorated with period antiques and an area rug. The room was small, with a wall hook to hang his clothes. It came with a porcelain basin and washstand for personal grooming. The place would do for now. Kaiser unsheathed the blessed sword masked as a walking stick and stared at the silver blade. The weapon was an ancient masterpiece that helped him hunt down and kill vampires. The blade had significant engravings and scuff marks visible. But the sword wasn't his only weapon for battle. Kaiser opened the steamer case containing a small arsenal of weapons. Each weapon was vital in fighting the supernatural and was blessed with the holy blood of Christ. Kaiser picked up a weapon called the "Hunga Munga." It was a handheld weapon with a pointed metal blade, a curved back section, and a separate spike near the handle. It could be used in hand-to-hand combat or thrown with a spinning action.

Then there was his "Cross-Blade Necklace." It was a necklace that doubled as a small weapon. The blade was a bit too small to damage a vampire, but it was still a valuable weapon since it was completely hidden.

Kaiser moved to the window and drew back the curtains to look outside. The room had a clear view of Main Street and was within walking distance of everything. It was still daylight out, and from his window, he watched several chained slaves march by in the mud. Kaiser sighed and wondered who the actual monsters were in this country—vampires or chattel slavery.

It was a lovely afternoon, and Kaiser was dressed differently in a wool tailcoat, a silk necktie tied in a flat bow, and a top hat. He was a well-dressed gentleman ready to take in the town and assimilate with everyone else. He exited his room, clutching his signature walking stick with the silver handle.

Moving through the hotel, Kaiser finally got a chance to take in the place and was delighted at the convenient arrangement of the area, the gorgeous furniture in the parlors, and the extent and beauty of the dining hall. Such richness, lavish expenditure, and excellent taste. He decided to dine in the dining hall before going into town to explore and investigate. He sat at a nice table among several parties, eating a meal in the hotel's dining room. Kaiser sat alone, but he was observant of the people around him. He noticed a few black crepes accessorizing the background.

Excellent cuisine was an essential component of hospitality. Hence, the hotel hired a gourmet French chef whose menu drew large crowds and ongoing accolades. Kaiser decided to have the green turtle soup, the filet beef with mushrooms, and a variety of fruits.

After his meal, Kaiser went out for a stroll. The streets were well-populated this late afternoon, with many people out strolling. Most were white, but there were a few free Blacks, along with enslaved Black people who traveled with their white masters. Some were physically downtrodden field hands. However, a few well-dressed slaves apparently led an easier life than their counterparts.

Kaiser crossed the road and headed toward the local tavern. He walked into a decent place, though a bit crowded and smoke-filled. It was lively, and Kaiser somewhat stood out. With his walking stick, he approached the bar to order a beer.

"*Heh low*, sir," Kaiser greeted the bartender with his thick German accent.

"What can I get you?" asked the man, who was tall with a dark beard.

"Your finest pint will suffice," Kaiser responded.

The man looked confused by his words "pint" and "suffice."

"What did you say?"

"I'll have a beer," said Kaiser.

"Why didn't you say that in the first place?"

The bartender turned to get his beer while Kaiser continued to take in the tavern with keenness. The bartender soon returned with his beer. Kaiser quickly paid the man and moved away from the bar. His purpose was to try and connect with a few locals. He needed to interview them subtly about the massacres on plantations. But most importantly, he needed a personal guide who was knowledgeable of the land and could be somewhat trusted. Unfortunately, that would be hard to find.

Kaiser took a sip of his beer and noticed the attention he was receiving from a few customers. They perceived him to be a man of wealth and importance because of his attire. The ladies smiled his way, but the men sensed he would become somewhat of a threat to them. Nevertheless, Kaiser continued to be polite with manners and his catchy smile.

"You might be in the wrong place dressed like that," said a young woman.

Kaiser smiled her way. "And why would you deduce that?" he asked.

She smiled. "Your fancy clothes with your fancy words. Where are you from?"

"Germany, my fine lady."

"Germany? You're a long way from home, aren't you?"

"I am, but I'm here in America on business," he explained.

"What kind of business?" she asked him.

"The kind of business that one usually does not understand," he replied. "But might I have the pleasure of knowing your name?"

The young lady smiled and replied, "Dorothy."

"It is a pleasure to meet you, Dorothy."

"Likewise."

Dorothy wore a Victorian silk dress with sloping shoulders and wide pagoda sleeves. She had gold hair, high cheekbones, and a freckled face, and she was pretty and engaging.

"And what is your name, sir?" she asked him.

"Kaiser Adelberg," he answered.

Dorothy looked at him with puzzlement. It was a confusing name to her. She liked him immediately. There was something about Kaiser that was warming but intriguing at the same time. His accent was alluring, but he was handsome with a flare to him.

"Mr. Kaiser, answer me this. Are you a gambling man?" Dorothy asked him politely.

"I happen to partake in the leisure here and there," he replied. "Why do you ask?"

"I know of a place you might like. It's private, with a better class of people to associate with and better drinks. But if you like a particular taste in company, they have that too," she mentioned.

Kaiser grinned. "This place does sound intriguing. You lead, I'll follow."

"Buy me a beer first, and I'll take you there," said Dorothy.

"Of course," Kaiser grinned.

Chapter Seventeen

Akasha's fangs found his flesh and sliced into it, the neck of a white male, the soft warmth giving way like a ripe melon, filling his mouth with thick, enjoyable blood. The victim shivered in Akasha's firm grasp as he drew in deep, gulping mouthful after mouthful, reveling in the strength and the life that filled his veins, jolted his limbs, and granted him his semblance of life. The man of the small farmhouse began to moan faintly as his body was growing limp. There wasn't anything he could do to stop it. His death was inevitable—and painful. Akasha gorged on his flesh like a predatory and hungry lion. He became a messy eater with this one, literally ripping the victim's neck apart.

It was gruesome to see, especially for the victim's family. His wife and teenage daughter stood frozen nearby, watching as a husband and father was viciously drained of his life. The mother cloaked her arms around her daughter as fear paralyzed and tormented them. Their eyes were clouded with tears and dread. A shotgun was by the husband's side, a weapon now considered useless against the supernatural.

The mother held her daughter tightly, wanting to protect her. Her mouth went dry, and she was too frightened to scream. They were simple people living in a basic two-story, old farmhouse. They didn't own any slaves. She believed her husband was a hardworking farmer, a good man. *So why is this happening to us?* The devil had surfaced from hell to attack their family.

Finally, after finishing the feasting on the man, Akasha stood from the body and looked at Solomon. His mouth was coated in blood, and his eyes were dark and soulless.

"I told you, you must feed to survive," Akasha told Solomon. "Pick which one. The younger, the sweeter it is."

Solomon stood there expressionless. He stared at the two women. The mother's eyes were wild with terror, and the daughter's eyes widened with panic. They were in their long, white nightgowns, barefoot and helpless. It was the middle of the night when the attack happened suddenly.

Solomon was an intimidating presence. He was taller than Akasha and muscular. His dark skin glimmered in the shadows, his eyes were black like obsidian and soulless like Akasha's, and he produced sharp fangs. He was hungry and trying to fight his hunger for blood, but it was an unwinnable battle.

Noticing Solomon's hesitation, Akasha stepped closer to him, scowling.

"They mean nothing to us but food," Akasha growled. "Replenish or die in pain and agony, Solomon. Because I can guarantee you that the more you resist your thirst and your exact calling, the more it will rip you apart on the inside. Fresh blood is necessary for our survival, for you especially. You're young, still vulnerable, weak. The blood will allow you to regenerate any wounds you may acquire and sustain living flesh. If not, you will rot like a corpse. Fresh blood moving through our bodies allows our flesh to stay alive."

Solomon could feel something burning inside him. It felt like a pit of fire inside his chest and stomach. He could smell the mother and daughter's blood as if he could smell Irene's cooking. It was becoming irresistible.

"I want you to feast on the young girl," said Akasha. "Her blood is sweet and ripe, perfect for your first time."

Solomon stared at the girl. She was fifteen years old with smooth olive skin, raven-black hair, and perky tits peeking from underneath her nightgown.

"Don't be weakened by her age, Solomon. She is one of them. Kill her and survive," Akasha exclaimed.

The mother continued to clutch her daughter tightly, wishing she had the strength of God to protect her child from these monsters. However, they were human, and fighting to save her daughter would be futile. The mother's face was awash with tears, and the only thing she could do was beg for mercy.

"Please! Leave my daughter alone. Kill me instead. She's an innocent girl, and she doesn't deserve this. Just let her go," the mother cried out.

"You hear that?" Akasha asked Solomon. "That's the sound of desperation and weakness. They want mercy from us, but when have they ever given our kind any mercy?"

Akasha grew angrier. He stormed toward the mother and daughter and quickly shredded the daughter's nightgown from her skin, rendering her completely naked. Then he pried the daughter from her mother's arms and flung her across the room. She landed on her side, hurt, while her mother howled in horror, defenseless to protect her offspring.

"No! No! Don't hurt her! Please!" she screamed.

Akasha wrapped his hand around the mother's slim neck and lifted her off her feet. She struggled to breathe as she was suspended in the air. Akasha glared at her, nearly toying with his food. The mother continued to kick and fight, but to no avail. If he wanted, Akasha could easily snap her neck. But he wanted her alive when he began to devour her blood. It was more fulfilling to drain their life when they were aware of it.

Therefore, the moment he placed the mother back on her feet, Akasha didn't hesitate to plunge his fangs into her neck, seizing her body tightly by her arms and draining her of her natural life, bit by bit. A wave of pain exploded through the mother and crashed through her body. The life in her eyes began to fade.

The daughter's face drained of color, seeing her mother being killed.

"Mother!" the girl cried out in anguish.

Akasha drank and drank. He sucked at her neck until there was nothing left to suck, and then he dropped her to the ground, where the mother fell in a crumpled heap. Akasha smirked. Her blood was refreshing.

He looked at Solomon and shouted, "Kill her now and feast!"

Solomon stepped closer to the girl, still with hesitation. It was hard for him to accept what he finally was—a monster. All he ever wanted to do was love Irene and escape with his wife to the north, to freedom. He wanted a family and to live his life on his terms. Solomon didn't want to belong to anyone. Now, his future was uncertain. It was hard for him to understand though he was alive . . . He was the dead, or the undead. It was sorcery or witchery, maybe voodoo magic.

Akasha glared at Solomon.

"You are not human anymore, Solomon. We do not eat food for nourishment. Inside of you, food is digested and transformed into energy. Their blood is ingested and absorbed directly into you for life, power, and strength," he proclaimed.

Akasha crouched closer to the girl, seized her by her lengthy hair, and yanked her head back, exposing her thin, long neck. The girl flinched and whimpered, and tears trickled from her eyes.

"You can smell how sweet her blood is," Akasha said. "Take her blood, drain it into you, and your transformation will be completed. Do it now!"

Akasha lifted the girl to her feet like she was a rag doll. Her nakedness would have appealed to most men, but to Akasha and Solomon, she was merely food. And instead of rape, she would be devoured.

The teenage girl continued to tremble and cry in Akasha's firm grasp as he held her by the back of her neck. Akasha continued, "They will come for you, so you need to be strong and ready."

"Who will come for me?" Solomon asked him.

Akasha didn't answer his question directly; he refused to. Instead, he replied, "Enemies that want to wipe our kind from existence and who are strong enough to do so."

He squeezed the back of the girl's neck tighter, causing her to wince and cry out in pain. He was hurting her.

"Kill her!" Akasha screamed.

Solomon knew he didn't have a choice. He stared at the girl and displayed his fangs; her end came. He glanced at her parents' contorted bodies sprawled across the cold, wooden floor. Then he thought, how many times have their kind killed, tortured, raped, and maimed slaves, men, women, and children without a second thought or a conscience. White people took away everything he'd loved. White men lusted after their wives and the young girls on the plantation. They tormented and mocked their husbands with abuse, humiliation, and debauchery. Solomon missed Irene wholeheartedly and would do anything to get her back. Now, he had the power and abilities to do so. It was time to find his wife and live the life he dreamed of in the north.

Akasha was right. He would need his strength to find Irene.

Solomon's eyes blackened, and his fangs seemed to grow longer. The scent of the girl's sweet blood rose stronger, and his hunger became excruciating. The side of her neck throbbed as Akasha's claws pressed into the nape of her neck.

"Yes. Feed on her, my brother. Become stronger for our kind," Akasha uttered.

With that said Solomon released his fury and sank his teeth into the girl's neck. She immediately seized in shock, and her eyes widened in terror. It was the most painful thing that ever happened to her. The pressure of Solomon's bite was crippling. She felt his fangs and mouth sucking blood. Knowing her blood was draining from her, her body reacted, and she urinated on herself. She wanted to collapse, but Solomon kept her upright, fulfilling his hunger while killing her.

The monster in Solomon could care less about her pain, not as long as her sweet crimson fluid continued to flow into him—pumping him full of stolen life and vitality. As Akasha did to her parents, he drank and drank until there was nothing left of her. Then he released her from his grasp, and her body crumbled to the floor. She was dead. But Solomon felt more alive than ever.

Akasha grinned. "Now, you are complete."

Solomon had never felt anything like it before. He pivoted and walked out of the farmhouse into the cool night air. His entire body continued to rewire itself, and his teeth had changed. He'd lost his molars and gained sharp fangs. His heart had stopped. He didn't need to breathe anymore. Solomon stepped off the porch barefoot and stared at the sky with enchantment. His change was weird at first. Things were happening. He could hear, taste, smell, and feel more, and there were things he could now experience that his human mind would not have been able to process. He was geared for the hunt. Solomon had changed from a herd animal to a predator.

Chapter Eighteen

Kaiser followed Dorothy toward the Supper Club in Blue Ridge, Georgia. It was a regular three-story home among other lovely homes on an affluent street. Dorothy opened a small garden gate in front of the house, and they walked up the small steps toward the front door. Kaiser remained observant, knowing he was in unfamiliar territory with a stranger he needed to trust.

Dorothy knocked on the door, and soon it opened to reveal a young, beautiful, Black woman dressed in a French maid's outfit.

"Bonjour," the woman greeted.

Dorothy smiled. "Bonjour, mom petite femme noire. We are here to see Dante Noris."

The Black girl in the French outfit continued to smile and uttered, "Enter."

She opened the door wider, stepped aside, and allowed them into the house. Immediately, Kaiser and Dorothy were greeted by the hostess of the place, a blond, leggy woman named Renee.

"Good evening. I'm Renee. Can I help you?" she asked, staring at Kaiser and taking in his neat and distinguished appearance.

Kaiser took it upon himself to greet Renee with a handshake and a smile. "My name is Kaiser Adelberg, and it's a pleasure to be in your company this evening."

Renee smiled. "Your accent is intriguing. Where are you from, Mr. Adelberg?"

"Germany," he replied.

"Well, welcome to America. I'm sure Dorothy has mentioned that we are a private club with a particular palate and regard," Renee mentioned.

"I've heard, and it's why I'm here."

Renee continued to smile. "Then follow me."

Kaiser and Dorothy followed Renee through the entryway and into a dining room. It was a lush, fancy restaurant and lounge area. It was charming with a crystal chandelier and bar, and there were well-dressed white men with pretty Black girls dressed in the most elaborate ladies' fashion of the day. Some white men were with young Black girls as young as thirteen years old, and some white men hosted three Black girls for their pleasure and entertainment. The men drank whisky and wine while the girls drank sarsaparillas.

"So, what do you think? Is it what you're looking for?" Dorothy asked him.

Kaiser felt somewhat disgusted by what he saw—seeing young and old, wrinkled white men with young, pretty Black girls that they would fornicate with tonight. Yet, he kept a smile on his face and masked his true feelings.

"It's an intriguing place," he replied calmly.

"Do you see anything you like?" asked Renee.

A white male in his sixties and a young girl descended from the club's prominent staircase. He was fastening his trousers as she was collecting herself. What went on above was apparent as the man joined the other regulars with a pleasing smile. A billiard game was being played nearby, and a poker game was on the other side of the room.

Kaiser grinned at the host and said, "If it's not a problem, I would love to partake in the poker game."

Renee grinned. "The buy-in can become costly, Mr. Adelberg."

Kaiser displayed a leather wallet with lots of paper money, and Renee continued to grin. She was impressed.

"Then follow me, Mr. Adelberg."

He followed her toward the poker table, where several men sat and were intensely involved with the game.

"Gentlemen, I want to introduce another player to the game," Renee announced. "This is Mr. Kaiser Adelberg from Germany."

The players barely looked his way, instead remaining focused on the game. Then, finally, Kaiser took a seat at the table, set his walking stick aside, and placed his cash in front of him. The dealer acknowledged him by replacing his money with chips; now, he was in the game.

"Welcome to America," a distinguished gentleman named James said.

"It's the land of the free, I hear," Kaiser replied sarcastically.

A few gentlemen chuckled at the slight remark. Kaiser took in all their faces. A few were older than him by ten or twenty years.

"So, Mr. Adelberg from Germany, what brings you here to America?" a man named Donald asked him. "Is it business or pleasure?"

"Business," Kaiser replied.

"What kind of business would bring you here to our grand country?" James asked him.

"I am looking for someone," he replied.

"A runaway nigger? I didn't know niggers could swim that far from Germany, yet, swim at all," James joked.

The men laughed.

Kaiser didn't. He responded, "Something was stolen from me, and I'm looking to retrieve it."

"Well, I wish you the best of luck," said Donald.

Kaiser played poker with them. Unbeknownst to them, Kaiser was a skilled player at the game. Still, his ruse was to gather information about the killings on several plantations in the area. First, however, he needed to gain their trust somewhat, but it was easier said than done. Also, he wanted to earn some extra cash, though he didn't need it. He was a wealthy man, but what he wanted was to subtly punish these bigots for their cruel acts against humanity by taking from them what they loved most—money.

He remained calm and maintained a poker face by relaxing his facial muscles. He threw his opponents off by sometimes smiling, acting confidently, and conversing with the other players. Most of the time, he could trick his opponents into folding prematurely by acting cheerful. Kaiser's winnings were growing.

"I've heard there's been quite some trouble stirring here with the locals," Kaiser said.

"If your implication of the locals means niggers, don't worry about it. We have it under control, Mr. Adelberg," said James.

"Besides, that trouble has traveled north, and the niggers we believed to be involved with that mess, let's just say, they won't be a problem to our community anymore. Lots of good white folks are dead," Donald proclaimed.

"The niggers in Germany, are they considered a problem there?" James asked.

"Germany has come a long way, my dear good friends. Fortunately for the country, under the Second Republic, a decree-law written by Therese Huber has abolished slavery in the remaining colonies," he said.

"Abolished slavery, huh? Are you one of those treacherous abolitionists, Mr. Adelberg? Is that your business here?" Donald asked. "To continue stirring up our niggers to revolt and go on and kill good white folks, including children?"

"Your business in this country is your business," Kaiser replied.

"You never answered the question. What is your business here in America?" James now demanded to know.

"You wouldn't understand it," said Kaiser.

"Entertain us tonight at the card table. You've piqued our interest," James added.

Kaiser locked eyes with the men with a slight grin. He wasn't nervous. He'd seen evil and power, and he figured they wouldn't be able to comprehend what he was about to tell them. These men were dressed nicely, but he felt their mannerisms were barbaric and primitive. They were hypocrites, able to enslave Black men and women and comfortable having sexual affairs with young Black girls.

"I'm something of a bounty hunter," he mentioned.

"You're telling me you hunt runaway niggers?" asked another gentleman named Pete.

"Not quite. I pursue the supernatural," Kaiser explained to them.

Every man at the card table stared at him, dumbfounded.

"What do you mean the 'supernatural'? Do you mean ghosts? Are you a ghost hunter, Mr. Adelberg? Or are you a bit touched in the head?" James mocked.

Everyone laughed.

"No such thing. These beings are very much physical. They're strong, fast, and dangerous. And they can kill everyone in this room within a heartbeat," Kaiser replied.

"So, you do hunt niggers?" said James.

Kaiser was disgusted by the word and their prejudice, but he kept his cool and humbly replied, "No, I hunt evil. Sometimes, it's hard to tell the difference between what I hunt and what I see daily."

The disparaging remark caused James to glare at Kaiser with some resentment. He took a pull from his cigar, and they continued to play poker.

The game went on.

Soon, a $3,000 pot was on the table between Kaiser and James. James looked at his hand and felt confident. He held his cards with a young, Black beauty draped around him.

"I raise you five hundred," said James.

"I see your five hundred and raise you another three hundred," Kaiser replied, tossing the last of his chips into the pot. "And I call."

It was becoming a showdown between the two men at the table. Everyone was watching, waiting to see who would come out on top.

"Sorry to tell you this, Mr. Adelberg from Germany, but the pot isn't fat enough yet for you to get comfortable," James said.

"I'm all in," said Kaiser.

James smiled. "Too bad. One final raise."

James signaled for one of the young Black beauties to come their way. A petite Black girl came and stood by James. James wrote down something on a piece of paper. Then he handed it to Kaiser. He took it and read it with confusion.

"What is this?" Kaiser asked.

"It is this prime piece of Black beauty bill of sale," James answered.

"I have no use for her," Kaiser replied.

"You mean to tell me you have no use for pleasure? She's currency, worth about $900. She'll do whatever you desire, Mr.

Adelberg. Isn't this why you're here at the Supper Club?" James questioned him. "So, what will it be? Match or fold?"

The spotlight was on him, and Kaiser didn't want to raise any suspicion about himself. However, Kaiser grinned and replied, "I don't want to disappoint a man in his hometown. It would not be polite. So I'll match."

With that said, Kaiser removed a pure gold crescent ring from his finger and placed his attractive and pricey silver walking cane into the pot. James picked up the ring to inspect it.

"That ring is pure gold and worth more than your young beauty," Kaiser informed him.

James smiled. "Impressive . . . a gold ring from Germany and a silver cane. It doesn't get any better than this, right, boys?"

They laughed.

"Now, let's see those cards, Mr. Adelberg," said James. He displayed a straight flush. Then . . . *Whoa!* Everyone at the table gasped.

Kaiser kept calm and displayed a royal flush. Everyone was taken aback. It was the best hand possible, featuring five consecutive cards of the same suit in order of value from ten through to ace. James's smile dropped immediately into shock and a scowl.

"You are a damn cheat!" James shouted heatedly.

"I resent the accusations, sir. I'm no such thing," Kaiser exclaimed.

James sprang from his seat in anger and shouted, "You're nothing but a card-cheating son of a bitch! *That's* what you are!"

"You lost, sir. Accept it and move on," Kaiser replied nonchalantly.

"I will do no such thing!"

James removed a small Derringer pistol from his pocket and pointed it at Kaiser. Everyone in the club grew still, nervous, and quiet. James was known to lose his temper and become belligerent.

However, Kaiser remained calm, his eyes trained on James and the pistol.

"You're not leaving this place with a damn thing," James hollered.

The move was uncalled for, and Kaiser frowned at being threatened. However, it happened quickly. Before James could react and pull the trigger, Kaiser countered swiftly by unsheathing the silver blade and slicing off James's hand entirely. His severed hand fell to the table with the gun still attached. It was shocking, and James hollered in extreme anguish as he clutched his severed hand and stumbled back.

"Ohmygod!" someone cried out.

Kaiser kept calm and stated, "Americans and y'all uncouth violence."

Everyone in the room was in absolute shock. Kaiser remained calm and in control. He placed the silver blade back into its casing. Then he collected his winnings while James had fallen to his knees in agony, blood gushing from his wound. No one dared get in Kaiser's away. He stared at James's young pony that he'd won in the bet and uttered, "Come with me."

The girl nervously followed behind Kaiser as he exited the Supper Club. Dorothy didn't know what to think of the situation. It seemed surreal. She'd brought him there. Now, he'd made her look like a fool. Everyone was staring at her.

Kaiser stormed out of the Supper Club with the young Black girl in tow. Once they were a few feet away from the place, Kaiser turned to her.

"What is your name?" he asked the girl.

"Melody," she replied timidly.

"How old are you, Melody?"

"Sixteen."

"Well, Melody, you're a free woman. I won you. Now you can leave and go home."

"My home was with Masser James," she said.

"He's no longer your master. You're free to live your own life the way you want," he replied.

She couldn't comprehend her sudden freedom. So instead, she stood there confused and deserted, like a lost puppy.

"You bought me, and I'm yours," she said.

Kaiser sighed. He didn't want to own her. He despised slavery. But he saw how brainwashed she was. Then suddenly, he heard Dorothy shout, "Hey!"

Kaiser turned to see Dorothy charging his way, scowling.

"What is your problem? You embarrassed me back there. I brought you to a decent place to have a good time, and you cut off a man's hand," she scolded. "Do you understand what heap of a mess you placed yourself in?"

"That was a vile place, Dorothy, and that man got what he deserved," Kaiser said.

"He has friends, you know."

"And I'll be ready for them too," he replied.

Kaiser was finished conversing with her. He turned and marched away, with Melody following behind him. The only thing Dorothy could do was stand there completely dumbfounded. Something was unnerving about him. She moaned, turned, and went the other way.

Chapter Nineteen

The next day, Kaiser woke up on the hardwood floor. He'd given Melody the bed for the night. It would have been frowned upon to let a slave sleep in the bed while he took to the floor. But Kaiser was a complete gentleman. The girl was young and most likely the victim of unspeakable horrors; therefore, giving her one night of rest was rewarding.

Kaiser walked to the window and peered outside. It was a sunny morning, and the main street was active with everyday people, buggies, and carriages. Fortunately for Kaiser, he didn't see an angry mob outside the hotel. However, last night was unpredictable, and he briefly displayed the warrior that he was. He didn't want to attack James, but the one thing Kaiser wouldn't tolerate was his disrespect and threats.

Kaiser continued to peer out the window and soon fell into deep thought, thinking about the horrors he'd witnessed over the years of being a vampire hunter. He was shirtless, and his body was marked with scars. Some were so old he'd forgotten how he attained them. Yet, he was physically fit and capable of handling himself anywhere. The last thing he wanted to do was attack a human being. It was frowned upon by the Holy Command. But some men were so vile, dogmatic, and aggressive that Kaiser called them monsters in the day. There was a thin line between the iniquity of humanity and things that went bump in the night . . . unstoppable creatures that could harm and devour towns and threaten humanity. The only difference between vile men and monsters was a heartbeat.

There were things that human civilization couldn't possibly comprehend. There would be turmoil if the truth ever came to light about how frail humanity was. The Holy Command was humanity's front line and cutting edge of defense, and they worked alone and in secret.

Melody had finally awakened. She sat up in the bed and stared at Kaiser as if dreaming. Kaiser turned to her and grinned.

"Are you hungry?" he asked her.

She nodded. "Yes."

"I'll get you some breakfast," he said.

He donned a shirt and left the room.

Kaiser came back to the room with breakfast and questions for Melody. He placed the tray near the bed, and she began to eat.

"Are you not hungry too?" Melody asked him.

"I'm fine. You enjoy."

He watched her for a moment. Her skin was copper brown, like a windfall autumn leaf, and she had dazzling, champagne-brown eyes and half-moon cheekbones. She was beautiful.

"Where are you from, Melody?" he asked her.

"New Orleans," she answered.

"Isn't that a long way from here?"

She nodded. "It is."

"Do you have any family, Melody?"

"The only family I know is Massa James. He takes care of me. He treats me fair," she replied.

"He treats you like some kind of Jezebel," said Kaiser.

"He bought me when I was young. My parents, they dead. He raised me and brought me to Georgia. I was his for years; now, I'm yours."

"You belong to no one, Melody," Kaiser replied wholeheartedly.

"Then what I'm to do, huh? All I know is Masser James. He puts me in these fancy clothes, and I gets to travel. I eats good and live good, better than any slave," she proclaimed.

"But you're still a slave," Kaiser uttered grimly.

Kaiser stared at her, knowing though she was physically free, she was still a slave in her mind. Melody had been a sexual puppet to white men for years, and James Welling was her pimp. Kaiser had no idea what to do with her next. Though he won her playing poker, he had no papers on her; there was nothing on Melody to indicate she was a free woman. If she went out on her own, she would most likely end up back where she started . . . probably worse off.

Melody continued to eat and remained comfortable on the bed.

"I've heard there's been a few violent uprisings in this area," Kaiser mentioned.

"They weren't an uprising, suh. It wasn't a mob of angry slaves that killed those white people. It was one man," Melody replied.

Her reply attracted his attention more. "What do you mean it was one man? How do you know this?"

Melody looked like she didn't want to continue with the conversation. But whatever it was, it spooked her.

"Noah, he said the devil himself sprung from hell and killed those white people," Melody replied. "He says there was no stopping him, not even a blast from the overseer's shotgun. He says white peoples' chickens are finally coming home to roost, and the devil himself came to collect."

"Who is this Noah?" he asked her.

"He was a slave on the Cullens' plantation a few months back. Saw it all happen. He says he looked the devil himself in the eyes, and the devil stared right back at him, fire and brimstone burning behind him."

"Where can I find this Noah?" Kaiser asked.

"He be up for auction today," she replied.

"Auction, huh?"

Melody nodded. "Yes, suh."

"Okay, then. We have work to do, Melody. I want you to tell me everything you know about this auction and Noah. I may need his help."

Melody smiled. "Yes, suh. Much obliged to you, suh."

It was another sunny afternoon. And like the day before, well-dressed buyers were clustered around the platform. Tons of white buyers, sellers, and enslaved Black people were there to buy and sell in the open market. The buyers lit their fresh cigars, got their catalogs and pencils, and looked excited to bid on the next batch of niggers being sold off.

With Melody towing behind him, Kaiser made his way into the crowd. He blended in with the nicely dressed and well-off men looking to purchase a nigger for the right price. However, Kaiser was willing to let no one outbid him. This was important. He clutched his walking cane and waited for Noah to be auctioned off. Melody was his guide. She pretended to be his slave, standing gingerly by his side.

Several slaves were sold to the highest bidder. Kaiser waited patiently in the crowd of buyers. Some men tried to strike up a conversation with him, and there was small talk here and there. His accent stood out, but Kaiser remained focused and calm. It bothered him that he was participating in the vile act of auctioning a human being into slavery. But he had to play the part since he already looked like a wealthy buyer.

The following slave they brought onto the auction block was Noah. He was a tall, half-naked Negro with powerful arms, the blackest skin Kaiser had ever seen, and nappy hair. He was a beast of a man, intimidating but docile at the same time. The expression on his face was deadpan. All eyes were on Noah, and Kaiser knew it would cost him. But he was determined to buy Noah at any price.

"Look here, my fine gentlemen. I bring you a healthy and strong buck named Noah. He's twenty-four and good for the fields or any hard labor you bring forth to him. He's young, can breed, and the nigger may look intimidating, but he's as docile as a mule. I'll start the bid at nine hundred. Do I hear nine hundred for this strong, healthy buck?" the auctioneer, Andrew, called out.

"Nine hundred," Kaiser shouted.

"Nine hundred. Do I hear a thousand, fellows?" the auctioneer speedily shouted.

"One thousand!" a man exclaimed.

"I hear one thousand. Do I hear $1,100?"

"$1,100," Kaiser countered.

"$1,300!" a different voice shouted from the crowd.

"$1,300 coming from Mr. Rockwell. Fine bid, Mr. Rockwell. We have $1,300. Do I hear $1,400? Gentleman, do I hear $1,400 for this young buck?"

"$1,500!" Kaiser bellowed.

"$1,500 from the well-dressed, distinguished fellow," the auctioneer smiled. "It's $1,500. Do I hear $1,600 for this strong, breeding field buck? Gentlemen, we have $1,600. He's a fine nigger. OK, $1,600 going once, going twice, sold to the gentleman with the cane," the auctioneer cried out, pointing to Kaiser.

Kaiser nodded his head and remained nonchalant. He'd bought his first—and last—slave, which was a gut-wrenching feeling for him. Noah was removed from the platform and brought to Kaiser. Melody grinned. Kaiser stared at Noah, who remained quiet, chained, and doubtful about his new master.

"You'll be fine, Noah. I promise you that. Melody told me about you, and I need your help," Kaiser said.

"Don't know how much help I can be to you, suh. I's a field nigger, as the man said," Noah uttered politely.

"I hear you come from the Cullens' plantation and that one night, you saw something horrific . . . the devil himself," Kaiser stated.

The mention of this made Noah jittery and scared. "I's don't know what you talking about, suh. I've seen no such thing."

Kaiser knew he was afraid to speak about what happened on the plantation. He'd come across a vampire, and there weren't too many people that lived to tell about it.

"That nigger is a good purchase, Mr. . . . . ?" a stranger uttered to Kaiser out of the blue, interrupting their chat.

"Kaiser Adelberg," Kaiser spoke.

The two men shook hands.

"Mr. Adelberg. I've seen Noah do fine work on Mr. Cullen's plantation. You outbid me respectfully, Mr. Adelberg," uttered the stranger.

"I know a good worker when I see one," Kaiser said, playing the role.

"I do myself. I've been looking to purchase a few field bucks, and you got one of the best ones," said the stranger.

"We'll see," Kaiser replied. "If you excuse us, we're on our way."

The stranger smiled and nodded. "Mr. Adelberg, where are you from? I haven't seen you around him before."

"Virginia," Kaiser lied.

"Virginia? I find it odd that you would travel some good ways from Virginia to purchase one nigger," said the stranger.

"I was simply passing through on business, happened to come across this auction, needed a nigger to bring back with me. No wrong with that, right?" Kaiser proclaimed calmly but surely.

"No. No harm in that at all," said the stranger, who chuckled.

Kaiser didn't trust the man. There was something about him that seemed off. Still, he remained calm and agreeable. It pained him that he had to utter "nigger" not to seem odd and fit in. And it also pained him that he fueled the town's economy with this purchase, but he needed Noah. After Noah's help, he planned on freeing him along with Melody. Maybe they'll both travel north together and carve out a better life for themselves. Until then, Kaiser had to pretend to be their master.

Kaiser knew he needed to leave Blue Ridge, Georgia, right away. Though word around town was that the uprising had traveled north, no Black men or women were still safe on the road. Negroes were hanging from trees that stretched for miles. The South was becoming a dangerous place, not only for enslaved people but for white folks too. But this vampire wasn't going to stop. He was bloodthirsty and strong, and there was no stopping him. And the backlash behind this vampire's actions would cost hundreds of lives.

Chapter Twenty

The horse-drawn wagon slowly moved down the main street with all eyes on it. What it carried as cargo had the townspeople horrified. Old Man Will was in charge of transporting the bodies into town. It was early morning, and the news of several patty-rollers being brutally killed spread faster than a cool breeze. Old Man Will brought the wagon to a stop near the sheriff's office. The townspeople watched as Will climbed down from the wagon with a sorrowful look. He huffed as the sheriff, Bill Madison, and his men approached the wagon cradling his Winchester rifle.

"Is it all of them?" the sheriff asked him.

Old Man Will nodded and replied, "I believe so. Damn shame what happened to them. I've never seen anything like it before in my life."

Bill Madison frowned. He shot an uneasy glance at his men standing behind him. The bodies were covered. Bill was given the task of identifying these men who were found nearly ripped apart in the woods. He stepped closer to the wagon and removed the covering to reveal Foxx and his men's contorted corpses. It was gruesome to see. Limbs ripped apart, blood drained, flesh torn open, and their faces frozen with absolute horror. Its sight made several men queasy, including one man who threw up near the wagon.

"What kind of animal would do this to these men?" Old Man Will asked the sheriff.

"Got-damn niggers, fucking savages they are!" one of Bill's men griped.

"You believe niggers did this?" Old Man Will asked the sheriff. "I've been around a long time, Sheriff. Saw my fair share of violence, but nothing ever like this."

"I don't know what to believe," the sheriff replied.

"I say we get our guns and round up a mob of good, God-fearing, Christian men, and we hunt these niggers down and give our fallen brothers the justice they deserve!" a man named Catcher cried out.

"I agree! It could be us dead in that wagon," someone replied to Catcher.

Curious, the townspeople gathered around the wagon to get a glimpse of the dead men. It wasn't very pleasant to witness, and the troops were rallying. People were scared. They continued to receive word of unspeakable attacks and murders against white folks throughout the South. If it was a slave revolt, they wondered why haven't the militia or the army brought it to an end by now, and the niggers responsible had not yet hung from a rope?

Sheriff Billy Madison frowned. Foxx was a good friend of his, and it bothered him that niggers slaughtered him like he was some pig. *But how?* Foxx would never allow niggers to get the best of him. He once was a skilled soldier, a feared man, a remarkable tracker, and a cautious man. The men he hired were equal to his skills. But unfortunately, the sheriff's friend looked like he was the victim of a bear attack.

Suddenly, they heard a woman shriek. Everyone turned from observing the bodies to see Milly Henderson running toward the wagon. She was wearing a fitted bodice with a floor-skimming wide skirt. Milly ran to the wagon while hiking up her dress to avoid tripping over it. She was grief-stricken and cried out, "Joseph!"

Immediately, the sheriff intervened. He stepped forward and grabbed Milly into his arms to prevent her from seeing her husband's mutilated body.

"Milly, no. You don't want to see him this way," said the sheriff.

"No! No! I need to see him. Please, Sheriff, that's my husband!" Milly cried out.

She and Joseph had been married for two years, and he was the love of her life. Now, she was a widow.

The sheriff held Milly back as she cried like a baby.

"He can't be dead!" Milly continued to cry out.

Everyone stood around and watched the sheriff try to comfort the grieving Milly. She was a likable girl, twenty-two years old, with a fresh, pretty face. Her husband's body was a nightmare to see. His jaw had been nearly ripped off, and there were deep gashes to his neck and face.

"I want to see him, hold him, and kiss him. I loved him," Milly sobbed.

"You don't want to remember him this way, Milly," said the sheriff. "It's not pretty."

She dropped to her knees with her hands in the dirt. An older woman hunkered toward Milly and placed her arms around her for comfort.

"It's going to be okay, Milly. Come with me. The sheriff is right. You don't need to see him like this," the woman said.

She lifted the grieving wife to her feet and escorted her away from the wagon. Once Milly was gone, an armed local named Westfield shouted, "What are we going to do about this, Sheriff?

You have a grieving wife who lost her husband today. A few good men are dead because of savages running amok."

The armed white men around him agreed and roared for revenge.

"He's right, Sheriff. This must end right now," another local townsman named Steven expressed.

"This is South Carolina, and we are proud people that will not live in terror. No more! These niggers need to pay with their lives!" Westfield exclaimed.

"I hear Cornwell Walken had one of his niggers recently run off but killed his overseer before he did so; strangled the man with his bare hands. And Foxx was hunting him down, and now he's dead too," one of the locals mentioned.

"What is this nigger's name?" the sheriff asked.

"I hear his name is Solomon. And he's becoming a problem. The nigger done escaped twice from Walken's farm."

"We need to find this nigger and whoever's with him and lynch them!" Steven shouted. "Are you with us, Sheriff? No more! No more loss of good white souls to these savages!"

The sheriff nodded. They raised their rifles and shotguns into the air and were riled up to implement revenge.

Everything seemed back to normal on the Walkens' plantation. Enslaved people were hard at work, tending to the cotton fields and other chores throughout the plantation. It was a warm fall day. But the work on the plantation remained backbreaking and tedious. Cynthia Walken exited her home in her evening dress, carrying a glass of cool lemonade. The lady of the house was all smiles for the afternoon. Her house nigger, Gloria, who was shy and sheltered, followed behind her. Cynthia stood on the wide front porch and observed the bustling activity happening on the plantation, taking casual sips from her drink, while Gloria stood docile behind the lady of the house, ready to implement whatever command she gave.

"I must say, it is a beautiful day today, isn't it, Gloria?" said Cynthia.

Gloria nodded. "Yes, ma'am, it is."

Cynthia turned to stare at Gloria, clad in a one-piece frock. She smiled and said, "I hear you are with child."

Gloria nodded. "Yes, ma'am. I am."

"Well, congratulations to you. More nigger children on this plantation are always a blessing from God. Don't you agree?"

"Yes, ma'am. I do."

"You are young and fertile, Gloria. And a fertile young nigger girl is a valuable commodity to this generation. You are pretty too, Gloria. You must woo the hearts of all these young niggers on this plantation. And might I ask who your baby's father is?" asked Cynthia with a raised brow.

"Ma'am, it's Brody," Gloria shyly responded.

"Brody, huh? He's a tall, strong, and striking nigger." Cynthia smiled with suspicion.

Gloria nodded and slightly smiled. But Cynthia's eyes suddenly burned into her house nigger, as if she knew her slave wasn't telling her the truth.

"You wouldn't lie to me about who the father of your baby is, right, Gloria?" Cynthia questioned.

"No, ma'am. I wouldn't," Gloria lied.

"Good to hear, Gloria. Because I like you. We took you from the fields and made you comfortable in our home, Gloria. And I can be a reasonable woman to my niggers, but I will not tolerate liars and any deceit in my home. Do you understand me, Gloria?" Cynthia proclaimed wholeheartedly.

Gloria nodded. "Yes, ma'am. I do."

"Good," Cynthia uttered with finality.

Cynthia smiled, then turned away from her house nigger and stared back at the slaves active in the fields and everywhere else. She took another sip from her lemonade while Gloria diverted her eyes to the floor in shame—and scared. She was pregnant by Master Walken. He took advantage of her many times when they were alone. He found her irresistible. She was seventeen, pretty, and vulnerable. Gloria felt trapped and used. Their sexual affair was meant to be kept secret from his spouse. Cynthia was a jealous and vengeful woman when it came to her husband. And Gloria knew if the truth came out about their affair, then it would be her paying the price for her husband's sins—not him.

"Mr. Colemon, how are you feeling today?" Cynthia cheerfully called out.

"I'm feeling better, ma'am. Thank you for asking," he replied.

"Well, it's good to see you back on your feet and running things again. It hasn't been the same since you were injured."

"It's good to be back, ma'am," Colemon replied.

Once again, Colemon was back on his feet and was the plantation's overseer. But there was something different about him; he seemed fragile, angrier. He allowed a nigger like Solomon to get the best of him. But it angered Colemon that Solomon had run off and hadn't been captured yet, and worse, Irene had been sold off. He wasn't allowed his revenge. Colemon felt humiliated and denied. Therefore, he took out his anger and aggression on the enslaved people on the plantation.

While Cynthia and Master Walken were enjoying their day lounging on the porch, drinking lemonade, and conducting business with locals, Colemon found himself seething inside. He was angry at Mr. Walken for selling off Irene and allowing Solomon to escape a second time. He'd promised himself that if he ever saw Solomon again, he would skin that nigger alive.

Colemon wanted to assert his authority and dominance over the enslaved people. He believed they were mocking him behind his back. He couldn't stop thinking about Solomon assaulting him, and he wanted to make an example out of someone. Colemon noticed Marcus unloading feed bags from the wagon. He started to watch Marcus like a hawk. He wanted the opportunity to strike, and it soon came when Marcus clumsily dropped one of the feed bags to the ground.

Immediately, Colemon stormed his way, glaring at Marcus, and shouted, "You are one clumsily nigger, Marcus."

"I'm sorry, Massa Colemon. It just slipped from my hands," Marcus nervously replied.

"I warned you, didn't I?" Colemon exclaimed.

"Yes, Massa Colemon, and I's sorry. It won't happen again. I's promise," Marcus uttered uneasily.

"I know it won't, nigger!"

Colemon reached for a large stick and immediately brought it down against Marcus's head. Helpless, the only thing Marcus could do was try his best to defend himself from the attack and beg for the overseer's mercy. But Colemon wanted to take out his anger and aggression on a fifty-five-year-old man. Marcus fell to the dirt as Colemon continued to strike him. The attack was unexpected and unprovoked, and everyone watching was fearful as the victim was incapable of fighting back.

The only thing Marcus could do was cower and pray for the overseer to stop soon. But Colemon became so enraged that it seemed like he would kill the slave as he repeatedly hit him in the face. There was rapid swelling and blood. Marcus tasted blood in his mouth as he developed a sharp, stinging pain right between his eyes.

"You're nothing but a got-damn, lazy nigger. And I will not tolerate any disrespect here on this farm!" Colemon shouted.

"Massa Colemon, please!" Marcus cried out frantically.

But Colemon implemented welts all over Marcus's body until he heard, "That is enough, Mr. Colemon!"

Finally, Colemon stopped striking Marcus to turn around to see Cornwell Walken glaring at him. Colemon was gasping heavily, scowling. He dropped the stick from his hand while Marcus lay by his feet, severely beaten, bleeding, and nearly unconscious.

"The nigger got out of line, Mr. Walken. He needed to be disciplined," said Colemon.

"You've disciplined him enough," Cornwell replied.

Colemon pouted. Then he walked away without uttering another word. Master Walken stared at Marcus's battered body. He lay there on his side in the dirt. It was horrible to see, but it was their life on the plantation. His nigger was still alive, and that was the only thing that mattered to him.

"Nancy and Karen, attend to this man immediately. Make sure he's back on his feet within two days, you hear me?" Master Walken ordered the two young girls.

The girls nodded. "Yes, sir."

Cornwell pivoted and walked away as if the man were a sick hog.

The girls hurried right away to attend to Marcus. And though they were ordered to treat his wounds, they would have done it without the master's orders. Marcus was close to them, and he didn't deserve to have been beaten like he was some wild animal. So, the girls helped Marcus to his feet and gently escorted him to his shack.

Meanwhile, as Cornwell returned to the big house, he noticed a horse rider approaching his plantation. It was a messenger bringing him some news.

"How can I help you?" Cornwell asked the young lad.

"I was told to inform you there will be a town meeting tomorrow late afternoon," said the rider.

Cornwell nodded.

He watched the young lad ride off his plantation in silence.

Chapter Twenty-One

Mr. Walken arrived in town in his carriage. He brought it to a stop near the South Carolina meeting hall. Wearing his cutaway coat, best trousers, top hat, and walking stick, Cornwell Walken looked the part of a statesman. He followed behind the men in dark pants and expensive shoes, marching toward the pillared entry to the building.

The main room was crowded with folks, the majority prominent and biased white men interested in politics, ideology, and dogma. Cornwell Walken entered the town hall meeting and soon found his friend, General Mathews. He dressed fashionably in checked blue pants, a grey vest, a black frock coat, a blue cravat, and a bowler hat. The general pulled on his pipe and smiled at Cornwell when he noticed him in the room.

"Cornwell Walken, always a pleasure seeing you, even on, unfortunately, such offensively and urgent matters," he said.

The two men shook hands.

"Good to see you, General," Cornwell replied.

"And how's my nigger Cherry?" the general joked. "I might require her company after tonight's assembly. Wild niggers and their shenanigans have me worked up, I must say. And some nigger company might do me well."

Cornwell wasn't in a laughing mood.

"Maybe I need to take her off your hands and purchase the nigger for my benefit one day," the general added.

The mayor, a local statesman, and Sheriff Bill Madison were all present and in charge of the assembly. Nearly three dozen men were gathered in the room. A gavel slammed down on a sounding block to silence the raucous disorder in the large assembly room. Finally, the noise subsided for the statesman, Robert Gideon, to announce, "I've received word from Washington, gentlemen."

Everyone was listening.

"It is what we have all been waiting for. Congress has passed The Fugitive Slave Act into law. From now on, nowhere in the United States will a slave find safe harbor!"

The room erupted with joyous cheering, and everyone started to drown out the statesman. Men, primarily slaveholders, tossed their hats into the air and smacked each other's backs.

Statesman Gideon continued with, "Gentlemen, you are free to pursue your property, with the aid and protection of the law, wherever your niggers may be. No longer will our niggers be protected in the North."

"Damn sure, right," someone shouted.

"And these damn abolitionists need to burn in hell for messing with our way of life," another man hollered.

"Hear! Hear!"

The general smiled at the news, but Cornwell remained deadpan.

"What's the matter, Cornwell? Are you not excited about the Fugitive Slave Act? I'm sure you would be ecstatic about the news since you have several niggers run off from your plantation in the past three months," the general mentioned.

"My business is my business, General. So I'm taking care of it," said Cornwell.

"It would be in your best interest to implement swift justice with some subtleness," the general uttered.

Statesman Gideon slammed the gavel on the sounding block again to get everyone's attention. Once he had it, he proclaimed, "Gentlemen, along with good news, unfortunately, I'm the bearer of bad news. It has come to my attention that Mr. Lincoln Latham, his wife, and young daughter were murdered inside their home."

Where there were once cheers and celebrations, the assembly room fell deathly silent as everyone was brooding over the news. First, the slaveholders were saddened and then angered by the news. A few of them knew Lincoln Latham.

"What are we going to do about this slave rebellion?" Mr. Rockwell shouted out. "It's been weeks, and it's spreading like a disease. If a group of untethered niggers continue to create chaos and turmoil in our great state of South Carolina, then I fear we are becoming a primitive society."

"I hear in Maryland and Delaware, there's a nigger named Moses freeing slaves from their owners and taking them north," a man named Abraham exclaimed.

"It is spreading. It started in Georgia, and it's making its way north. How are we supposed to protect our families, properties, and land if this nigger uprising continues and grows larger? Do we know how many niggers are involved in this uprising?" someone asked.

The room continued to erupt with loud, idle talk and hearsay. Fear, doubts, and uncertainty mixed with anger and hatred. The statesman, the mayor, and the sheriff had their hands full. Robert Gideon tried to bring order back to the assembly room, but questions were being thrown out that he could not answer, nor the mayor or sheriff. Their fear was palpable. Their fear of being killed in their sleep by savage niggers quickly overshadowed the joyous news of the Fugitive Slave Act.

It was evening when a group of men in black coats and hats exited the doors to the building and stood at the pillared entryway. The town hall meeting had ended, but their fears and concerns were relevant. Cornwell and General Mathews followed behind the group of men into the street.

The general lit his pipe and took a deep pull. Then, finally, he uttered freely, "Well, I must say, that was an intriguing moment of complexity and quarrelsomeness. But of course, we are free to pursue our niggers when they escape north because it is law, but our niggers might cut our throats before it happens."

"It's good to see that you're taking this situation lightly, General," Mr. Rockwell said. "Are you not concerned like we are?"

"Oh, I *am* concerned, Mr. Rockwell. But I will not dwell on the fear of a nigger killing me while I sleep. That is giving niggers too much power over us," the general replied.

"I wish I could be as gallant as you, General," Mr. Rockwell returned.

"Oh, Mr. Rockwell, keep your doors locked, windows shut, and your niggers chained tightly. But if death is meant to be, then it is inevitable. I will not live in fear, gentlemen. I will continue to live gloriously with lust, wealth, and pleasure. God's earth is paradise to us, for He gave control over these simple beasts. And they are designed to lash out once in a lifetime, to bite the hands that feed them. But God gave us the intelligence and manner to bring order and command to these untethered niggers. It is our duty," the general proclaimed wholeheartedly.

"Well, I wish I could be calm like you, General," Mr. Rockwell responded.

Suddenly, the conversation shifted to Cornwell.

"It has come to my attention that one of your slaves named Solomon killed an overseer, has escaped twice from your plantation, and hasn't been captured yet," the sheriff, Bill Madison, uttered.

"He will be found, Sheriff. I'm sure of it," Cornwell replied with conviction.

"Five men have been murdered while trying to track him down, including a friend of mine," said Bill.

"I'm aware of that, Sheriff. Are you insinuating that my nigger Solomon is the culprit?"

"I'm afraid so. This nigger, he's dangerous. Do you have any idea where he might run off to?"

"I sold his wife a few weeks ago to a farmer in North Carolina. The couple became more trouble than they were worth. But Solomon has no idea where she is," Cornwell mentioned.

"Then he'll come to you to find out where she is," the sheriff stated.

"He will. From what I hear from your niggers, Cornwell, the man was absolutely in love with that nigger wench. He did not want to depart from her and will want to find her. And what is the most dangerous thing on God's green earth? A nigger with nothing to lose, no family," General Mathews proclaimed.

"You will need to protect yourself, Cornwell," Abraham chimed. "And not just from this savage nigger, but from angered slaveholders who will think it is only appropriate that you pay them restitution for their property loss if Solomon is behind these attacks."

Cornwell frowned. He was *not* having a good day.

Chapter Twenty-Two

The believed uprising was still happening throughout the South and was becoming worse. But this time, the rebellion carried a name with it—Solomon. The nigger from the Walken plantation. His name was spreading everywhere quickly, like a plague. So, of course, it was him, white folks assumed. He had already killed an overseer and badly injured another, and several patty-rollers were slaughtered while pursuing him. The tension through the South was thick; folks were afraid, and white, violent mobs grew. White men were arming themselves with rifles, shotguns, and pistols. And the repercussion behind their fears and attacks was the enslaved people.

No one was safe—man, woman, or child, black or white. There was constant danger coming from the vicious uprising or angry white mobs hunting down and killing enslaved people and free men. Near the border, South Carolina and parts of North Carolina had become a battleground for death and destruction.

Every Negro in South Carolina, North Carolina, and Georgia feared for their lives and their family's lives. It seemed like Armageddon was happening everywhere.

The night was young when a youthful slave girl named Ellen walked to the barn to check on her master Lee's livestock before she retired to bed. Carrying a lantern, she walked into the barn but stopped immediately, and her eyes widened in fear. Two local white men named Luke and Sam had liked Ellen, and now they were there to "comfort themselves"; in other words, rape her.

"What you doing out here so late, girl?" Luke asked her while moving closer.

"Evenin', suh. I was just checking on master's chickens before bed," Ellen said.

Luke smiled and replied, "I don't suppose you got a pass anywhere under that pretty dress?"

"No, suh. I belong to Massa Lee, and this here his property," Ellen replied.

Luke and Sam stepped threateningly closer to her. Finally, Luke chided. "You sassin' me, girl?"

"No, suh."

"You one of these niggers rebelling out here, huh, girl? You wanna cut my throat in my sleep?" Sam chimed in.

"No, suh. I was finishing my chores for the evening," Ellen said nervously.

The look in their eyes was familiar to her. Luke and Sam took a step forward, and Ellen took a few steps back. She was ready to run away but accidentally bumped into a third man named Laurence and a fourth man named Alex. Now, she was surrounded by them.

"You ain't goin' nowhere. Me and my boys, we need to unwind tonight and comfort ourselves with a pretty nigger like you," said Luke.

Laurence grabbed her from behind before Ellen could scream or escape and slammed his hand over her mouth. Her screams became muffled as the four men dragged her into one of the stalls. Ellen tried to resist, but Luke punched her, and she dropped to the ground.

"Listen here, girl. Hush up, and we gon' make it quick!" Luke exclaimed.

Ellen was forced on her back. Her dress was pulled up and torn as Luke was the first one between her legs and forced himself inside her. He was immersed in absolute pleasure with Laurence helping to hold her down, and Sam and Alex stood at the threshold to the stall, watching and smiling. Then, suddenly, something caught Sam's attention. It was Akasha approaching them in the dark. Sam frowned at him and removed a small ax from his side.

"What's going on, Sam?" Luke asked while still inside Ellen.

"We got ourselves a lone nigger out here," Sam replied.

"Well, take care of him," Luke uttered, grunting.

Ellen cried out, "Help me!"

"Shut up!" Luke shouted, punching her in the face, then he continued to fuck her.

Sam glared at Akasha and exclaimed, "What you doing out here, nigger?"

Akasha coolly approached both men, undaunted by the ax in Sam's hand.

"He asked you a question, nigger. What you doing out here?" Alex shouted. "This isn't your business, so I advise you to turn around and leave before we kill you."

Akasha could hear the other two men raping Ellen in the stall nearby. He stepped closer and caught a glimpse of a frightened young girl. She was helpless, with her face full of tears. Luke was on top of her like she was some rag doll. Ellen reminded him of his wife back in Africa a long time ago. He knew she was dead now. Only memories of her remained, treasured reminiscences of a youthful, abundant, and full life from long ago fading from him as he became this dark, monstrous creature hell-bent on revenge. Looking at Ellen being fucked by these white devils, a boiling rage stirred inside of Akasha. They took what they wanted, whenever! They felt privileged to attack and rape Black women without any consequences. But tonight, they would pay the ultimate price for their lust and savagery.

The human features on Akasha's face quickly transformed into something demonic. Instantly, he had soulless dark eyes, sharp fangs, claws, and hellish skin. Alex was the closest to him, so immediately, Akasha lashed out with lightning speed and sank his fangs into the side of Alex's neck, paralyzing him with fear and pain. Though Sam was horrified at what he saw, he tried to aid his friend and attacked Akasha from behind with the ax. He plunged it into Akasha's neck . . . but with no results. Instead, Akasha quickly pivoted and lunged forward, slashing Sam across his chest with his razor-sharp claws. It was a gaping wound. Sam fell helplessly to his knees, crying out in agony. His demise grew closer as Akasha stood over him.

"Oh God!" Sam cried out.

"God cannot help you!" Akasha growled.

Luke and Laurence were immediately shocked at what they were seeing. Their friend, Sam, was being ripped apart by this creature, with his blood gushing from him like a fountain. Luke leaped from between Ellen's legs and wrestled with collecting himself, hurriedly pulling up his trousers to fasten them. Laurence took off running from the barn. Akasha allowed him to escape as he set his eyes on Luke, who was now the one afraid and cowering in the barn stall.

"What is this?" Luke hollered.

"Judgment day!" Akasha responded chillingly.

Akasha lunged forward at frightening speed, tackling Luke backward to the ground, nearly knocking the man unconscious. Then his sharp fangs tore into the side of Luke's neck like it were paper-thin. Luke's screams echoed from the barn as Ellen rose and watched her attacker being brutally killed.

Laurence sprinted through the woods like he was a runaway slave. What he saw back there was so horrifying that he nearly peed on himself. Unfortunately, he didn't get too far. He stopped dead in his tracks abruptly. The woods were pitch black, and a branch snapped under someone's foot. It didn't come from him. His heart stopped, and he sucked in air. Laurence spun around. In the distance, two small red dots were glowing. But they weren't dots. They were a pair of gleaming, red eyes trained on him, watching his every move.

Solomon loomed closer with his fangs showing. Laurence knew this man was a monster.

"Please, it wasn't my idea," Laurence begged.

In a flash, Laurence's entire body became suspended in the air. Solomon held him up by his neck. His strength was unreal to this man.

"I have a family," Laurence cried out.

"So did I," Solomon replied before killing him.

A moment later, Solomon joined Akasha in the barn stall with his mouth coated with the victim's blood. Solomon glanced down at Ellen, who was shaking in fear. Luke's body was sprawled across the ground in a pool of blood. There were a few pieces of him strewn about.

"What are you going to do with her?" Solomon asked Akasha.

Akasha moved closer to Ellen. Like everyone, she was afraid, believing she was next to die.

"You need not be afraid of me. I'm here to change your life and give you absolute strength and power to overcome and defeat your enemies," he proclaimed.

Akasha took her hand into his and gazed into her eyes.

"Become calm and become my warrior of the night. Then you will be unstoppable and their worst nightmare—no more rapes or fears, only power and vengeance . . . and total freedom. But you must accept death to become alive fully," he continued.

Ellen locked eyes with Akasha. There was something comforting about his speech. She was eighteen, and the only thing she knew was slavery and feeling helpless all her life. She'd been raped by white men before, young and old. It started when she was fourteen. Her parents had been sold off, her brothers killed, and her baby by Master Lee was stillborn.

"Will you accept death to live?" Akasha asked her.

She nodded. "Yes."

Akasha grinned. Then he slowly sank his fangs into the side of her neck to turn her into a creature of the night. Ellen didn't resist. Instead, she closed her eyes and allowed the transformation to happen. Solomon stood to the side and watched. Akasha was starting to build his army of the undead.

Ellen emerged from the ground naked. She had no idea how long it had been, but she felt different . . . changed. Like Solomon before her, a wave of awkwardness hit her quickly. She didn't care that she was naked. However, her physical state was altered. She started to hear and see things with precision, and there was a sudden increase in strength. Akasha and Solomon were staring at her. Solomon approached her and covered her nakedness with a blanket. Akasha told her, "Now, you must feed, or you'll die."

It didn't matter if they were men, women, or children. Several Black bodies of all sizes hung like ornaments on the branches of massive oak trees along the roadside. It resulted from violent white mobs looking to seize revenge across the countryside. It was a horror show. Militiamen scoured the country searching for Solomon and rebellious slaves, heatedly looking to end the uprising spreading through the South like wildfire. Life on many plantations had been uprooted and changed. Crops had been ruined because of fires and violence. Homes were destroyed, and enslaved people were escaping from their enslavers and the bloodshed by the dozens. They were scared. It didn't matter if you were innocent or not. If your skin was black, you were endangered of being murdered.

Hickory Grove, South Carolina, was a hundred miles from the border of North Carolina. It was a growing city with small farms and extensive plantations growing cotton, corn, sugar, and rice. Most enslaved people lived on extensive plantations. But most Southerners in the town didn't experience a degree of wealth. A few men were indentured servants, able to come and go with decent pay. And though the contrast between rich and poor was greater in the South, there was peace and tranquility in the caste system . . . until the sun had set that evening. Then the sins of slavery were coming back to haunt them, everyone believed.

A shopkeeper named Wallace DuPont stumbled out of his supply store, holding his side while clutching his shotgun. He had been gravely injured as blood soaked through his shirt. He fell to the ground on his hands and knees with the shotgun spilling from his hand. He immediately caught the townspeople's attention as they came to aid him.

"Wallace, what happened to you?" a woman asked him.

He couldn't speak as terror was written on his face. Quickly, Wallace was surrounded by caring folks, including the sheriff.

Something was wrong. They saw the blood and the shotgun nearby, and they all grew worried.

"Have you been attacked?" the sheriff asked him.

But Wallace remained quiet. Something did attack him. He released an ugly groan and then doubled over in the dirt. Suddenly, everyone heard an ethereal howl inside Wallace's supply store. They've never heard anything like it before.

"What was that?" another man questioned.

"Maybe there's some kind of animal inside the store," someone else suggested.

The supply store was dark, too dark for everyone's comfort. Nevertheless, the sheriff and his deputy decided to check it out. They cautiously approached the entrance to the store carrying a lantern.

"Whoever is in here, come out now," the sheriff shouted.

There was no response. Both men moved farther into the store while everyone looked on from outside. Wallace was now dead, and a few folks were mourning his death.

The sheriff and his deputy pushed forward into the darkness. Quickly, a shape flashed behind them, unseen. Startled, both men spun around.

"What was that?" the deputy asked.

Whatever it was, it seemed enormous, and it was fast. The sheriff and deputy removed their Colt Buntline Special .45 revolvers, believing they would stop whatever threat came their way. They continued exploring the source of the sound and movement, but there was still nothing. They moved to the back of the store, where they came across a pair of gleaming black eyes sizing them up in the darkness. The deputy raised his pistol at them. Then they were gone.

"Something ain't right," the deputy uttered. He didn't want to be in the store any longer.

Another shadow rapidly crossed behind them, which was much closer this time. Then it was gone. It seemed like something was toying with them. The men grew tense, with the deputy quivering. Suddenly, a low, rasping chuckle came from over their shoulders, harsh and hungry. They pivoted quickly, with the sheriff dropping the lantern at the sight of Akasha looming menacingly toward them. Both men aimed their pistols at him.

"Stop where you are, nigger," the sheriff hollered.

Akasha continued.

Speedily, Akasha ripped his clawed hand across the sheriff's neck. His blood sprayed through the darkness as he staggered backward, closely grabbing his wound. The deputy screamed and then fired his pistol repeatedly at Akasha, but to no avail. Finally, Akasha lunged at the deputy, attacking him. Immediately, the deputy's head was wrenched back and forth. This mighty creature, Akasha, sawed his way through the deputy's neck as they both fell. The man's neck snapped as they hit the floor. And the deputy was rendered nothing but dead prey.

When Akasha exited the supply store covered in the men's blood, looking demonic with his claws dripping in crimson, the townspeople were immediately horrified. They'd never seen anything like it.

"Your sheriff and deputy are dead," Akasha uttered in a chilling voice.

He stepped closer to them as they all took a step backward. It seemed like the ground trembled with every step he took. His soulless, black eyes glared at every white soul before him, making men and women quiver where they stood.

"You all will be helpless against what's coming," Akasha continued.

"He killed the sheriff and the deputy," a man hollered.

The crowd grew angry but remained intimidated by Akasha's demonic appearance. They were ready to lynch him. This nigger dared to taunt them after killing three people. But not a single one attempted to attack him—not until someone from behind pressed a gun barrel against the back of Akasha's head.

"You move, nigger, and I'll blow your head clean off!" a young man named Marvin growled.

Akasha smirked. He was too cool to react quickly, but his energy was noticeably different as he stared at the crowd with a smirk.

"Kill that nigger, Marvin!" a man shouted angrily.

Unexpectedly, with a speed that no one could comprehend, Akasha pivoted, shattering the shotgun into two pieces. His claws heatedly slashed against the man's neck, nearly decapitating him. Everyone was shocked and horrified. They ran, but many wouldn't get far. Akasha grinned—*Let the massacre begin.*

A middle-aged white woman named Mary attempted to hide inside her home. This was it. The nigger uprising had reached their town. She was terrified. She desperately searched her home for a weapon. Then out of nowhere, she heard someone say, "I see you."

Mary froze. It was a woman's voice. She wildly looked around but saw nothing.

Again, a young woman's voice taunted her with a sibilant, slimy whisper, repeating, "I see you."

"Please, leave me alone!" Mary screamed.

"Your blood smells so sweet. Can I get a taste of it?" The woman's voice continued to taunt her.

Mary cowered in the corner, not knowing what to do next. She was afraid and felt trapped. Then, all of a sudden, Ellen loomed into her view. She was young and beautiful. But Mary knew there was something dangerous about her. Her eyes were cold, and her demeanor frightening. Ellen coolly approached her and ran her nails across her cheek threateningly. Mary shivered while Ellen grinned.

"Don't worry, I'll make it quick," said Ellen.

"Please!" Mary begged, quivering.

Seeing a white woman begging for her life made Ellen feel powerful. She could smell her blood, and her fear was alluring. Before Mary could say another word, Ellen plunged her sharp fangs into the side of her neck, brutally killing her.

The town was under attack, and Akasha, Solomon, and Ellen were unstoppable. The fear in the townspeople's faces was palpable like daylight. A few men tried to stand against the uncanny, ungodly trio, only to be cut down like weeds. Akasha grabbed a man and ripped open his face. Another man emptied both barrels of his shotgun into Solomon—only to gasp. Then the shotgun was torn from his hands, tossed away, and he was brutally killed. A couple dropped to the ground, howling in pain and blinded by darkness. The husband clutched his broken right leg while his wife screamed for his help. He dragged himself crying in pain toward her, fighting like a banshee against Ellen. The husband lunged for his wife, and he was able to grab her hand, but Akasha quickly dragged her away to her death. Then he too was pulled underneath a house, screaming in agony.

Nearly two dozen decapitated and twisted white bodies were sprawled across the town. It was a bloody massacre. The trio tried to kill as many people as possible. The townsfolk couldn't run or hide. It was judgment day. It would become the uprising they wouldn't be able to suppress.

Suddenly, something changed with Solomon. He watched as Akasha and Ellen attacked the children. He watched as a twelve-year-old girl was ripped apart by Akasha like she was a rag doll. After he drained her blood, he tossed her carcass into the dirt. Solomon wanted justice for his people, but something was disturbing about Akasha's motives. He'd been hunting and killing with his maker for several weeks now. Yet, he still felt alone and confined.

Everyone in the town was either dead or somehow had escaped the horror. Solomon stood in the center of the town and saw the destruction they'd created. He stared down at the body of a lifeless nine-year-old girl. It was disturbing to see. This wasn't him. He thought about Irene and knew it was time to find her. He could find her, but he was changing into a monster. He could no longer enjoy the warmth of the sun. His body was indifferent, and he was always hungry.

This ability was starting to become a curse for Solomon.

Chapter Twenty-Three

It was early morning, and the sun beamed through the clouds and lit up the tiny shack. The rising sun cast a rosy hue across the morning sky, indicating a new day. The golden light was everywhere, covering natural and man-made creations. The day was becoming full of beauty and filled with the promises of a new beginning—if you were white. But it was another day of survival and hard work for the enslaved people on Randall's farm.

Loud moaning escaped from Randall while he was on top of Irene. He was inside of her, sweating and finishing. He was rough and clumsy. It looked like something between an awkward rape and a virgin attempting his first sexual encounter. Irene lay on her back and pretended not to be there. She continually turned her head from Randall but remained as still as possible while her master huffed and puffed on top of her. If there was such a thing, she was vicious with her passive-aggressiveness. There was a fuss and fight, tears and disgust in the beginning. But weeks later, Irene mastered becoming a statue while Randall had sex with her.

Soon, her master was rocked by an orgasm, ejaculating into her, sliding into that scale of absolute pleasure. His deep breathing was above her. There was a moment of Randall coming back to his senses, with the desire for sex slowly diminishing. Finally, Randall climbed off Irene while she remained still, not even looking his way. Her eyes cast to the ceiling, and her nakedness was covered with his sweat and residue. She heard him fiddling around her shack. He told her, "You need not lie around here all morning, Irene. You got chores to do. Get now!"

"Yes, Massa Randall," she replied.

Randall exited her shack. Irene lay there briefly before she finally lifted herself from the bed. She immediately went to her wash area and scrubbed his sweat and odor from her body. Afterward, she dropped to her knees and prayed to God. Solomon was on her mind. She missed him and feared that she would never see him again in his physical state. Solomon had a warrior's spirit. And knowing her husband, Irene believed he would run off again to try to find her. He was stubborn but determined to pursue what he believed in—freedom. The memories of her husband kept her strong and moving forward because she believed they would reunite someday, either in this life or the next.

Randall's plantation was smaller, but the work was more demanding. He wasn't as wealthy as Cornwell Walken. He grew tobacco, had a fat wife, and had no morals. He was often drunk, and he provided the bare minimum for his slaves to survive. He had repulsive and coarse manners and didn't have a sense of kindness or justice. Randall McHenry would outsource several of his slaves to nearby farms. But he wasn't shy in inflicting abuse and rape on Black women and the men he enslaved. When drunk, he would lash out at enslaved people with a whip, enjoying the sound of their screams. He frequently made degrading comments about Black women, dehumanizing them and framing them in animalistic terms. To Randall McHenry, Black women were objects to be taken advantage of—and for now, Irene was the prize in his eyes.

Irene donned her usual attire for the day, a one-piece frock and a sunbonnet. She stepped out of her cabin and stopped. Though it had been weeks since her arrival, the place still felt strange and new to her. She'd never been this far from home in Franklin, North Carolina. But no matter what state she was in or how bigger or smaller the plantation was, everything remained the same with slavery: Black people were inferior, subhuman, and dehumanized.

Irene smiled at Penny, exiting her shack to begin another workday with her mother. Irene had become close with Penny. They were about the same age. Penny was bright, hardworking, and tough. She was Randall's sexual tryst before he bought Irene. However, Penny knew it wouldn't be long until Massa Randall pivoted back to climbing on top of her daily to please himself. Penny was a pretty girl with brown skin and childbearing hips.

"Massa on top of you again this morning?" Penny asked.

Irene huffed and said, "Like routine, like a rooster crowing in the morning."

Penny chuckled. Then she replied, "It won't be long now until he gets bored with you and comes back to climbing on top of me again," she said. "I be reckoned he'll get you pregnant soon, if you not already."

"Pregnant?" Irene uttered in disbelief, placing her hand against her stomach.

"Massa Randall, he filled the bellies of many pickaninnies on this farm with his seed. Some babies he keeps, some he sold off. He's an immoral and lustful man," Penny said. "Massa Randall has done already sold off three of my offsprings; the fourth was stillborn. We's buried him nearby."

It disgusted Irene. The thought of being pregnant by a man she despised suddenly made her sick to her stomach. But she was helpless to stop him.

With the sun again high in the sky, the enslaved people worked the tobacco fields and the farm. Then, finally, the men and women in the fields began to sing a spiritual hymn. It was the only thing that distracted them from the tedium.

Irene hung clothes near the tree line. Master Randall sat on his porch in the distance, drifting in a rocking chair and smoking a pipe with a bottle of whiskey by his feet. Irene could hear her fellow Negroes singing in the fields, expressing their deepest religious emotions of souls touched by Christ, and it kindled a flame in their hearts and gave them some hope. Irene paused and closed her eyes. She felt the bright sun against her face, thinking about Solomon. She thought about her husband every day. She focused on the good memories with Solomon, though they were subjugated. *Oh, how he used to touch me and look at me*, she thought. She dwelled on their deep intimacy when they were alone. Irene missed how he used to hold, comfort, and protect her. She yearned to feel her husband's deep strokes inside her while being on top of her.

Irene loved him. They had something so special that not even slavery could impede their passion. And though they were separated, her heart was stamped with memories of Solomon and his dogmatic ways about freedom. If given a second chance, she would have run off with him rather than stay behind, being afraid. She understood his motivations clearly. The only thing Solomon was truly afraid of was losing her. And he would rather die first than be separated from the love of his life. Irene was deep in thought about her husband. It was painful. A few tears started to trickle from her eyes as realization hit her. He was gone.

Suddenly, something snapped Irene out of her daydream. A runaway slave quietly appeared from the tree line into her view. He was crouched and hiding. Irene gasped.

"Sshhh!" the runaway hushed her.

Irene froze.

"Please, I's need ya help," the runaway said.

He looked gaunt and exhausted. His clothes were torn, his skin was plagued with abuse, and his eyes were sunken in from being malnourished.

"Help me," he whispered to Irene.

Irene quaked visibly, but she returned to hanging the clothes.

"You need to get on from here now. I can't help you," she replied quietly.

"I need to hide. They gon' kill me. They killing us all," the runaway pleaded.

Irene glanced back at Master Randall, still sitting in his rocking chair, enjoying his pipe. She wanted to help him, but she had no idea how. Her hands were tied. It was daylight, and the farm was busy with the overseer riding his horse and Master Randall and his family nearby.

"Turn back around and keep running. You not safe here. Massa see you, and he'll tan ya hide fo' sure," Irene said.

But the runaway man remained stubborn, crouched, and hidden. He had nowhere to go.

"Go on now, get!" Irene uttered sternly.

"Irene!" she heard him shout. "Who are you talking to?"

Randall stood from his rocking chair and stared in Irene's way. She froze in fear.

"Answer me, girl. Who are you talking to?" Randall shouted again.

"No one, Massa Randall . . . just to myself," she replied.

"Now, don't lie to me, Irene!" he exclaimed.

The runaway remained crouched. Suddenly, there was the sound of barking dogs in the distance. He knew they'd found him. The man leaped to his feet, pushed by Irene, and ran toward the farm. Randall was shocked by the runaway.

"What in the hell?!" Randall shouted.

The runaway was weak, but he still moved fast. Irene watched him try to escape as he feared for his life. It was as if she were watching Solomon flee for his freedom again. Next, three canines sprinted toward him, and bringing him down didn't take much effort. Several men on horseback followed the barking dogs, patty-rollers tracking him down. The disturbance caught the attention of everyone on the farm, including Randall's overseer, Hawk.

"Gentlemen, what is this?" Randall asked one of the trackers.

"We been lookin' for this nigger for days now," a tracker named Jessie replied. "He a slippery nigger. But we got him."

"What's he done?" asked Hawk, the overseer.

"Caught this nigger concealing a firearm, shot a white man dead a few days back. We believe he's part of the uprising happening south," another tracker named Casey replied.

"I heard that's happening some miles yonder from here," Hawk uttered. "Is it reaching Franklin County?"

"Nearly twenty white folks killed ninety miles from here. They attacked the town in the night and killed nearly everyone, including children. They said a nigger named Solomon is behind it. Got an army of niggers behind him," said Jessie.

"Solomon?" Randall repeated the name.

When Irene heard her husband's name mentioned, she gasped in shock. He was still alive. However, she kept her composure. She was afraid that if they found out Solomon was her husband, they would kill her for his sins. And though the news was grim, Irene was grateful for it.

However, the news of the uprising spread north to North Carolina towns. Everyone feared it was coming to them, and they were willing to take extreme measures to prevent it.

"You think you're smarter than us, don't you, boy?" Jessie shouted at the captured runaway. Next, he rushed forward and kicked the man in his face.

The captured runaway winched in pain as his mouth became coated with blood. They stood over him with the canines snarling while being held back by their leashes. These German shepherds barked, snapped, and growled at him. The fear in the runaway's eyes was clear-cut. First, Jessie spat at the runaway's feet with disgust. Then he looked at Randall McHenry.

"You wanna keep your niggers in line and behaved, Mr. Randall, then we need to set an example. You need to show what happens to unruly niggers right here on your property," said Jessie.

Randall glared at the runaway slave, still wincing in pain. Then finally, he stepped closer to him and exclaimed, "You think you can kill white women and men and get away with it, you filthy nigger, huh? I'm talking to you!"

The runaway slave cowered at Jessie's feet and groveled. "I's a good nigger, please. I didn't harm no one. I'm just scared!"

His pleads and simplicity fell on deaf ears, with his death already determined. The enslaved people on Randall's farm had gathered nearby to watch the horror show. Master Randall didn't believe in forgiveness when it came to his slaves, and though the runaway man didn't belong to him, the man was still a nigger that needed to be taught a lesson.

"Jessie, go on and show my niggers what will happen to them if they ever decide to uprise in North Carolina," said Randall smugly.

"Gladly. Will do," Jessie replied.

Jessie looked at his men holding three large, snarling dogs on leashes. Then he uttered, "Send this runaway to nigger hell!"

Casey smiled. He was the first to release his canine from its leash and yelled, "Git 'em, boy!"

The other two men did the same. They let loose their leashes holding their dogs back, and the dogs charged toward the runaway on his knees. Immediately, it was a bloodbath. Randall, Jessie, Casey, and the other white men didn't blink an eye as the slave was being torn to pieces by the vicious dogs. However, Irene and the other enslaved people were scared and sickened by what they saw. Irene had never seen a man ripped apart by dogs before, and she cried at the sight.

"Ohmygod!"

While the runaway slave was being torn apart, Randall glared at his niggers. He shouted, "Let this be a warning to every last one of you niggers. You create trouble on my land or anywhere in North Carolina, and this will be your fate!"

Irene was horrified. She fell to her knees in tears, and she thought about Solomon. It scared her to think this could be her husband's fate if they ever caught him. The man's dreadful screams still rang in her ears.

Chapter Twenty-Four

"You hunt monsters?" Noah asked Kaiser.

"I hunt vampires," Kaiser replied.

"What's a vampire?" he asked.

"They're creatures of the night. They're strong, fast, and dangerous. It's what you saw that night when your owner and his family were killed."

"What I saw that night was the devil," Noah replied.

Kaiser couldn't contest Noah's answer because he believed this specific creature was something demonic. It was killing people. It wasn't to feed but to create chaos and destruction. It was angry and vengeful.

Melody was asleep in the cart, and Kaiser and Noah struck up a friendship. They started to learn from each other. Noah recounted his horrors of being a slave in the South to Kaiser, and Kaiser informed him about vampires.

"Most vampires only need to feed a couple of times a week to maintain their health. But a wounded vampire must feed more often as blood is required for healing," Kaiser proclaimed.

"They drink blood?" Noah asked.

Kaiser nodded. "Unfortunately. But as a vampire ages, it requires less blood to maintain normal functionality."

Noah was listening, but most of the conversation went over his head. Everything was new and strange to him. A few days ago, he was an enslaved person up for auction. He moved around in leg irons and witnessed his family sold off. Now, he was considered a free man with Kaiser and learning about the supernatural.

Kaiser continued. "The reason behind this is not entirely clear, but it likely has to do with the fact that a vampire's gift and special abilities intensify over time. Thus, the older a vampire gets, the stronger its power becomes, and the less mortal its body is."

Still, Noah couldn't believe what he was hearing.

"How do you kill it?" he asked.

"These creatures are hard to kill. So, if you were ever to come across one, run. But the fact that you've seen one and lived to tell about it is remarkable," Kaiser said. "Sunlight kills it, fire . . . maybe silver, and decapitation. And that's *if* you can get close enough to kill it."

"Why would God create such a monster?" asked Noah.

It was a good question. "Where there's good, there will always be evil. The world is filled with mysteries, my friend. It's still young, and many places and things are undiscovered."

"My world has always been slavery," said Noah sadly.

"It will no longer be," Kaiser replied. "After you help me with this mission, you are free to go wherever you please, start over, and become the man God intended you to be."

Noah smiled.

They headed toward the Cullen plantation in Georgia as they continued to converse. It was once a thriving commerce with dozens of enslaved people. Now, it was in ruins. The big house was where Akasha slaughtered his first family after awakening from his lengthy hibernation. It became the catalyst for the devastation that was happening across the South. And it was once the place Noah called his home.

Kaiser brought the cart to a stop near the big house, and both men climbed from it. Melody had finally awakened from her sleep and looked around. Something that once served as a symbol of wealth and prosperity was now a place haunted by tragedies. And not with the massacre of the Cullen family but with generations of chattel slavery.

"No one's here," she said.

Noah took a deep breath and stared at the big house. This abandoned plantation stirred some deep and horrible memories for him.

"He stood there," Noah pointed out, in front of the big house. "And he stared at us with those eyes. I never will forget those eyes."

Kaiser took in the area with soft eyes. He walked toward the big house and entered slowly. Noah and Melody chose to remain outside. Everything was still, and there was a certain stench that he couldn't deduce. Kaiser figured the vampire that killed everyone was long gone, but he knew the main vampire liked leaving underlings behind. And with the day sunny and bright, Kaiser went exploring through the forsaken place.

He kept his walking cane close and ready. He cautiously moved through the lower area of the house first, sweeping dark corners and spaces. Then he moved upstairs toward the bedrooms. Fortunately, he didn't come across any underlings left behind. During the day, they would stay hidden or buried somewhere dark. Kaiser stood in the center of the home and closed his eyes. Though the attack happened weeks ago, he could sense the evil there. This vampire left behind a scent that only he could pick up. It was intense, vengeful, and young—coming from Africa nearly a hundred years ago. While vampires plagued Europe and Africa for thousands of years, America was still almost untouched and unfamiliar with the species. But with the arrival and awakening of this vampire, things were about to change. Vampires liked to remain hidden and low-key. Many didn't want to attract any attention to their kind. Still, this particular one was unleashing an intense fury in the South that the backlash was becoming detrimental to Blacks and whites. It would only be a matter of time before civilization in the South tore itself apart.

"Who are you?" Kaiser said to himself in the empty room. Finally, he turned and exited the premises with Noah and Melody standing by the wagon.

"Everything okay, sir?" Noah asked him.

"Is there a cave nearby?" Kaiser asked Noah.

Noah nodded. "Yes, sir. Ellison's Cave."

"Take me to it," said Noah.

It was nearly dark when Kaiser reached Ellison's Cave. The area was quiet and creepy, but it didn't stop Kaiser from exploring inside. It was the deepest cave in Georgia. Ellison's Cave was rare and beautiful but dangerous too. It featured the deepest, unobstructed pit in the U.S. and other deep holes and pitches. So, Kaiser knew that he had to be careful with every step he took as he traveled farther into the pit of darkness alone. He soon came to an area where a deep drop prevented him from traveling further. But Kaiser knew this was where this vampire had awakened from its hibernation. It was dark, hidden, dangerous, and the conditions treacherous. Unfortunately, there weren't too many humans brave enough to travel farther into darkness and the unknown.

Kaiser had many questions that needed answering, like what made it sleep for so long and its true purpose here. But the one question that needed answering was what happened to the vampire hunter sent to hunt down this creature over a hundred years ago. Unfortunately, the deep drop prevented Kaiser from traveling further into the cave. So, he turned around and headed back the way he came from.

When he emerged from the tight crevice, it was already dark. He looked at Noah and Melody and said, "It's late. We'll camp here tonight."

South Carolina seemed hotter than Georgia as November was approaching. The sun's scorching heat made Noah and Melody's throats dry and their skin full of sweat and perspiration. Noah drove the wagon down a dirt road while Kaiser was asleep in the back. It had been a long journey, a dangerous one too. Every county from Georgia to South Carolina seemed to have been through war or was preparing for one. The roads were dangerous, and the trio was fortunate to have traveled this far.

"Yuh believe him when he say we gon' be free soon?" Noah asked Melody.

She nodded. "Yes."

"Yuh trust him?" asked Noah.

"He kept his word this far," Melody replied.

"He believes in monsters," said Noah.

"And why not? We see them every day, Noah . . . monsters," Melody said.

"What I saw that night on Massa Cullen's land was de devil, I's swear it. We all swear it. He ripped that overseer n' his boy apart. And I's never forget those eyes. They looked right at me," Noah stated.

Noah reflected on that night. It stuck with him like a nightmare he couldn't wake up from. He was a masculine man but became childlike when bringing up the massacre of the Cullen family.

"I was twelve when Massa James first raped me," Melody said out of the blue. "And he marked me with his brand."

She pulled down the sleeve of her dress and lowered her left shoulder to reveal her branding. It was frayed but burnt into her skin. It was a permanent symbol, leaving behind a raised scar. She covered it again.

"I was twelve years old," she repeated. "Twelve. Massa James on top of me for a year, almost every day. And when he done with me, he had others climb on top of me doin' to me what they pleased. He would dress me nice and pretty and present me to his friends. He would rent me out for the evening, and I believed it was how things were supposed to be. I made them feel special in the bedroom, so I started to feel special. They liked me. I would be on my back with them inside of me, and I felt I's could be their equal, not a slave. But then, one night, one of the Massa's friends had trouble with his man parts. He tried to perform, but he couldn't. So, he blamed me, and he beat me. He beat me and cursed me. Massa James found out, and he beat me too. He says it's my job to make his friends feel good and not embarrass them."

Noah glanced at her as a sudden sadness swept over Melody.

"Fo'd a long time, I believed it was the way things were supposed to be . . . until Mr. Kaiser tells me different," Melody added.

They both shared their horrors while traveling down the dirt road. Suddenly, Noah spotted something ahead. It was trouble. Several armed white men had implemented a roadblock. And on the side of the road, they had captured three slaves, apparent runaways. They were bound and muzzled and looked to have already been thoroughly beaten. Noah's eyes widened with panic. "Shit!" The men saw the wagon approaching with two Blacks driving it. They confronted Noah and Melody by pointing their rifles at them right away.

"Mr. Kaiser, you need to wake up, sir!" Noah exclaimed.

"What are you niggers doing on that wagon?" one of the men demanded.

"We's just passing through, sir. That's all," Noah calmly replied.

"Do you know a slave named Solomon?" another man asked them with his rifle trained at Melody.

"No, sir. Never heard that name in my life," Noah replied.

"You lying to me, nigger! You part of this got-damn nigger rebellion, killing good white folks out there?" they shouted.

"No, sir! We's traveling with Mr. Kaiser. He's in the back sleeping. I can wake him for you," said Noah.

Noah glanced at the three runaways on the side of the road and knew their fate. They would be lynched. And it would be his and Melody's fate too, if Mr. Kaiser didn't wake up.

"Mr. Kaiser, you need to wake up, sir!" Noah hollered, trying to keep calm.

As if on cue, Kaiser awoke to find the predicament they were in. He was surprised to see four armed men.

"Oh my, I see we're in quite a pickle here," Kaiser uttered.

"And who are you?" they asked.

"Good day to you, gentlemen. My name is Kaiser Adelberg. We are simply passing through your fine county on our way to Virginia for business," he announced, and his German accent immediately stuck out.

"Virginia is a long way from here. And are these your niggers?"

"They are," he responded.

"And do you have papers for them?"

"I assure you, gentlemen, we come here with no attention of malice or difficulty in your fair county. My driver and his companion are not part of any rebellion," he said.

"And we supposed to believe you?" they replied.

"I know these are troubling times, gentlemen, and we are strangers passing through. But we mean you no harm. I agree, niggers should know their place. And these are *my* niggers, and they know their place," said Kaiser convincingly.

The men nodded. Fortunately, Kaiser had the bill of sale for Noah, which he presented to the men. They quickly glanced over it, glared at Noah, and back at the sale.

"And the girl?" they asked.

"Fortunately, I won her in a poker game," said Kaiser.

"I would like to win a pretty wench like her myself," one uttered, grinning. He stared at Melody with a look she was far too familiar with.

Kaiser chuckled. "And she is worth the wager." His relaxed demeanor pacified the men.

"Okay. You check out. But you need to be careful when riding with niggers and not fall asleep around them. Someday, they can catch that nigger disease called rebellion and gut you in your sleep," they said.

"Duly noted," Kaiser replied.

However, before allowing them to pass, the four men had unfinished business with the captured runaways. And now that they had an audience, it was time. Three nooses were placed around the runaways' necks and fastened. Then the men were hoisted into the air without a second thought. There were a few convulsive struggles and suffering, and then two human souls were gone to judgment. Their bodies swayed from the tree as a display of punishment.

Finally, the men cleared the roadblock, and their wagon was free to move through. But the trio was left with the memory of two men hung and the third runaway near his end. It was hard for Kaiser not to intervene. He could have easily killed all four men in a heartbeat. But he was forbidden to kill any humans unless they endangered his life. His assignment was to hunt down this vampire or vampires that created havoc in the South. But the longer he stayed in America, the more the lines were blurred between good and evil.

"I apologize for the derogatory language back there. But I had to convince them," Kaiser said when they were far from the roadblock.

"We understand, Mr. Kaiser. It could have been us lynched," Noah replied.

Unfortunately, this was America.

Chapter Twenty-Five

They had two hours of sunlight left, and Kaiser felt there was a malevolent entity nearby. They'd arrived at another plantation in South Carolina where another attack had happened weeks ago. The moment Kaiser steered the carriage onto the sprawling land, they ran into more company. Conner and his men were on the plantation looking for runaways they believed were hiding on the abandoned property or nearby. They inspected every square inch of the place when they spotted the wagon. Seeing Kaiser, Noah, and Melody, the men immediately approached the wagon with frowns and hostility.

Kaiser sighed. He was growing tired of the regular confrontation with armed, racist Southerners. Life was becoming difficult in Georgia, South Carolina, and North Carolina. There was destruction, hunger, lawlessness, violence . . . and blockades. Many African Americans were becoming refugees, homeless, and being hunted down.

"Hold it there, now. What are you and these niggers doing on this property?" Conner asked.

Kaiser knew he had to put on a show while traveling with Noah and Melody. But unfortunately, they were in hostile territory.

"Good day to you, gentlemen," Kaiser greeted them politely while he tipped his hat at them. It was to show them some respect. "We mean not to cause you any trouble. My name is Kaiser Adelberg, and I'm here on official business."

"And what business would that be, and with these two niggers?" asked Conner.

"I'm what you might call a bounty hunter, gentlemen . . . And like yourself, I'm searching for a specific nigger myself . . . a dangerous man," Kaiser mentioned.

"What is this nigger's name?" Donald asked.

Kaiser knew what name to mention to rile them up and make it believable. "His name is Solomon."

"Solomon. That nigger's name has created quite a stir lately in these parts, and we want a piece of him ourselves," Conner uttered. "Heard he attacked two overseers, killed one, and then killed the five men looking for him. God bless their souls. Now, he got niggers uprising against the South, disrupting our way of life. But God almighty, when we find this nigger, it will be some biblical shit with him."

His men concurred.

"And might I ask, where are you coming from, Mr. Adelberg? And what's the use with these two niggers?"

"These are my niggers bought and paid for. They are my help with tracking Solomon," Kaiser replied.

"Help?" Donald chuckled. "You trust these niggers?" he questioned and raised his pistol to Noah's head.

"They've never been a problem, gentlemen. I trust them."

"Well, I lost a brother named Billy a few weeks back. He was torn apart like some hog while tracking some nigger," Donald added. "And you know what? I don't trust your story, Mr. Kaiser. You seem like a nigger lover to me."

The tension grew thick, and now Kaiser began to feel his life was endangered. He locked eyes with Donald, and if so be it, he was quick with the draw with either gun or blade. It was either them or him. Noah and Melody became nervous and held hands inadvertently. *We gon' die here*, Noah thought. White folks were restless, antsy, and trigger-happy. The way these white men stared at Noah made him uneasy. Though he was innocent, he was still considered a threat. But something happened, a distraction.

A young boy came running from the woods with fear written across his face.

"Help me!" the boy shouted. "It killed my dog!"

Everyone turned to see the young boy sprinting toward them like the devil was chasing him. Conner, Donald, and the others became alert and were familiar with the young boy running toward them.

"Samuel, what happened? What did you see, boy?" Conner asked him.

Samuel was dripping with sweat and fear. He dropped to his knees in front of the men, the color drained from his face, his throat tightened, and he felt like he might throw up.

"What did you see, boy?" Conner reiterated.

"He looked like he saw the devil himself," Donald uttered.

"Talk to me, Samuel. What did you see?" Conner demanded, becoming impatient.

The boy was trying to grab back his senses and compose himself. He had everyone's attention, including Kaiser's. Conner stood over him, waiting to hear something.

"Down at Taylors' mansion. I-I just wanted to explore it since it was so big, and I had never been inside before," Samuel began.

"And what did you see inside there?" asked Conner.

"She . . . She grabbed me . . ."

"Who grabbed you? Was it a nigger?" Donald chimed.

Samuel nodded. *It was.*

"How many did you see inside there?" Conner asked.

"I . . . I don't know. It attacked my dog and killed it," Samuel said sadly.

"It . . . ?" Kaiser uttered. "What do you mean, 'it'?"

Conner glared at Kaiser and exclaimed, "This isn't your business. This is *our* land, and we will find these niggers and deal with them the right way."

Conner then turned to his men, several with rifles and pistols, and shouted, "You hear that, boys? We got niggers hiding out at the old Taylors' mansion! Probably that nigger Solomon is hiding out there too."

"Yeehaw! We gon' finally get some justice for our fallen brothers," Donald exclaimed. "Y'all hear me?!"

The men quickly mounted their horses and rode toward the mansion, forgetting Kaiser and his company. Noah looked at Kaiser. "What we gon' do, sir?"

"Follow them," Kaiser said.

Noah grabbed the straps to the reins and hurried the horse and cart behind the men.

The Taylors' mansion was once a grand place that captured the very essence of Southern charm. It was three stories with eight fireplaces, seven bedrooms, and many more rooms to get lost in. It sat on seven acres of land and once was the epitome of Southern wealth. But then, it became an abandoned place with haunted stories of a husband who went crazy one night and murdered his family along with a dozen of his slaves. Now, it was a creepy and monolithic place that had been abandoned for nearly two years.

There were two hours of daylight left in the day. Conner and his men were galvanized with animosity and hate as they dismounted their horses, believing runaways, murderers, and Black savages were hiding inside.

Conner stood seething outside the antebellum mansion, armed with a rifle and a pistol holstered on his side. Behind him were his men, equally seething and ready to attack niggers. They stormed toward the mansion through the gateway and didn't hesitate to kick open the front door to make their way inside. They were eager to implement retribution on any enslaved person they found hiding inside the dwelling.

Kaiser and his companions had arrived in time to see the men disappear into the mansion. Noah brought the wagon to a stop near the gate. They stared at the place in awe, and Noah and Melody were immediately creeped out by its size and look. Kaiser hurriedly removed himself from the wagon, clutching his walking stick. He drew a Colt Paterson revolver from his possessions and handed it to Noah.

"Take it, and keep watch outside," he demanded.

"You gon' inside there, sir?" Noah asked. "Those men sure didn't take a liking to you, and I don't want no harm to come to you, sir."

"I'll be fine, Noah. And if my hunch is correct, those men are in grave danger—maybe already dead," Kaiser replied.

Noah and Melody looked spooked. During their long journey from Georgia, Kaiser constantly preached to them about monsters and vampires. They existed. There were things out there that were hard to explain and only believable when seeing them themselves. It was challenging to comprehend a vampire in a civilization that didn't believe in monsters. Europe and Africa were plagued with them, but America was still a new country.

But America was about to have a rude awakening. The supernatural was on their soil. Like a malignant virus, it would spread no matter what.

Kaiser nodded to Noah and said to him, "I'll be fine."

He spun and marched toward the disturbing manor, clutching his walking stick and armed with his Cross-Blade Necklace and abilities. He entered the place via the foyer and slowly continued farther inside, knowing what to expect.

Conner and his men slowly moved through the manor with candlelight illuminating darkened areas. Though it was late in the day, the place's interior seemed extra dark and eerie. They walked through the dark portrait corridor, where two marble busts were at the end of the hall. Finally, they reached the grand ballroom, which had a fireplace, crystal chandelier, dining room table, dance floor, and pipe organ. It was a gateway to the outside, in addition to stairs and balconies leading to different stories of the manor.

"We'll split up here. Donald, Charles, Louis, and I will continue looking around down here. Ya check upstairs," Conner suggested. "You find these niggers hiding, don't kill 'em yet."

Three men nodded.

The endless hallway on the second floor was shadowy and eerie, lined with doors that seemed to go on infinitely. The hallway was lined with ancient macabre décor, cobwebs, and disturbed tattered wallpaper. The three men began to look into every room. When they reached the last door to their right, they heard a quiet sobbing from the room. The men exchanged looks and warily proceeded to the room. The door opened slowly to reveal the source of the sobbing. It was a little Black girl in the corner, bent over a grown man's motionless, bloodied body. The girl turned and looked at them. Her mouth was covered in blood, and surprisingly, the man was alive, and it was *he* doing the sobbing. The Black girl was a vampire.

All three men stood there in shock and horror at what they saw. The girl placed a clawed hand on the man's jaw and ripped him apart while she eyed them creepily.

"I'm done playing with this one. You want to play with me now?" the girl uttered chillingly.

The three men freaked out. They had no idea what they were looking at or what she was. A man was dead. Then, quickly, the girl's face morphed into a preternatural snarl. Her canines extended, tapering to razor-sharp points.

"Holy Mother of God!" one of the men screamed.

Being freaked out, he raised his rifle to fire, but she was faster. She careened toward her first target and powerfully smashed into him. They both fell to the floor, and he was dazed for a moment. It was hard for him to believe a girl who looked twelve years old could be that strong. Next, he felt the side of his neck ripped open by her fangs, and he screamed.

"What is she?" the second man yelled.

Their friend was already dead. Suddenly, the tables were turned on them. *They* were now the hunted. Unfortunately for them, the girl wasn't alone. A figure blurred behind them, and both men pivoted and fired at something but hit nothing. Next, they could hear the girl eating their friend. Then they heard a faint voice on the second floor.

"I see you."

Their terror mounted with every step, and their hearts hammered in their chest. Something was watching them in the dark. These men clutched their rifles tightly and became parched with fear. Then suddenly, it attacked them with such speed and brute force, tossing them back and forth violently. An ear flew left, a hand went right, skin was ripped open, and their blood sprayed everywhere. Their bloodcurdling screams traveled.

Connor, Donald, and two other men heard the gunshots and spine-chilling screams. And it wasn't coming from Black people. So, instead, they moved around on the second floor and came up empty with their search.

"What the heck was that?" Conner questioned.

There was something about the mansion that didn't sit well with anyone. The place was odd and hair-raising. It felt like they were being watched, and not an ounce of daylight percolated inside. They wondered, *Why is it so dark in here?*

They would soon find out.

Out of the blue, a figure appeared before them. It was a Black male. He was young, shirtless, and thin. Conner and his men quickly aimed their rifles at him, and Conner shouted, "Stop right there, nigger!"

But this Black male seemed undaunted by their guns. He stepped closer to them. And when these men got a good look at this nigger, every last man became ghostly white. It was a demonic visage. This creature stared at them with these unearthly bloodred eyes, his pupils oscillating hypnotically. His tongue flicked, lizardlike, and his fingernails were sharpened into claws.

"God almighty!" Charles shouted.

Quickly, it moved fast and attacked Charles, and he went down. This creature gnawed at his flesh ferociously while the others gazed on helplessly and in shock. Donald attempted to fire at it but became so nervous that he missed completely. When he tried to fire again, he was attacked by a second creature without warning looming nearby. It was another male dragging him away like he was prey.

Conner and Louis became overwhelmed with fear. Suddenly, storming into the old and ruined Taylors' mansion wasn't such a great idea. Their bravado diminished faster than a heartbeat.

"What is this?" Conner frantically screamed.

Gunfire continued.

When Kaiser stepped into the mansion, he immediately recognized what it was—a vampire's nest. It was a place for vampires to dwell in packs and where they would sleep and bring their victims. It was spreading. The awakened dead was a disease that humanity in the states wasn't prepared for. This nest was a breeding ground for disaster, cataclysm, and death.

Kaiser heard the screams of men dying inside the place. But unfortunately, there wasn't anything he could do for them. It was too late. But what he could do was prevent this pack from feasting on the locals again and turning the town into a buffet. This pack of vampires was becoming completely mindless and totally carnivorous. They'd been turned by a tainted vampire that didn't come from the pure blood or the true bloodline—*the Mark of Cain*. And over time, they would become mindless, bloodsucking demonic creatures where there would be no humanity left in them.

When Kaiser entered the grand ballroom, he saw the vampiric creature feasting on Charles. Its body spasmed, its face was contorted, and it let out a satisfied breath. Suddenly, it noticed Kaiser watching him. It stood immediately and lunged toward Kaiser, moving at superhuman speed—practically a blur. Kaiser, with matching speed, unsheathed his blade and reacted. The silver blade punched into the vampire's heart. This hellish creature howled from the grave penetration and started to convulse. Kaiser glared at it, then retrieved his sword. It dropped dead at his feet. Then, sensing danger rising from behind him, Kaiser, in a flash, swung his sword downward and sliced off the parasite's right hand at the elbow. The limb fell to the floor, and the creature squealed in pain. Then Kaiser took off its head with a mighty swing of the blade.

Kaiser displayed how fierce a warrior he was, moving like lightning with strength like Samson. He sensed more in the mansion, and the men inside were most likely dead. He moved through the corridor poised with his silver blade. Two more creatures charged at him. The first slammed into him, and Kaiser flew backward forty feet, tumbling over a table, slamming into the wall so hard that it cracked. The male charged at him with frightening speed, but Kaiser pivoted from its attack and countered by piercing its heart from behind. The touch of his silver/holy blade meant immediate death to the creature. The second male lunged his way, howling with rage. Kaiser spun again and quickly cut the vampire clean in half.

Shit!

When Kaiser finished killing the vampires, he was shocked to see Conner was still alive. The man had cowered in the corner. He couldn't believe it. They were demons and monsters, *not* niggers. It would have been easy to leave him behind and allow these creatures to tear him apart. But Kaiser wasn't there to judge him.

"Get out of here now!" Kaiser yelled at him.

Conner was too afraid to move. He'd witnessed his friends ripped apart by these creatures and feared he would be next. Kaiser frowned. *How brave these men are when they believe they're pursuing runaways and the enslaved.*

"This is hell!" Conner yelled.

More vampires were coming. Kaiser had no idea how many were inside the place. He had to think fast. He grabbed an oil lamp and flung it at the long drapes covering the window. It immediately caught fire.

"We need to go," Kaiser said to Conner, pulling him to his feet.

The fire started to rage. They heard the howling of others coming their way as Kaiser helped Conner to the front entrance.

But blocking their way out was a female vampire. Her bloodred eyes glared at them as fangs protruded from her mouth. Conner became so scared he trembled and fell to his knees.

"Ohmygod!" he screamed.

It charged at them, and Kaiser found himself wrestling with a feral-faced nightmare. She reared its head back, jaws stretching wide. While he fought with it, Kaiser shouted to Conner. "Run!"

Fear nearly paralyzed Conner, but he managed to stand and escape to the front door. He ran into Noah and Melody, waiting patiently by the wagon. Conner appeared ghostly white to them, his eyes huge from the horror he had witnessed. They had never seen a white man look so scared and spooked before, and both wondered where Mr. Kaiser was.

"Run! Run! Run for your damn lives!" Conner shouted to them.

What is happening? they wondered.

Then the loud disturbance at the entrance swiveled their attention. What appeared to be a female came flying out of the manor, and it fell to the dirt . . . a vampire. There was an hour of daylight left, and the reaction was instantaneous. Conner hurried far away from her while Noah and Melody were about to witness something they couldn't comprehend. The vampire began to scream, exposed to direct sunlight. She squirmed around on the ground as her skin blistered and blackened. It was suffering in great pain and became diminished from power. Sunlight was torture to it. It was painfully dying. Then she burst into flames and burned.

The sun was the brightest regularly visible celestial body in Earth's sky, the second being the moon. Now, Noah, Melody, and Conner saw with their own eyes that vampires exist. They stood there in awe.

"Where is Mr. Kaiser?" Noah asked Conner.

Conner was visibly trembling and disturbed.

Finally, Kaiser emerged from the burning mansion. He looked like he'd been in the fight of his life. His silver blade was still visible, and his clothing was torn and dirty. Noah smiled. Kaiser glanced at the dead vampire on the ground, its charred body in the fetal position. He kneeled beside her and closed his eyes to pray for it. He then stood up and looked toward Noah and Melody. Seeing it was believable.

"Sunlight is one of the basic weaknesses of nearly all vampires. They are naturally weak against the sun," Kaiser proclaimed.

The three of them, including Conner, had witnessed what they were up against—the supernatural.

"Our fight will get worse. There are stronger forces out there," Kaiser added.

Chapter Twenty-Six

Militiamen scoured the swampy woods in South Carolina, where cypress trees were otherworldly gorgeous. The swamp had become a temporary haven for runaway slaves. A group of torch-wielding rebels galloped through towns and cities in North and South Carolina. Angry white mobs grew by the dozens and scoured miles of countryside, searching for Blacks to kill. News of the tragedy in Hickory Grove, South Carolina, had every man, woman, and child fearing for their lives and livelihood— whether you were Black or white. The South was tearing itself apart with fear, violence, and hatred. President Millard Fillmore imposed martial law in various areas of the United States.

It was the beginning of a civil war.

Akasha and his group watched the slaughter of many in a town called Duncan. The sun had long ago set, the night was brisk, and below the hill, they witnessed wielding torches, heard the sound of gunfire, and heard the screams of people dying. Akasha's group had grown to seven vampires. The look on his underlings' faces was satisfying and bloodthirsty. Indeed, the chickens had come home to roost. This is what they wanted: chaos and rebellion. Akasha crouched near the edge of the foothill and stared at a town burning. What he felt was enthralling. The desire to see America being destroyed was happening. While the South was in chaos, he was gradually building his army of the undead. When the fires stopped burning, and the plantations were overwhelmed with ruin and ashes when enslaved people were either killed or uprising to survive, civilization in the South was crushed. Akasha planned on reshaping this country in his making. He would turn white men, women, and children into either slaves or food for his kind.

Ellen joined him near the slope. She wrapped her arms around him romantically and grinned.

"Can we feed now?" she asked him.

"No," Akasha replied. "Wait, and let it burn . . . Let *them* burn."

Ellen nodded.

Below, everything was aglow in flames. Menacing flames danced in their soulless eyes, uncontrolled, spreading unevenly and quickly. More than three dozen homes and businesses burnt down, leaving many homeless, and some people even lost their lives. In addition, the fire burned natural crops and vegetation exceptionally quickly. Duncan, South Carolina, was becoming hell on earth.

Solomon stood apart from everyone and watched the blaze below becoming unpleasant and dangerous. Both races were dying in the blaze. He remained deadpan while the others gloated. *What are we doing?* he thought. Akasha noticed his aloofness and walked toward him.

"Death brings them unity," Akasha uttered with sarcasm. "Do you feel for them?"

"Why kill the children too?" Solomon asked.

"Have they ever had any mercy for our children?"

Solomon didn't answer him. He knew the answer and frowned.

"Their offspring will eventually grow and become them again, maybe crueler. What I want is to eradicate their bloodline forever. They took something special from me. Now, I'll take away everything special to them," Akasha proclaimed.

Solomon turned to stare directly at Akasha. It was eating away at him. He said, "I need to find her."

He and Akasha locked eyes.

"She will not understand you. You are a monster to her now, no longer human, but one of us," Akasha said.

"I made a promise, and I intend to keep it."

"And what about your promise to me?" Akasha mentioned.

Solomon stood there quietly, brooding. He stared down at the town burning and thought about his future. What he wanted was freedom, not this.

"As long as they live with control and power, you and she will never be at peace. This country is a plague and a curse and must be purged. To have absolute freedom means the end of their kind," Akasha uttered with contempt.

Solomon huffed. By now, the others were glaring at him. They had no conflict with Akasha's endgame. Although all of them had suffered because of slavery, each one could tell a horror story that could rival the next. They owed Akasha their lives, and they could fight back and win because of him. Because of him, they were unstoppable and knew what power felt like. As Akasha had promised them, the women no longer feared being raped and abused. The men now had the strength and abilities to protect what they loved and implement their revenge.

Solomon, however, was becoming a different story. He'd become one of the first Akasha had turned. And although his thirst would become unbearable, the thought of never seeing Irene again became insufferable. She was out there somewhere, probably scared, hurt, and alone.

"I love her. And I need to find her," Solomon proclaimed wholeheartedly.

The statement angered Akasha. He once was in love with someone, but that was over a century ago. Now, his only purpose was vengeance. The two men continued to stare at each other. Akasha wanted his loyalty, and the thought of Solomon veering off from the pack for love was betrayal, and it angered him.

"You leave us, and you will die," Akasha warned him.

Solomon was willing to take that chance. He felt he'd gone from one master to another. This wasn't freedom; it was still bondage in his eyes.

"This isn't freedom, Akasha. This is hell," Solomon growled.

"Hell?" Akasha replied disputably. "I gave you life to fight back."

"But not like this," Solomon replied.

Akasha moved closer to Solomon, his soulless eyes never leaving him. The tension between them grew thick. The other vampires circled them, and if so, they were ready to attack Solomon if Akasha gave the command. They were all unquestionably loyal to their maker—their master—unlike Solomon. But Akasha cautioned them back with a wave of his arm. He didn't need or want their help. So, they stood by idly, uncertain of what would happen next.

"You're either with us or against us in this fight," said Akasha.

Solomon glanced at the faces of the other vampires, and it was clear every last one was with Akasha. He was alone. Solomon's hesitation was his answer. Enraged and with frightening speed, Akasha grabbed Solomon's throat with one hand and lifted him from the ground with a sadistic smile.

"I saw promise in you, Solomon," Akasha stated. "You've become a disappointment to me."

Akasha hurled Solomon to the ground, kicked his face viciously, and then towered over him.

"Now, you will die," Akasha growled.

No vampire was more important than his cause, and Akasha didn't want a weak link in his pack.

Solomon struggled to his feet. Then he speedily threw a fist at Akasha, who caught the fist and tossed Solomon back to the ground. It was obvious that Solomon was no match for Akasha. This fight was futile.

"I gave you life, strength, and a second chance. I gave you a purpose: revenge toward those who enslaved you. But you mock us and deceive us. So now, I will take back what I pledged to you. Life!" Akasha roared.

Solomon lay on his back, defeated, and stared up at Akasha. He expected to die tonight. There would be no more mercy from his maker. Both of their fangs and claws came out, the moon was full, and death was inevitable, they both thought. But suddenly, gunfire rang out, and a round splintered into a tree near Akasha's head. Every vampire turned toward the gunfire to see an army of militiamen charging their way, nearly twenty men. It was unexpected.

"I see we have company," Akasha smirked. He looked at Ellen and exclaimed, "Now, we feed and kill."

Ellen grinned. *It's about time.*

It was seven vampires against twenty armed white men. The odds were against them. But they remained undaunted. The undead charged toward the living, and what followed next was a massacre and bloodbath. Claws ripped open skin and clothes, necks were snapped like twigs, and fangs sank into flesh. Men were being ripped apart limb by limb in front of their comrades, and the terrible screams that followed echoed like a howling wind.

Unbeknownst to the other vampires, Solomon decided to run in the opposite direction. The charging militiamen were the blessing he needed to escape the pack. While they were busy fulfilling their lust for blood and violence, Solomon ran down the slope at full speed, crashing into trees and tumbling toward the bottom. Finally, he reached the end of the hill unscathed. He could hear the battle happening atop, and by the time they realized he hadn't joined their fight, Solomon planned on being long gone from everyone.

He continued to run through the woods at an incredible speed. It was like he was something else, a swift animal on four legs. The burning town soon became distant behind him. Solomon looked south, and with the night still young, he headed in that direction. Cornwell Walken's plantation was twenty miles away, and with a few hours of night left, Solomon ran toward the plantation.

He was special now, but he had his limits. However, there would be no stopping him from finding Irene. Solomon understood that freedom from slavery was achieved only when individuals started to feel and understand they would prefer death to being a slave. And Solomon wanted to be a free man with his woman despite his change.

Freedom was his human right—no matter what he'd become.

Chapter Twenty-Seven

General Mathews poured himself a glass of scotch and downed it quickly. He then looked at his good friend, Cornwell, and griped, "Cornwell, would you have me drink alone tonight? After all, I *am* a guest in your fine home."

Cornwell Walken huffed. "How can you be so calm during a time like this?"

"It's simple. A drink here and there, along with some good nigger company," he laughed.

"I'm amazed at how you find this madness funny, General. Towns are burning, and white people are dying from a nigger uprising that cannot be suppressed."

"A good reason for you to have a drink with me, Cornwell," the general replied amusingly.

The general poured himself another glass. Then he took a seat in the armchair across from Cornwell. He sat back, crossed his legs, and enjoyed the scotch. They were conversing inside Cornwell's study. The fireplace was burning where it was warm enough to become a place of comfort. However, Cornwell was apprehensive.

Hickory Grove was forty miles west of his plantation. The thought of an entire town being slaughtered was a nightmare. This revolt was happening too close to home.

Cornwell started taking extreme measures to ensure his family and property were safe. He placed nearly every enslaved man in leg irons and a slave collar, especially at night. He wanted to restrict their movement on his land. The only time their shackles were removed was during the workday. Cornwell didn't want to take any chances. There were now two overbearing overseers: dogs and guns. Life on his plantation had become extraordinarily harsh and challenging for every slave, man and woman.

"I fear this nation will become a mirror of the French regimen in Haiti, being overthrown by savages. The state of our livelihood will be in jeopardy, General, if this uprising doesn't end," Cornwell said.

"Cornwell, you give these niggers far too much credit. We are not the French, and a handful of savages will not bring down the South. Our civilization is built on advancement and God's will," the general replied.

"God's will," Cornwell chuckled. "You underestimate them, General," Cornwell countered.

The general took another swig of scotch and said, "What about this nigger Solomon? If he is in charge of this madness, he'll return here for revenge. You took away the one thing he truly loved. You should have lynched that nigger after his first offense."

Hearing the name Solomon, Cornwell poured himself a drink and sighed. "He was one of the best blacksmiths in the county . . . maybe in all of South Carolina. That nigger helped me get rich. He was profitable."

"But now he's become your worst nightmare," the general replied.

Cornwell sighed. *Where did it all go wrong?* he thought. He gave Solomon a good life, a beautiful wife, a good position, becoming a blacksmith on his land, and some liberty. Though Cornwell had his share of Black women, Irene was unscathed. But he was naïve to believe that he could ever give Solomon his best life while still being a slave.

The two men continued to talk and drink in the study. Suddenly, they heard screaming—a woman shrieking. Then Cynthia screamed from another room. Immediately, both men leaped from their seats and hurried out of the study to see what was happening. Cornwell feared the worst . . . Slaves were barging into his home and attacking his wife. His first reaction was to grab his gun for protection, but he had to see what was happening with his wife first. The general was right behind him.

"Cynthia!" Cornwell cried out.

Both men turned the corner. They entered the great room to find Cynthia alive but angry and troubled. She gripped a bloody kitchen knife, and by her feet was the body of Gloria, their young and pregnant house nigger. Her throat had been cut, and a pool of blood was on the floor.

Cornwell was confused.

"What is going on here, Cynthia? What happened? What has she done?" he asked her.

Cynthia refused to drop the knife. She needed it for protection.

"Cynthia, what did you do? What happened?" Cornwell asked again.

"I can't trust her anymore. She wanted to kill me, to kill us!" Cynthia exclaimed. "I know she's part of that nigger rebellion."

"Cynthia, it will be okay. Just drop the knife," Cornwell replied coolly.

"They are all foul with hate for us. They all are black animals to leave us gutted like pigs in our sleep," she shouted.

Something snapped inside Cynthia. She glared at her husband and shouted, "You think I didn't know? It was *your* baby she was carrying. You think I don't see it, Cornwell. She lied to me. *You* lied to me. You would rather entertain these nigger whores than me. *I* am your wife!"

She was becoming unhinged. Cynthia gripped the knife tighter, held it above her head, and prepared to use it again.

"Cynthia, I've made sure our family, home, and property are protected," said Cornwell. "Our niggers are securely chained and put away until morning. And Gloria was no threat to us."

Tears streaked down Cynthia's face. "She was a threat to *me*!" she shouted.

"Cynthia, put the knife down so we can talk," Cornwell said civilly, moving closer to her.

"Why, Cornwell? Why betray our marriage for this nigger? What is yer fascination with her? You can't remain the Sabbath without her under your eye. Your affair with that Black wench makes you a filthy, godless heathen, and my bed is too holy for you to share," Cynthia wholeheartedly proclaimed.

"Cynthia, you talk nonsense," said Cornwell.

"You are a no-account bastard!"

The general smiled at the couple's quarrel. Then he replied, "You, my friend, have more to worry about here than a nigger rebellion."

Cornwell cut his eyes at the general. "Now is not the time for humor, General."

"I see that," the general replied.

"You should leave," Cornwell suggested.

However, dogs barking outside suddenly interrupted the commotion happening inside. Something was happening.

Chapter Twenty-Eight

The moonlight gracefully traveled through the night, lighting the rising path. Even in the velvet dark was the light of the stars, perhaps a promise of hope. It was the light Solomon craved . . . hope, for without it, what was his world? Would he become a creature of the night, forever becoming a predator, imagined or real? And though he was mighty in the dark, he sought after his light, his beacon of hope and happiness, the chance to stand up and be strong, to see the beauty and be beautiful. Maybe becoming not the monster that created him.

The moment Solomon stepped foot onto the Walken's plantation, wild memories of his past flooded him rapidly. Months had passed. Yet, it felt like yesterday when Irene was taken from him. Solomon gazed at those bright friends of the moon and their pattern that seemed so fixed and yet, ever-changing—distant lights to call his heart, to inspire dreams of other worlds. The moonlight brought a comforting beauty to the bloody night.

Movement on the plantation was still. No candles were burning in any windows of slave shacks, and no one was around.

An ominous feeling flooded the place. Solomon walked around the slave quarters, and then he stopped in front of his old home. He stared at the shack with some haunted nostalgia. It was empty or abandoned . . . Nothing had changed. The place was constructed of wood with no steady foundation. Solomon unhurriedly ascended the short steps onto the rickety, small porch and opened the door. He wanted to see her—and he did. There was Irene, smiling brightly and waiting for him to arrive. He imagined his wife placing her tender arms around him, hugging him intimately, then kissing him with her sweet lips.

"*I love you*," she whispered to him.

"I love you too," he replied.

He didn't want to pull away from her. Solomon stood in the center of the shack and visualized her. It felt like she was there, embracing and comforting him. He wasn't a monster to her, but her husband. She was okay with the monster he'd become, tending to his sadness with her love. She kissed the scars that plagued his skin. Their love was rare, and it was evident that she missed him. Irene had always been faithful, protective, and nurturing. Their love was like the sun, bright and glowing like a beacon no matter where they were. It would always shine, stay with them in quietness, and become their comfort even far apart.

But then Solomon was reminded of the terrible things that happened there and how Colemon wanted to take something special from him because of his lust. And with the blink of an eye . . . Irene was gone. The stillness and darkness gripped Solomon, and anger poured through him. Finally, he was alone, and hatred was all that was left.

Under a sky of perfect midnight velvet, under stars so brilliant that they drew the eyes heaven-bound, Solomon marched through the slave quarters with purpose. He arrived at the barn and effortlessly opened the door to find many enslaved people, mostly men. They'd been herded into the shed and pressed together, sleeping, and chained to one other like they were cattle. It was inhumane.

Solomon stood there quietly, staring at the expressions of his fellow slaves, all of sudden awakening to his sudden presence. Many didn't expect to see him again, alive anyway. But there he was, an ambiguous figure in the night. He was different.

"Solomon, is that you?" a voice cried out.

Solomon searched for the familiar voice through the sea of faces. Marcus stood to greet his friend. Solomon smiled slightly to see his old friend, but his friend wasn't the same. Marcus was a broken man, and his body was more scarred now than before. He was weak, abused, and nearly rail thin. He was becoming a dying old man.

Solomon approached Marcus while the others stared at him in awe. Their oppression manifested via leg irons and slave collars. For Marcus, Solomon was a sight for sore eyes.

"I's thought yuh be far north by now," said Marcus.

"Not without her," he replied.

Marcus smiled. He understood their love.

"Masser got us chained at nights n 'here, fear we rise up like we's been hearing. But they lookin' fo' you, Solomon. They believe yuh behind this chaos happenin' in the South. They see yuh here n' lynch yuh fo' sure," Marcus said.

Solomon wasn't worried. "I'm here to free you, all of you," he responded.

"They killin' people everywhere, fo' no reason but being Black," Marcus added. "They say the killin' won't stop til they get you."

Solomon seethed. His mission to the plantation was to torture Master Walken and have him reveal where and to whom he'd sold Irene. But now, he saw firsthand the backlash his violent actions with Akasha had created. The disparity and brutality against his people were disheartening. Solomon continued to stare at the faces of each Black soul in his presence, and what they'd been through the past few weeks was hell on earth.

"You free, Marcus. No more slavery for you . . . for any of you," Solomon exclaimed.

Everyone looked at Solomon with confusion, not knowing what he was talking about. He'd gone mad for sure this time, they believed. However, Solomon was prepared to show all of them what he'd become . . . a monster. First, he crouched closer to Marcus's leg irons. Then he effortlessly broke his chains and released him from any constraints.

Marcus was amazed. "How . . . How yuh do that?"

Solomon stared at him and replied, "I'm different now, Marcus."

"Different . . . Different how?" Marcus questioned.

Solomon ignored his question. He continued to free the others from their chains and iron collars. They were thankful and relieved.

"Go," Solomon said to them. "You all are free."

But they were apprehensive. *What now?* They didn't have his abilities, and worse, they were mentally shackled to the plantation. Cornwell Walken and Colemon made it clear to them what would happen if they tried to escape or uprise. They watched Colemon and his cronies mutilate Black men and women to strike fear into every enslaved person on the plantation.

"They afraid, Solomon, Massa Colemon did horrible things while you were gone," Marcus explained.

"You won't have to worry 'bout Colemon or any other massa no more," Solomon replied.

Solomon pivoted and marched away. There would be no stopping him. Being haunted by his past and missing Irene, he was wordless with rage and focused on his revenge. He wanted them dead, all of them, every last one.

Colemon lived in a separate house away from the big house near the slave quarters. Solomon was desperate to find Irene, but first, he needed to finish what he had started with the overseer. This time, he would get it right.

Solomon stopped at the edge of the log cabin and glared at it. He was infused with emotions. A lantern illuminated the window of the place. Someone was inside.

"Colemon!" Solomon shouted. His voice boomed into the night.

The cabin door opened, and Colemon loomed into Solomon's view, wielding a shotgun. He glared back at Solomon and was both shocked and delighted. Finally, he could get his revenge on him.

"You must be one helluva a stupid nigger to come back here, Solomon!" Colemon exclaimed. "You black sonovabitch, I'ma tan ya hide and lynch you, boy. Yuh black ass will swing from a tree!"

Solomon stood there seething and undaunted by his threats. It was because of him that Irene was gone. He hated everything about him and what he represented. Colemon scowled and positioned himself with the shotgun to fire. Solomon charged at him as Colemon opened fire.

Boom . . . Boom!

The second shot struck Solomon and propelled him back into the dirt. Colemon grinned. *Got that nigger!* he thought. He stepped off the porch and moved closer to the body, believing Solomon was dead. Hearing gunfire, the second overseer, Kevin, came running toward the skirmish, clutching his rifle and looking for a confrontation.

Colemon smiled his way and uttered, "Shot me a wanted nigger tonight."

"Is it him, Solomon?" Kevin asked.

"It's him. Nigger came back here to finish what he started," Colemon replied proudly.

It appeared that Solomon was dead, lying facedown in the dirt, not breathing.

"There's no blood," Kevin pointed out.

Kevin was young and eager to see the damage a shotgun blast could do to a Black man. So he crouched closer to Solomon, wanting to turn him over and get a good look at him. But instead, he wondered how one nigger could create so much trouble.

"You be careful with that nigger," Colemon warned him.

"He deader than a doornail," Kevin mocked. But then, his smile faltered into agony when Solomon rapidly sprang from the ground and plunged his sharp fangs into the boy's neck. Colemon's eyes grew wide when he saw Solomon was still alive. He wrestled with firing his shotgun again while Kevin had his throat completely ripped out. Finally, the boy dropped dead into the dirt as Solomon rose again to attack.

"Wh-what is this?" Colemon screamed in disbelief. "I hit you, nigger!"

With his fangs, dark eyes, and claws showing, Solomon looked demonic, and fear immediately gripped Colemon.

"What are you?" Colemon shouted.

Colemon fumbled with the shotgun to put down Solomon again, but he wouldn't get a second chance. This time, Solomon planned on killing him, and there would be no recovery. When Colemon attempted to aim the gun at him, Solomon lunged at him with such speed that the impact nearly broke Colemon's bones. Colemon slammed into the dirt with an "*Oomph.*" Solomon was perched on top of him.

"You took everything from me!" Solomon roared.

"Damn you, you black bastard. Go to hell!" Colemon screamed back.

"You first!" Solomon exclaimed.

It would be Colemon's last words. Solomon wrathfully thrust his sharp fangs into the side of Colemon's neck and began tearing away. Colemon screamed and hollered from the pain. Solomon wanted him to suffer, and he did. Solomon was too powerful of a beast who wanted bloodlust revenge. Colemon's eyes began to dim as he felt the side of his neck being painfully shredded to pieces, with his blood pooling into the dirt.

He was soon dead. Solomon stood from the mutilated body with his mouth coated in the man's blood. He was still in his demonic form. Finally, revenge was his, but he felt adrift and angry. He screamed from the top of his lungs. When he returned to his senses, Solomon saw they were watching him. The enslaved, including Marcus, now saw Solomon in his most proper form—a vampire. They were afraid of him, although he wasn't a threat.

What now?

Solomon locked eyes with Marcus, and absolute anger, pain, agony, and misfortune were in his eyes. The night seemed still and tense. Would his peers try to attack him from fear and misunderstanding, or would they run from him? However, it was Marcus who approached him with an emotional gaze. Solomon stood there.

"They can't hurt you no more, Solomon. You's free to move on n' find her," said Marcus. "We okay. Go."

Solomon nodded. Then he pivoted and stormed toward the big house.

Chapter Twenty-Nine

While Gloria's dead body lay on the great room floor, Cornwell and the general scrambled through the big house to retrieve pistols and rifles to protect themselves. Cornwell knew his worst nightmare was coming back to haunt him. He heard the gunfire in the distance, knowing what it meant. Trouble had reached his land, knowing it was Solomon or others. And he wasn't taking any chances. He tossed the general an infantry rifle and gripped a Colt revolver. Cornwell looked at the general and uttered, "That nigger steps one foot into my home, and I'll blow him away."

"I reckoned this is judgment day for us," the general replied. "Civilization against savagery."

Both men were armed and believed they were ready.

"They're coming for us, aren't they, Cornwell? The niggers are coming to kill us," Cynthia ranted, charging into the room.

"Everything's going to be okay, Cynthia," Cornwell assured her.

"How? How will it be okay?" Cynthia screamed back. "They want to slaughter us!"

"I won't allow that to happen," Cornwell replied.

His wife was frantic and becoming more unhinged. She worriedly paced around the room and ranted, "Got-damn niggers! What did we ever do to them? *Oh God!*"

She believed it was judgment day for them too.

"Stay in this room. Lock the door, Cynthia. We'll be back," Cornwell exclaimed.

The general followed Cornwell out of the room, leaving Cynthia behind in a deep state of fear. She fell to her knees in prayer, but terror weighed her down. The room was slightly dimmed and lit by lanterns. Cynthia remained on her knees in prayers.

"Our Father, who art in heaven, hallowed be thy name; thy kingdom come; thy will be done on earth as it is in heaven. Give us this day our daily bread and forgive us our trespasses as we forgive those who trespass against us, and lead us not into temptation but deliver us from evil . . ."

The second she uttered "*evil*," the window shattered, and a dark figure hurtled into the room. Cynthia shrieked and froze in panic. Whatever it was, it remained hidden somewhere inside the room. She wanted to know what the hell she was alone with. She soon found out when Solomon revealed himself and attacked her.

Hearing his wife screech like no tomorrow, Cornwell and the general doubled back to the room and pushed open the door . . . to find Cynthia gone. The window was smashed, and both men stood there in shock.

"Where did she go?" General Mathews uttered.

Right away, they heard her screaming, and it came from outside.

"They took her! They took my damn wife," Cornwell hollered in a panic.

Both men ran wildly outside to try to retrieve her. But she was nowhere to be found.

"Cynthia!" Cornwell screamed.

"Cornwell, help me!" they heard her screaming in the distance.

"It came from the slave quarters," the general said.

The two men ran toward the slave quarters, hoping to find Cynthia there. When reaching the courtyard, Cornwell and the general were shocked to see that every enslaved person had been unchained and was now free. Cornwell panicked and raised his rifle at the group of people that now surrounded him.

"I don't know how you niggers got free, but I will send every last one of you to hell right now!" Cornwell shouted.

Cornwell glared at the sea of faces scowling back at him. The rifle was not a threat to them. He was one, and they were many . . . ready to die if necessary. They were the subjugated and tortured souls who had enough. Solomon gave them the unforeseen courage to rise up and confront this barbaric institution called slavery. He may have seemed demonic, but to them, he'd become their impulsive savior. He'd unleashed them from their chains, and the overseers were dead.

"I'll kill you all!" Cornwell shouted. "Where is she?"

"Still alive," Solomon responded, stepping out of his old shack.

Cornwell pivoted with the rifle and aimed at Solomon. Then he shouted, "Give her back to me, or I'll kill you where you stand, nigger!"

It was nearly laughable to Solomon. Cornwell tried to show courage but trembled with the rifle, knowing he was outnumbered.

"Everyone, let's remain calm here and reasonable," the general voiced. "All of this hatred is not God's will. However, I can assure you that we can come to some kind of compromise."

"You speak of reason, compromise, and God's will?" Solomon replied, glaring at the general. "Where was God's will when we were in chains? Where was reason when we were beaten and tortured? Where was a compromise when you raped our women?"

Cherry stepped forward from the crowd, glaring at the general. She was a shell of herself, having been raped and abused multiple times by the general.

"My sweet Cherry," the general smiled. "Haven't I treated you fairly?"

Cherry scowled at him. The horrors he put her through—rape, abuse, humiliation—she had become his sexual puppet. He'd done things to her that were unthinkable. Now, she had the upper hand, but she started to cry. Seeing him was painful.

"I always liked you, Cherry. And I don't want to kill you. But I will if I have to tonight," the general said. Then he aimed the rifle at her chest.

However, following Solomon's courage, she didn't flinch. Instead, she continued to lock eyes with the blue-eyed devil, seething. The general was prepared to take her life. But unlike Cornwell, he remained poised, held the rifle firmly, and wasn't bluffing. Cherry was ready to step forward and confront him . . . but someone beat her to it. Andrew charged toward the general, raising a short ax above his head, and hollered.

The general fired.

Boom!

Andrew's chest exploded, and he dropped facedown into the dirt, dead. A second man charged at the general, and he too lost his life as a bullet tore through his head. A third man charged, screaming. The general tried to let off a third shot but stumbled doing so and was punched in the face and quickly overpowered.

Cornwell followed in the general's footsteps, discharged one round from the rifle, and hit a woman in her side. Then the crowd overpowered him and brutally brought him to his knees.

"Get your damn hands off me!" the general shouted as he squirmed and struggled.

The threat had been nullified, and now, both men were at the enslaved people's mercy. Cherry removed the short ax from Andrew's hand and walked toward the general with pent-up pain.

They held him hostage and vulnerable on his knees, and the only thing he could do was fret.

"Cherry, there's no need for you to do this. Whatever you are feeling, I'm sorry about it," the general pleaded.

But there wasn't anything he could say or do to change her mind. She remembered that hurtful night they made her strip completely naked and forced her to have sex with Andrew for their twisted entertainment. Cherry gripped the ax tighter and scowled at her rapist and abuser.

"My sweet Cherry . . ." the general said, then smiled. It would be his last words.

Cherry raised the ax and hacked into his neck. Then she straddled his body, raised the ax again, and chopped into him with measured focus. She repeated the brutal act until she decapitated him. Then she finally rose, holding the general's steaming head by the hair. For a moment, everything was still, no one breathing. This was their moment of liberation. Cherry then tossed the man's head into the nearby brush.

Cornwell was beside himself with fear and grief. Seeing the general brutally hacked was terrifying. He believed his wife was already dead, and he was next. He remained on his knees and surrounded.

"You niggers will pay for this!" Cornwell cried out.

Solomon turned, entered his old shack, and soon returned with Cynthia. She was unconscious in his arms. Cornwell gritted his teeth and threatened, "You touch one hair on her head, and I swear to Christ almighty, I will kill you—all of you. The full force of the militia will rain down like a swarm of biblical locusts on each one of you!"

But it was an idle threat.

Solomon dropped Cynthia onto the ground and growled. "Where is my wife?"

"She's gone," Cornwell replied. "I made sure you would never see her again, Solomon. You were my best and most skilled worker. I gave you everything."

"Everything but freedom," Solomon responded.

"Let her go and take me," Cornwell pleaded. "My wife has nothing to do with this."

"You beg for ya wife's life, but take away mines," Solomon replied.

"I'm sorry about that. It was only business," said Cornwell.

"It was to punish me," Solomon corrected him.

"As I said, it was business."

Solomon decided to show Cornwell his actual appearance. So, he crouched closer to him, and his appearance changed dramatically in the blink of an eye. Cornwell came face-to-face with Solomon's dark, soulless eyes and sharp fangs—and was horrified.

"You have no idea what I became!" Solomon growled. "Where is she?"

Fear rose behind his eyes as Cornwell trembled at the sight of Solomon. Immediately, he tried to shuffle away from him, but there was nowhere to go. He was surrounded by everyone he owned and mistreated.

"Please! Please, ohmygod! What are you?" Cornwell cried out.

"Where is my wife?" Solomon repeated.

Cornwell cowered in the dirt but soon answered. "She's in Franklin, North Carolina. A man . . . A man named Randall McHenry purchased her. That's all I can tell you."

Solomon glared at his former master. He wanted to rip his throat out, but he didn't. Instead, he stood above him, pivoted, and calmly left. He would leave Cornwell Walken and his wife to the fate of his slaves. It was judgment day for them, and their doom came swiftly. While Solomon walked away, every man, woman, and child circled the couple with malicious intent.

Chapter Thirty

"**H**e wants to create chaos here, implement civil war within the institution," Kaiser said.

"Chaos? But why, sir?" Noah asked.

"This being, it's angry, and it wants vengeance. Most vampires like to keep a low profile and only kill when needed. They're all over Europe and Africa and underground. They come from a wealthy civilization of the undead with their own laws and rules," Kaiser explained.

"Then why do you hunt them, sir?" Noah asked.

"It is somewhat complicated, Noah. But I hunt the ones that go rogue and break the rules. And I hunt what are called 'Reapers,'" Kaiser continued to explain.

"Reapers . . . ?"

"They're like a violent plague, equivalent to biblical locust yearning to devour everything it comes across . . . always hungry. They're violent and bloodthirsty, and they will become primal, mutant, and mindless beasts over time. They're a threat to civilization," Kaiser said.

"Are they what yuh fought back at de mansion?" Noah asked.

Kaiser nodded. "Unfortunately. If not killed, they'll continue transforming with a ravenous thirst for blood. I've seen them wipe out entire towns in a night."

"Why would God make such an evil?" asked Noah.

"The face of the Lord is against evildoers, to cut off their memory from the earth. For the evil man has no future; the lamp of the wicked will be put out," Kaiser quoted. "God, He doesn't exist without evil. It's the way this world is."

"And what 'bout slavery? God created that too?" Noah asked.

"Man created slavery, not God."

"But God watch it happen every day. He has de power to stop it, but He don't," Noah countered.

Noah was smart, and Kaiser knew he'd chosen the right one to be by his side. He would have been his equal had he been born in any other country besides America. And though Kaiser saw Noah as his equal, a human being created by God's law, society saw him as three-fifths of a man—someone who was not free but counted as three-fifths of a free individual for the purpose of determining congressional representation. It was to increase the political power of slaveholding states. It was sickening, but it was the law in this country.

"There's a balance in this world: good, evil, right, wrong, light, dark, humanity, the supernatural, and the Holy Command keeps that balance," Kaiser continued.

"This Holy Command you speak of, do they all look like you?" Noah asked.

Kaiser smiled. "Fortunately, no, they don't. We have agents in Africa, Europe, and England; I'm the first in this country. Our primary goal is to protect humanity, not judge it. However, sometimes, that has become difficult to do. Man can often be the cruelest animal."

Noah knew wholeheartedly how cruel man could be. He had the marks on his back to testify to it. If there's true evil in this world, it lies in the heart of humanity.

"The world is a dangerous place, my friend. But it can become a lot more dangerous if people stand by and don't do anything about it," said Kaiser.

Noah nodded, agreeing with him.

There was a gorgeous, big sky with a sunset looming over the horizon. It was a beautiful day, but things weren't too beautiful in the South. Every day, traveling through the towns of South Carolina was becoming much more dangerous. Folks were angry and vengeful. A white man traveling freely with two Negroes could become a death sentence for everyone. Everybody was up in arms.

A funeral procession of a well-known town figure was taking place. Several men, the pallbearers, carried a coffin up the hill toward the graveyard. At the same time, a white preacher walked out in front of the procession. The deceased was the victim of the violent uprising spilling from town to town, and the first mourner in line was the prominent figure's wife. She wore a fancy black dress, a wide-brim black hat, and a black veil.

Noah brought the wagon to a stop far away from the procession. The last thing he wanted to do was interfere with it.

"Shol I turn 'round, sir?" Noah asked.

Kaiser sighed. Everywhere he went was becoming a battlefield. There were nearly a hundred armed militiamen in town ready for war, and no Black man or woman was safe.

"We'll camp in the woods tonight. It might be safer for us," said Kaiser.

"Yes, sir," Noah agreed.

They decided to go back the way they came because it was too dangerous to proceed ahead.

"Everywhere we go, sir, white folks angry n' scared," said Noah.

"They have a right to be," Kaiser replied.

"And patrols got de roads block, make it difficult fo' us to continue ahead."

"We'll keep with our story, Noah, and keep our heads down."

"But this thing ya lookin' fo', this vampire. What happens when you find it?" asked Noah.

"I'll destroy it."

"And ya think everything go back to normal when you do, sir? You kill it, but then they will continue to hunt us and kill us. White folks ain't gon' believe in no monster. To them, we de monsters, sir," Noah uttered.

Unfortunately, Noah was right. When this supernatural being was dead, the way of life for Negroes in the South could become worse for the enslaved. The backlash behind Akasha's actions was becoming detrimental. In hindsight, the damage had already been done even if Kaiser had killed it.

The campfire lit a glow near the trio that night. It warmed the night air and appeared to echo the starlight. The night brought such a silence that the campfire crackling was all that could be heard. Flames sent red sparks dancing into the breeze. Kaiser, Noah, and Melody sat on a mossy log, their faces toasted warm and relaxed. Kaiser continued to enlighten them with his tales of the undead or the history of vampires.

"The Mark of Cain. It was said to be placed on Cain by God as punishment for killing his brother, Abel. The Mark is the originator of evil, violence, and greed. And Cain was condemned to a life of wandering in the dark and absent from the light.

The Mark soon became an alternate way for a human soul to be converted to a demon without sending a soul to hell and being tortured. It will render its host deathless, making the host truly immortal by the blood. Therefore, Cain became the first vampire. The Mark is a powerful entity. At first, it became God's protection and punishment. God stated that whoever kills Cain shall have vengeance seven times. And Cain, guilt-ridden and yearning to die to be reunited with his kin, decided to take revenge against God by spreading his Mark through his blood with the help of Lucifer," Kaiser explained.

It was confusing to Noah and Melody, but they continued to listen.

"With Lucifer's help, they created the horsemen of the Abyss. They were powerful demons handpicked by Lucifer from among the first fallen humans to be made into demons, the first of which was Cain. He became their commander, leading them to commit atrocities on earth. The Mark went from God's protection and punishment to corrupt humanity and turned God's creation into something demonic and cursed. The Mark makes the carrier practically immortal as its power is such that even death itself can't reap the person with the Mark," Kaiser added.

Noah shared a worried glance with Melody.

"The Holy Command was created thousands of years ago to combat this evil and keep the balance between humankind and the supernatural. Our advantage is the sun, the sword, and our faith. He calls us to His likeness, for He saith, He maketh His sun to rise on the righteous and the unrighteous. By the sun, we may understand not this visible, but that of which it is said, 'To you that fear the name of the Lord, the sun of righteousness shall arise,'" Kaiser exclaimed.

It was a campfire story that the two would remember forever.

"It's getting late. We need to sleep," said Kaiser. "I'll take the first watch."

Noah and Melody took up a position near the campfire and drifted to sleep in the dark woods, hoping to survive until the sun rose. At the same time, Kaiser stayed up and watchful until it was his time to sleep.

The night continued to remain quiet with Noah on guard. The pale crescent moon shone like a silvery claw in the night sky, and a blanket of stars stretched to infinity. Noah sat against the tree with a pistol near his side. But, unfortunately, he fell asleep. It was the middle of the night, and a branch snapped, indicating someone was approaching the group. Suddenly, a rifle muzzle was placed against Noah's cheek, and he was nudged awake. When Noah opened his eyes, he stared at a frowning white man.

"What ya doin' with that pistol, boy?" the male said.

A band of militiamen suddenly surrounded the group. Kaiser and Melody sprang awake to see the threat. Noah messed up by falling asleep.

"I asked you a question, boy. What ya doin' with that pistol?"

Noah froze in fear. He was too paralyzed to speak, the menacing atmosphere holding him in a tightening grip.

"You killing white people with that weapon? I'm talking to you, nigger!"

Kaiser slowly rose to his feet with his arms raised and having a slew of rifles aimed at him. He moved carefully.

"Gentlemen, there's been some misunderstanding. He's with me," Kaiser explained.

"You saying this nigger is with you, huh?" the front-runner asked. "You let your niggers sleep with guns?"

He was tall, and his face was blunt with harsh features like he'd been chipped from rock, all the rough edges left untouched.

The question left Kaiser stumped. How could he explain it to them? The group's front-runner snatched the pistol from Noah's side and inspected it . . . a Colt Paterson revolver.

"This is a nice piece of an arsenal, too nice for a nigger to have," said the head of the group. He pointed the revolver at Kaiser and asked, "What's your name?"

"My name is Kaiser Adelberg, and I've come here from Germany," he answered.

"Germany, huh? And what is your business here in my country with niggers?"

"I must say, it is complicated, gentlemen. One that takes quite some time to explain," said Kaiser coolly.

The front-runner cocked back the revolver and responded, "Well, you have one minute to give me a straight answer, or I'm gon' shoot you dead, and then these two niggers."

Kaiser locked eyes with him. His blade was out of his reach, and he knew the man wasn't bluffing. He counted over twenty men, not impossible for him to take down. Still, it was risky, especially if he wanted to save Noah and Melody's lives.

Kaiser kept calm, and his actions were innocuous. However, the tension grew thick, and Kaiser knew he had to make a hasty decision. It was now or never . . . live or die. Then, suddenly, a noise sounded far from the activity, and a blurry movement followed it in the dark. Whatever it was, it was fast and stealthy. The man in charge and his men swung around and aimed their rifles in the direction where it came from.

"What was that?" one of the men asked.

They weren't alone. Something was in the woods, and it was watching them. The front-runner glared at Kaiser and asked, "Who else is with you?"

"I assure you that it is only the three of us. Whatever's out there is a mystery to us too," Kaiser replied, feigning ignorance.

But he knew what it was, and it was stalking them—absolute death.

Another shadowy figure swiftly dashed by them, followed by a third. A few men began to panic. It seemed like they were surrounded. And then, out of nowhere, one of the shadowy figures decided to show itself. A branch snapped, and a young, thin Black male loomed into their view. He was barefoot with nappy hair, and his black skin was marked with scars from the bullwhip. His clothes were torn and tattered. He approached the group of men and was undaunted by their guns and rifles.

The front-runner stared at this young male confused, then uttered, "You must be one stupid nigger. Are you lost, boy?"

"Lost. No, I'm where I want to be," the man laughed.

Kaiser kept his undivided attention on this figure, knowing he was a vampire and, most likely, there would be a massacre if he didn't react immediately. He glanced at his silver blade concealed as a walking stick, knowing he had to snatch it from the ground as fast as possible. Noah and Melody were frozen with fear and bewilderment. *What is happening?*

"I like the smell of you," the young man said, grinning.

The front-runner stepped closer to the young, Black male and uttered, "You find something funny, nigger?"

He removed his sidearm, cocked back the hammer, and placed the gun's barrel to the man's head. The Black male didn't flinch. Instead, oddly, he continued to smile and taunt the front-runner of the militia. He repeated, "I like your smell. And I'm gon' enjoy devouring you soon."

Before the front-runner could take his life, the Black male's eyes inflamed red. He threw his head back, opening his mouth as razor-sharp canines extruded from his gums.

"What in God's name—"

He didn't finish his statement. Instead, with frightening speed, the male vampire clamped his mouth onto the man's throat and slammed him back against a tree. It began to rip out the front-runner's flesh and devour his blood. Terror washed over everyone's faces. Panic and chaos ensued, and gunfire exploded. Suddenly, many more vampires emerged from the woods and started attacking the militia. These creatures were everywhere, killing everyone they came across. The screams of men and the sound of gunfire danced collectively underneath the canopy of stars.

Kaiser reacted by diving toward his cane and quickly drawing it. His first kill came when a sharp-fanged vampire sprang from a tree branch to attack him. He wrestled with it for a moment, then plunged the sharp silver into the creature's chest and heart, killing it. He then pivoted quickly from the attack of a second charging vampire, a female. Kaiser grabbed it and launched his fist into the creature's gut, again and again, then he flung it across the woods, sending it smashing into a tree. Battered, the female vampire struggled to stand, but it soon met its demise. Kaiser cut off its head with one swipe of his silver blade. And he demonstrated that he was as fast, strong, and deadly as these vampires.

The attack continued, and the militia was being slaughtered. One man tried to raise his gun toward a rushing creature, but it gripped the man's hand and squeezed. The man screamed as his bones snapped like kindling, the gun falling from his grasp. He was then killed. Another man was lifted from the ground by his throat, dangling like a leaf in the wind, gurgling. And in the blink of an eye, sharp claws pierced his flesh, drawing blood, and he fell dead.

Kaiser continued killing these creatures. They were everywhere, but suddenly, Kaiser saw *him*, the one in charge. Akasha. It was him, the bloodline that created this massive disruption in the South. Akasha glared at Kaiser with his sharp fangs coated in blood. It was seething. He knew Kaiser was different than the others. He was skilled with a silver sword and fierce in combat, while the other men died with guns. Kaiser was ready to end this madness right now. He gripped his blade tightly, unafraid, and prepared to attack this entity.

However, he heard Melody and Noah scream, distracting him from Akasha. When he turned to find them, they were trying to escape several vampires. Damn! He thought he needed to save them, although he wanted to attack Akasha head-on. The last thing Kaiser wanted was for them to become casualties of a war he had pulled them into. So, he pivoted sharply and went to aid them. He whirled with the blade in his hand, charged at an approaching creature, and decapitated it. Men were dying left and right of Kaiser, and the militia's numbers began to dwindle rapidly. And it seemed Melody and Noah were a mile away from Kaiser. A war zone stood between them.

Noah picked up a large stick for his defense and swung it wildly at the sharp-toothed creatures. Melody hid behind Noah's bravery, but he was a mere man trying to fight demonic beings. Three male vampires were snarling and taunting the humans. They were ready to plunge their fangs into their hides and rip open their flesh with their claws.

"Leave us alone!" Noah shouted.

When it looked like their demise was about to come, a blade burst out of one of the vampires' chests. Kaiser rammed it from behind. It screamed and withered into a violent death. Kaiser battled the other two vampires while Noah and Melody watched in shocked amazement. When Kaiser took down the last vampire, he looked at the two fondly. He'd grown attached to them in the past weeks.

"Get to the wagon; I'll be okay," Kaiser said.

Melody smiled at him with gratitude. Noah took Melody's hand, and they were off to safety until—*BOOM!* The echoing gunshot made Kaiser spin around to find that Melody had been shot in the chest by one of the militiamen. It seemed unreal until Melody collapsed facedown into the dirt. Noah was shocked.

"Melody!" he cried out.

Kaiser ran to aid her, but it was too late. She was dead. Kaiser glared at the man who shot her and seethed. He gripped the blade's handle so tightly that it felt ready to snap between his fingers. Noah dropped to his knees beside her body, becoming overwhelmed with grief. They too had become close during their travel through the South.

"*AAAAH!*" Noah screeched.

"We need to go!" Kaiser hollered.

Noah didn't want to leave her side, but death was spiraling everywhere. The militia was dropping like flies by the swarm of vampires. Akasha was growing his army, becoming a force to be reckoned with.

"I can't leave her, sir!" Noah cried out.

"We need to," Kaiser shouted.

Gunfire continued to roar everywhere. And although Kaiser had killed several vampires, they seemed endless. And they weren't taking any prisoners. Men were being slaughtered like insects, like a child pulling wings from a fly. Finally, Noah came to his senses and decided to flee with Kaiser. They both sprinted through the woods on foot, with the battle between men and creatures raging on.

Chapter Thirty-One

Melody was dead, and Kaiser and Noah were devastated. The two men spent the past three days recuperating from the battle but continued to travel north. The roads became so dangerous that the men didn't ride together in public. Noah would remain hidden inside a covered freight wagon, sometimes concealed while Kaiser steered the horse. Roadblocks were becoming prevalent. Towns continued to burn, and martial law had been implemented throughout the South. Word started to spread from town to town about monsters and creatures like wildfire. People were afraid and alarmed. And something needed to be done. So, President Millard Fillmore sent 500 armed troops into the South to combat whatever threat was tearing civilization apart. The government believed this uprising was no longer a Southern problem but a problem for America itself. And if it weren't stopped, the country would be in jeopardy of collapsing.

A steam train arrived in Jonesburg, South Carolina, the second week in November. The cavalry had finally arrived. It was a sight. Hundreds of soldiers poured from the train into the train station, ready for battle. Each man proudly wore his military uniform—a dark blue woolen jacket, a blue overcoat, light blue trousers, a cap that was dark in color, and heavy shoes known as brogans. They carried rifle muskets and revolvers. The locals happily greeted the soldiers upon their arrival, and there was some jubilation on the streets of Jonesburg. A week ago, three towns had been attacked in the night, leaving dozens of folks dead, and homes and businesses were burned to the ground.

Awaiting the soldiers' arrival outside the train station were Rip, Trevour, and several fellas looking to hunt down Solomon and his niggers. They'd traveled a long way to South Carolina from Jeffersonville County, Georgia. Rip was a skilled tracker, and he would not rest until the head nigger responsible for such chaos and bloodshed swung from the end of a rope and was killed. So many white lives had been lost in the past two months that it felt like the country was at war again with the British.

"It's about damn time we received some help," said Trevour from his horse. "Strange times, when a man can't trust his own slaves."

"It's a damn sickness. I heard some nigger disease got 'em goin' mad like their animals," a man named Rubin uttered.

"They been animals, Ruben," Trevour laughed. "Can you really tell the difference if a nigger got it or not?"

"Still, I'm hearing it spreads through a bite, and if a nigger catches a fever or muscle spasms, or mental confusion, then it's best to put that nigger down right away," Ruben replied.

"Enough about that foolishness!" Rip griped. "We're here to do a job and protect our people, not talk about some nigger superstition. The army will hunt these fuckin' niggers their way, and we will continue to hunt them our way."

When Rip spotted the commander of the troops, he rode that way to greet him. Trevour and the other men followed suit.

"Commander Rogers, I assume," Rip greeted.

Commander Rogers was a middle-aged white male who moved with confidence that bordered on arrogance like he owned the place. He was of average height with a thick, black beard and was dressed immaculately in his uniform. He turned around to see Rip trotting his way on horseback. "And who are you?"

"My name is Rip, from Jeffersonville County, Georgia, and we are here to help."

"You are a long way from home," Commander Rogers replied.

"Me and my men have been hunting down these niggers in this rebellion for quite some time now. I figure you could use our assistance," he said.

Commander Rogers scoffed at the idea and replied, "It finally happened, huh? The niggers are taking over the South because of perpetual incompetence and tales of boogeymen in the dark."

Rip frowned.

Commander Rogers became more serious. He scowled at Rip and added, "I assure you, *I'm* the man to fear, *not* tales of boogeymen and niggers. My troops and I were sent here by the president to eradicate any threat he feels is against our great country. So now, you can head back to Georgia or stay out of our way."

Finished with his statement, Commander Rogers marched back to his troops and prepared for them to mobilize across South Carolina. He was determined to end this rebellion and bring things back to how they were in the South: harmony, stability, safety, niggers in their place, and wealth.

Rip headed back to his men, undiscouraged by the commander's words. *Ignorant bastard*, he thought.

"Trevous, you and Butch stay to the roads. Morris and I will take the woods. I know this nigger is close. Word is he's from a plantation nearby," Rip said.

Kaiser and Noah found an old farmhouse near the border of North Carolina and took shelter there. There wasn't anything around for miles—supposedly. It was vacant. It was late afternoon, and the two men loitered on the dilapidated porch. Noah sat at the foot of the steps, still brooding over Melody's death.

"Can't believe she's gone, sir. She was a sweet gal," he said.

Kaiser sighed. "The only thing we can do, Noah, is move on."

"How? Where's I go? Huh? Me a slave, and when they catch up to me, they gon' skin my hide fo' sure, sir. I's not like you, can't fight like you . . . I'm just some poor nigger helping some rich white man. You's says I free, but I feel trapped," he proclaimed.

"You are not trapped, Noah. Why do you believe that?"

"No matter de ending, sir, me and my people still lose, they still gon' continue a slave, n' I's still be a nigger in dey eyes. This uprising wit' these creature changes everything," Noah pointed out.

Kaiser knew he was right. When the time came for Kaiser to kill Akasha, there would be no rewinding the turmoil he created. Towns and cities were burning, and the tension between enslavers and enslaved people was thicker than a brick wall.

"Sometimes I's wonder who is de real evil n' why yuh hunt them when they killin' de same people who enslaved, beat, and killed men like me fo' years," said Noah.

Noah then stood up to remove his shirt and reveal the horrors of slavery to Kaiser. The deep scars that decorated his back told his chilling story.

"My massa was so cruel to his slaves that dey was almost crazy at times," Noah continued. "He would buckle us across a log n' whip us until we couldn't walk fo' three days. On Sunday, we would go to de barn n' pray to God to fix some way for us to be freed from our mean massa. My mother was sold away from me. I was so lonesome without her that I would often go 'bout my work n' cry n' look fo' her return. She never did come back. And it was not a vampire that killed Melody. It was a white man."

Kaiser listened to his story and heard his pain. Noah was becoming a broken man. Slavery had taken so much from him, and it continued to do so.

"Sometimes, I want to kill dem all, n' I can't help but envy these creatures. I understand they hate," Noah confessed.

"More hatred only guarantees more enmity, more pain, more death ahead, and never more healing or an increase in our humanity," Kaiser proclaimed.

"When will dey stop hatin' us?" Noah asked.

Kaiser sighed. How could he appease a man who spent a lifetime in slavery and perpetual pain?

Tears brimmed Noah's eyes. First, there was hate; then a wave of sadness hit him. A great pang gripped his heart.

Kaiser continued. "I've seen what hate, fear, and anger do to people, Noah. It can be passed like a dark flame from one generation to the next, perpetually inflamed and waiting for the next chance for genocide and war. This immortal I'm hunting, it's fueled by this hatred and anger."

"Do you believe that killing it will make the world a better place?" Noah asked.

"No," Kaiser answered honestly. "But it can't continue to kill and implement chaos. Change doesn't happen by violence."

"But you kill too," Noah countered.

Unfortunately, it was true. And Kaiser had no answer for him.

"How long ya been hunting vampires?" Noah asked.

"For nearly a century," Kaiser responded.

"A century? How long that?"

"A hundred years."

Noah was taken aback by his answer. "Hundred years . . . How dat possible?"

Kaiser stared at Noah deadpan and replied, "I'm somewhat of an immortal."

"Say what now?"

"I can live a long time like vampires and other supernatural creatures. But I'm not a vampire."

"Then what are you, sir?"

Kaiser sighed. It was too complicated for him to explain to Noah. So finally, Kaiser could only say to him, "My parents and my bloodline come from an alternate realm, a distorted version of this world."

Huh? Now, Noah was utterly confused.

"I age slower in this world than my own," Kaiser explained. "Alternate realms are worlds that belong to another dimension apart from ours. Entrances to these places are usually generated by ripping the fabric of time and space, opening a portal between worlds. However, these doors are generally only temporary. They can only be opened when a certain uncommon event or a large period of time has elapsed in our worlds, such as the passing of a century or a solar eclipse."

Huh? Say what now?

"I promise you, Noah, when this is over, I'll teach you things far greater than your expectations," said Kaiser.

Noah didn't know what it meant but didn't want to return to slavery.

"You gon' teach me, sir?" Noah asked sheepishly.

Kaiser nodded. "My time here in this country will end, along with my time in this realm. I see something in you that I like, Noah. You will travel with me back to Europe to train, learn, and become a human hunter."

Noah nodded.

"The Holy Command is not a place for hatred of men, but for balance, direction, and spiritual guidance. Hatred, Noah, is a disease that digs under your skin and forces fear into your veins, switching off any part of the mind that should protest. Hatred convinces you that others will come to harm those you love, and the only way out is to end their lives first. Hatred will bring you to thoughtlessly kill others and others to thoughtlessly kill you," Kaiser proclaimed truthfully.

He stood face-to-face with Noah, their eyes locked. Noah stood erect before Kaiser, ready to change who he was. He *wanted* to learn, and Kaiser was willing to teach him.

"I want to learn, sir," said Noah.

Kaiser smiled. "When this ends, we will leave for Germany."

Chapter Thirty-Two

Panic flared in Irene's eyes as she ran through the woods. She stumbled, picked herself up, and ran again. She was a mile away from the Randall plantation, and a mile was too close for her comfort. She had to get away from Massa Randall. Penny, her mother, and other enslaved people were dead. Massa Randall had gone crazy and decided to murder his fifteen slaves out of the blue. He took a rifle to Penny and then to her mother in a fit of rage. Randall subsequently went through the slave quarters to murder everyone, nearly succeeding.

"You niggers won't get me!" he would rant.

Irene immediately took to the woods barefoot and barely covered. She could still hear the gunfire coming from Massa Randall's rifle. He had help from his two sons. They were young, bigoted men that hailed rape, abuse, and murder of Black people. The world was going mad, and Irene wanted to escape it.

"Irene, she went into the woods, Pa," one of the sons uttered.

"Get that Black wench too!" the other son exclaimed.

Irene heard the German shepherd barking in the distance. She feared that dog, knowing what unspeakable cruelty it did to her people. She plowed through the thick trees as branches slapped her face and arms. She tripped over the carcass of a raccoon and was startled for a moment. However, she picked herself up again and continued to run. She remembered what Solomon once told her . . . "*When you decide to run, use the stars to get ya bearings.*"

The woods became alive with sounds, and the bright, full half-moon became a witness to her dangerous escape. Irene ran over tree roots and fallen limbs. She was so scared that she nearly peed on herself.

Irene continued tearing through the woods, pursued closely by her master, his two sons, and their dog. She could hear the dog barking behind her on her scent. Irene hardened her nerves and ran like lightning was striking her, with the North Star shining ahead, faint in the growing light. Finally, she caught her breath and approached a clearing in the woods. She soon reached rock formations, marking the graves of slaves and freedmen. It cast shadows in the moonlight. Ahead of her was a small wooden building, a church with a rough-hewn cross rising beyond the graves. She dashed across the open space toward the church, hoping there was help somewhere. She didn't want to die.

The church was abandoned and dark. She tried the door, and it opened. Irene hurried inside to hide, but she figured it would be fruitless. The German shepherd was on her scent, and her pursuers weren't far behind. She dropped to her knees behind a pew as her body shook with fear. Irene could feel nothing but blind terror, knowing what fate awaited her . . . indeed, rape, abuse, and death. *How could she protect herself?* Randall was determined not to allow her to escape and live.

Irene continued to hide behind the pew. She heard the men outside of the church with the dog barking wildly. They'd found her.

"We know yuh in there, Irene. Come out now and make things easy on ya'self," Randall ordered her. "Yuh get to join' the other slaves in nigger heaven tonight. Yuh hear?"

Irene whimpered with her eyes watering. She was crying for Solomon, and she was crying for herself. All of a sudden, she heard some commotion happening outside of the church. Someone was screaming, followed by gunfire, more and more, along with the dog barking hysterically. Then everything fell deathly silent. Irene remained cowering behind the pew with her attention fixed on the door. She had no idea who would come through it to harm her.

Irene's face was stained with tears as she watched the church door open, and a mysterious figure appeared at the threshold. She couldn't make out who it was, but he seemed alone. Then she heard him. "Irene . . . ?"

Irene heard his voice, but she wasn't sure it was him, her husband, Solomon.

"Irene, are you in here?" he called out to her.

She stood up from where she was hiding with apprehension. But when she saw Solomon there, she became overwhelmed with relief and shock, followed by absolute joy.

"Solomon," she cried out in disbelief.

Solomon grinned her way. "It's me. I'm here. I told you I would find you."

Irene ran into his arms with tears of joy trickling from her face like a human waterfall. It still didn't feel real to her. But she didn't want to let him go. "Thank God!" she hollered. They shared a passionate kiss, and their connection was unmatched.

"You are free, Irene. We are free," he proclaimed.

Solomon released her from his arms, and Irene took a clear and good look at him. She had no idea what he'd become because he remained in his human form. But Irene felt there was something slightly different about him.

"How . . . How did you find me?" she questioned.

"Nothing was gon' keep me away from you."

"Massa Randall and his sons, what happened to them?" she asked him.

"They dead, and they won't bother you no more," Solomon replied.

It was unreal.

One of the most painful things they both experienced was missing each other. There had been a silent ache in both of their hearts that had become unbearable. Knowing the other person was somewhere on this earth, but they had no idea where and couldn't protect or comfort each other, it felt like hell on earth.

Irene couldn't stop crying. She continued to feel extreme joy, but at the same time, she felt guilt too. The gleeful look in her eyes altered into sadness.

"What's wrong, Irene?" asked Solomon.

She didn't have a choice, so she decided to reveal to Solomon what saddened her. Irene took a few steps away from him to show her protruding belly, indicating that she was pregnant. Solomon was beside himself with emotions, both shocked and angry. The things he did to get to her—and now this. It felt like a betrayal to him.

Irene was teary-eyed. She uttered, "I'm sorry. It's Massa's child. He raped me."

Solomon scowled. He wanted a family as much as he wanted freedom, but now the woman he loved was carrying her slaver's child. He could kill a man, but how can he kill the unborn that was nurturing inside his wife's body? But they both had secrets to reveal. Irene exposed hers, and now, Solomon knew he needed to tell his. He wondered if Irene would accept the monster he'd become. Finally, Solomon dropped to his knees before her, remaining heartbroken and disturbed.

"Do you still love me?" Irene asked him with concern.

Solomon looked at her. *How can she ask me that or doubt that I don't still love her?* Neither of them had any control over what had transpired in the past months. They were born into slavery, with forces that tried to separate them. Solomon stood to his feet and took Irene's hands into his. They locked eyes, and no matter what, he wasn't going anywhere. He would be hers for life if she became comfortable with the monster he'd become.

"Irene, I love you. I will always love you. We's free now, and—" Solomon began, but suddenly, something else caught his attention.

There was something else lurking outside the church. Solomon knew it was a threat to them. He stood there in silence but alert.

"Solomon, what's wrong?" Irene asked him.

"We need to go. Now!" he uttered.

He took Irene's hand and attempted to leave the church. But the moment they stepped out into the opening, Solomon knew it was too late. They had company. He stopped and glared at the thick tree line, knowing what to expect. But instead, it was still and quiet, *too* quiet. The bodies of Randall and his two sons were sprawled across the ground. The dog too.

"Solomon, what do you see?" Irene asked.

He didn't respond to her question. Instead, he poised for the inevitable—a second confrontation. And like a ghost in the darkness, Akasha suddenly appeared from the woods. It seemed like he came out of nowhere. First, it appeared he came alone, but Solomon would be foolish to think that. Moments after Akasha showed himself, others emerged from the woods in their demonic form and approached the couple calmly but menacingly. Akasha had a small army of vampires, nearly three dozen.

Seeing these creatures, Irene became horrified. Once again, she was gripped by fear. She clutched Solomon's hand tighter and shrieked. "Solomon! What are they?" she exclaimed in horror.

Akasha grinned Solomon's way and uttered, "She still doesn't know what you've become, Solomon." Then he smiled at Irene and added, "Don't be frightened by us. Do you believe he can protect you?"

Solomon glared at his maker, demanding, "Get away from her!" He became a barrier between Irene and Akasha.

"How did you find me?" Solomon asked him.

"So much for you to learn, my brethren. There's a psychic connection between you and me, the creator and the subject. Where you go, I see," Akasha explained. "But I'm disappointed in you, Solomon. You're strong but still so weak and naïve. There's still so much to do, cleansing this country."

Knowing the backlash behind their bloody uprising, Solomon didn't want any part of it anymore. However, he had blood on his hands too. He felt it was creating more harm than good. Their people were being slaughtered by the hundreds across the South. The only good thing about him becoming a vampire was that he could reunite with his wife.

"I told yuh, I don't want any part of it. I just want freedom and peace," Solomon protested.

"You are a fool if you believe there will ever be freedom and peace in this forsaken country. You might as well cut her throat and yours if you seek the two," Akasha griped. "You will always be hunted by humans and by an adversary. Like I was hunted decades ago by a skilled hunter that weakened me. So, I fled to seek solace and strength in the darkness, then rose nearly a century later, fully revived but haunted by human memories. They will not rest until we are all dead."

Still, Solomon was ready to take his chances. "That is my choice, *our* choice to make," he rebuked.

Akasha was growing impatient with his protégé. Finally, he scowled and exclaimed, "Show her, Solomon. Show her what you have become, a monster of the night that tears men apart and drains them of their blood to survive."

Solomon glanced at Irene, who was now becoming concerned and baffled. "What is he talkin''bout Solomon?"

Solomon huffed.

"But if you seek harmony and peace, then I'll give you and her the peace you desire . . . in the grave," Akasha threatened.

The angry bond between them was evident. The other vampires circled the couple, but Akasha cautioned them back with a wave of his arm. He didn't need their help to deal with Akasha. This was going to be his pleasure.

"*Unapigana!*" Akasha uttered in a foreign language, shouting, "You fight!"

Irene gasped as Solomon's appearance turned demonic, matching Akasha's. His pupils widened larger and blacker, his hands became sharp claws, and his teeth became fangs and unsettlingly feral.

"Ohmygod!" Irene shrieked.

Solomon felt uncomfortable in front of his wife, how she looked at him and suddenly feared him. He felt ashamed. But no matter what, he was going to protect her. Solomon charged forward at Akasha, trying to grab him with surprising speed. Instead, Akasha backhanded Solomon, sending him to the ground. Solomon rose quickly and was poised for a lengthy and fatal battle. Akasha lunged for Solomon, knocking him into the church. Akasha was strong, fast, and experienced at killing.

Irene was taken aback by the fight. The other vampires had her surrounded. She was an enslaved person, as they had been, but she was still considered prey. And if Solomon didn't win this fight, she wondered what would happen to her.

Akasha snarled, then launched himself at Solomon and ripped at him repeatedly, battering his face and body mercilessly. Solomon desperately crawled and tried to get his feet under him. Akasha pulled Solomon by his nappy hair and thrashed him against the dirt. Solomon gasped for breath, fighting to suck in some strength. His mouth was bloody, staining the ground underneath him.

The other vampires watched closely and were, to some extent, impressed by Solomon's ability to survive against Akasha this long.

Akasha beat Solomon, pummeling him with his fists, gripped by an uncontrollable rage. Then he flung Solomon against the church walls so hard that they cracked and left an indentation.

Akasha hissed vindictively. He reached down and encircled Solomon's right hand in his clawlike fingers. He squeezed and squeezed relentlessly until Solomon's bone snapped.

"Aaaaaaaahh!" Solomon screamed.

"Hurts, don't it?" Akasha taunted.

Solomon wondered how much longer he could last. He fought not to feel the pain as his vision blurred. Akasha crowded him to finish him off, but Solomon summoned the strength to headbutt Akasha, knocking him to the ground. Akasha cursed and regained his balance, then charged like a wolf unwilling to give up its prey. Solomon was determined to keep the momentum on his side. With a brutal drive, he bolted toward Akasha, his right arm broken and limping but ready to strike again.

They traded blows, a brutal death match that seemed to defy gravity. Then Akasha dodged a punch and walloped Solomon into the ground again and again. The savage onslaught made Solomon's skull tremble from the impact. He needed to recoup. He tried to crawl away, but Akasha pulled him back. He towered over Solomon, grabbed his throat with one hand, and lifted Solomon from the ground with a merciless grin.

"When I'm done with you, I'll make your wife into my personal slave," Akasha growled. "But first, she's gonna watch you die."

He tossed Solomon to the ground and kicked him viciously in the face. "Ouch." It was painful, and Solomon struggled to remain conscious. *How can I win?* he thought. While he was facedown on the ground, in pain, dying, Solomon glanced at Irene. Her heart was breaking. Her eyes filled with grief and hope. He took it all in.

There was no way Solomon would give up and let his wife down. They'd been through too much for it to end like this. So, doing what he didn't think he could do, Solomon reached into his inner depth and summoned a lion's ferocity and strength. He wrenched himself off the ground and hurled himself at Akasha. They tumbled together, creating a chaos of fury and bloodlust. Finally, however, Akasha ended up on top and bared his fangs. This kill would be very satisfying. But Solomon wasn't about to relent. He had too much to lose with his face a mass of marks and suffering.

Solomon's eyes grew wide with rage. His black pupils intensely matched Akasha's.

"Enough!" Solomon roared.

He angrily reached up and grabbed Akasha's jaw with his broken arm and slammed his left hand into Akasha's mouth in a berserker's rage. And with velocity, Solomon decapitated Akasha with his bare hands. He then hurled his head, and it landed on the ground near the feet of his followers. Akasha's eyes closed; he was gone.

The other vampires gaped in awe. Akasha had lost.

Solomon remained on his back, still shocked and astonished by it all. He was unable to comprehend that he'd won. He slowly pulled himself to his knees and stared at Irene. She was pleased but still confused. Solomon glanced at the night sky above.

While one battle was won, another fight was quickly coming their way.

Chapter Thirty-Three

Akasha was dead. His followers were still in shock, some angry and confused. What would happen to them now?

Solomon remained on his knees, wounded, and stared at Irene. For her, something was far worse to learn from his win and transformation. But she went to him and kneeled beside him on the ground. Eventually, he would heal back to health and full strength, but his fight with Akasha took so much out of him. Irene embraced him desperately, still overwhelmed by his transformation and sacrifice. Finally, Solomon fought his way to his feet.

The others circled them. With Akasha dead, their hope and purpose seemed futile. But should they avenge his death and finish off Solomon? Clenching his jaw, Solomon glared at them and was ready to put up another fight if needed.

"He's gone," Solomon growled.

The vampires looked to the sky warily, tense, knowing the night would be soon gone. Finally, they realized they had to face a decision. Then torches carried by an army illuminated the woods. Soldiers were coming their way.

Commander Rogers and hundreds of armed soldiers carrying rifles, guns, and torches barreled the vampires' way like a swarm of ants on foot or horseback. They heatedly charged, and the vampires hissed their way, ready for a fight, although they were outnumbered. Their demonic form and strength didn't deter or frighten the soldiers. They raced from the trees, weapons aimed at the creatures, and fired. Each man hurried toward the undead, discharging gunfire. They believed this was evil they were battling.

Quickly, the undead clashed with the cavalrymen. The strength of the vampires was overwhelming, but every soldier pushed on, aiming, then firing.

Solomon was still too weak to fight. Irene helped him retreat into the church while chaos raged outside. They both crumpled to the floor in the middle of the church. Solomon shivered in agony while Irene held him in her arms. Meanwhile, gunfire and death continued outside. Men were dying, but soon, the soldiers would have the advantage.

Dawn was approaching.

Solomon lay still with Irene at his side.

"Get out of here before it's too late," Solomon said.

"I'm not leaving without you," Irene replied.

Solomon shook like an alcoholic going into delirium tremens. He needed blood, and he needed his strength to survive.

"You don't understand. The thirst . . . I don't want to harm you," he groaned. He clutched his stomach, experiencing phenomenal pain. It was tearing him apart.

"How can I help you?" she asked.

Solomon didn't want to surrender to his thirst, but they didn't have long. He tried to sit up, gripping Irene's wrist. He suppressed a shudder. Simply keeping himself from attacking her took every ounce of his tenacity.

"I need to drink blood to survive and find my strength," he admitted.

This was new and horrifying to Irene. *What are you? What have you become? What happened to my husband?* A million thoughts flooded her mind.

"Blood . . . ?" she stammered.

When she saw his fangs up close, she became frightened but faithful and remained by her husband's side.

"Is it my blood you need?" she asked.

He nodded. Yes.

"But I don't want to hurt you," he uttered.

Irene matched his gaze, steeling herself. But she was terrified. He'd sacrificed himself to save her; she knew she needed to return the favor.

"Take it, my blood," she said.

Solomon stared at her. He wanted what she was offering more than anything he'd ever desired. But he was afraid that once he began, it would kill her. However, he rose. He needed it.

"You saved my life; now I want to save yours," she said. "Where . . . ?"

He gaped at her neck. She nodded. *So be it.* She turned her head to the side, baring her neck, offering herself to her husband. The blood would taste so good, but Solomon hesitated. How could he trust himself not to drain her life completely?

"Do it, Solomon. Now!" she hollered.

He opened his mouth, and his fangs elongated. Then Solomon lowered his head and started feeding on his wife. Irene involuntarily stiffened as Solomon's teeth punctured her skin. He moaned, sinking his teeth deeper into her flesh. Irene's head rolled back. Her eyes were open and glassy, unseeing as a wave of ecstasy overtook her.

Solomon groaned as he fed on her.

Irene shuddered, her breath quickening. Her fingers dug deep into his back, clawing downward, tearing into him as tears streamed down her cheeks. To Solomon, she wasn't his wife anymore but blood nourishment. Before it was too late, he pulled himself from Irene with his pulse racing. She stared at him, wide-eyed as if waking from a trance. She touched the raw wound on her neck and was a bit shaken.

What happened?

Solomon rose to his full height. His strength had more than returned. He nearly felt like a god by the infusion of her blood. Yet, there was something dangerous in his gaze, an animal fury ready to compel him into darkness. He flexed his hands with his nails sharpened. Solomon locked eyes with the love of his life for a moment. Irene stepped closer to him and placed her hand on the side of his face. It was a tender moment between them—beauty and the beast. However, the moment ended when a soldier burst into the church. Solomon pivoted as the man hurriedly aimed at them.

Solomon pivoted and attacked him with speed and ferocity, tearing chunks of flesh from his neck, causing Irene to cringe.

"I'll come back for you," he said.

Solomon charged into battle with his fellow vampires. They were against him a moment ago, but now, an entire regiment was attacking them, and their survival looked bleak. Solomon tossed men left and right like they were toys. But he looked to the sky, and sunrise would be soon on the horizon. There wasn't much time. Solomon needed to retreat. No matter how many men he killed, there were too many soldiers to combat.

He spun toward the church, but to his horror, he saw vampires being chased into the church by soldiers with torches. They were being set on fire and burning. One of the soldiers shut the door to the church, and right away, they set it afire—with Irene still inside.

"*Nooooo!*" Solomon shrieked.

He raced toward the church and killed Rip and his men as they tried to stop him. But he was too late. The church had become fully engulfed in flames. Anyone inside quickly perished. Solomon's face darkened, and he became filled with thundering rage. All was lost.

Hundreds of soldiers died, along with a few vampires burned by men's hands. However, Solomon yearned to kill every last one of them in the small window of time he had before daylight. He raged on with insanity until he came face-to-face with Commander Rogers.

"Whatever you are, I'm going to send you back to hell," Commander Roger exclaimed.

Seeing bloodred, Solomon heatedly charged at the commander with such fierce intent that the commander was thrown off his horse into the air and crashed against his side. Solomon was on top of him when he tried to draw his sidearm, ripping out his throat. His blood spewed wildly. But killing him didn't satisfy Solomon. Irene was dead, and there was no bringing her back.

Solomon grieved and mourned on his knees. What was left of Akasha's legion began to scatter before dawn came. Solomon remained on his knees near the commander's contorted body. He wanted to perish along with Irene. There was no other reason for him to live. Then the faintest glimmer of predawn light started to brighten the sky. He hadn't seen the sun in months. Unfortunately for him, this would become his final sunrise.

The twinkle of light continued to emerge over the earth's curvature, spreading its dazzling radiance across the skyline. Akasha's flock began to ignite and burn toward the rising sun. Their skin was charring black as the sun stared down at them. It was beautiful and deadly, searing them with lethal radiance.

Solomon winced and gasped in pain. He fought back the tears. He could have lived forever, but he didn't want to breathe another second if he couldn't have Irene in his life. His eyes widened in expectation of the rising sun, his breath catching. Yet, he managed to smile and was prepared to die. His skin began to char as the sun reflected in his eyes.

"I will always love you, Irene," Solomon wholeheartedly proclaimed.

He figured the end would be divinely quick—not a slow burn of blazing agony, but a nearly seamless transition from life.

Chapter Thirty-Four

Chaos and carnage were strewn everywhere. The bodies of soldiers seemed endless. They had been torn apart. Their bodies were contorted from violence. And the bodies of the undead were crooked and completely charred as the sunlight became acid to their skin. The church had been scorched too. The flames had burned deep red and reduced most of the church to ashes, and everyone inside had perished.

Kaiser and Noah arrived in the one-horse carriage. The smell of the dead was thick, putrid, horrid. It became nauseating. He and Kaiser climbed from the carriage to inspect the scene.

"What happened here?" asked Noah. "They're all dead."

Words couldn't describe what they witnessed: an epic battle between men and creatures that lasted until dawn. Kaiser deduced that the vampires succumbed to the sunlight while fighting the soldiers. He'd seen it before: contorted, rotten, and blackened flesh. The sunlight was man's best weapon against them.

"Is he here among the dead, their maker?" Noah asked Kaiser.

Kaiser carefully walked through the bodies and inspected each one. Finally, he came across a charred body that had been decapitated. Kaiser kneeled closer to it and gawked at the remains of this creature.

"What happened to its head?" asked Noah.

Kaiser touched the scorched figure and closed his eyes. Even in death, he could sense how angry, determined, and strong this presence once was.

"There was a fight before the soldiers attacked," Kaiser deduced.

"A fight . . . ? And what happened to his head?"

Akasha's head was close by. Kaiser rose and walked toward it. He picked up the head and stared at Akasha's closed eyes.

"This is their maker," he uttered.

"Is this the end?"

There would be no epic battle between Akasha and Kaiser. Someone had beaten him to it, *but who?* Kaiser and Noah walked toward the burnt church and moved through the rubble. Were they all dead?

While Kaiser and Noah wandered through the wreckage of the church, several armed white men on horseback came from the woods into their area. Right away, both men became alert and wary.

"Jesus," one of the men uttered in disbelief. "What is this? What in God's name happened here?"

Immediately, these men set their eyes on Kaiser and Noah with contempt. They dismounted from their horses and approached them with hostility. The spearhead of the group, a man named Clarke, aimed a Colt revolver at Kaiser and exclaimed, "Who are you? And what's your business here?"

Kaiser didn't flinch. He locked eyes with the man and replied, "We happened to stumble onto the area like your group, sir. Me and my nigger Noah are both dumbfounded by this like you."

Kaiser hated using the word "nigger," but he had to convince them he was one of them. The man glared at Noah, standing quietly and passively behind Kaiser. Noah averted his attention to the ground. He didn't want any trouble.

"You sure he not one of them, trouble?" Clarke growled.

Kaiser stood firm between Clarke and Noah. He was willing to protect Noah by any means necessary.

"He's my property, and I'm sure. But I feel the niggers everyone is looking for lie before y'all feet right now, dead and scorched. So, therefore, I believe this is the end to any uprising," Kaiser proclaimed.

The men began to comb over the dead. There were so many. Clarke smiled. He believed it was over.

"With no trouble to you, sir, me and my nigger will be on our way," said Kaiser politely.

Clarke stared at them for a moment. Then he allowed them to be on their way. Kaiser and Noah climbed onto the carriage and rode off, not looking back.

"What now, suh?" Noah asked him.

"Now, we leave this country and give you a better life far from here," Kaiser replied.

Noah smiled—finally, a life of freedom.

Epilogue

1922

HARLEM, NEW YORK

The speakeasy in Harlem was bustling with people, music, liquor, women, and gambling. Harlem had become the epicenter for illegal booze, cheap women, and having a good time during the prohibition. It was a hot summer night in the city. Humid summer days melted into even more humid summer nights with thick air pressed upon people's skin. The full moon in the sky was a charming lady. It shined brightly, continuously witnessing humanity's sinful nights since the beginning of time.

A black Falcon Knight Roadster pulled to the curb and stopped on 145th Street. It was a flashy vehicle, one that represented wealth and style. The doors opened, and two Caucasian men exited the car. They were mobsters dressed in dark striped suit jackets with matching vests and pants. The passenger, Tony, wore a black band fedora hat and had a fat cigar in his mouth. He looked at the driver, a man named Vinny, and said, "This is the place, huh?"

"It is," Vinny replied, nodding.

"How much is he moving?" Tony asked.

"About fifteen to twenty thousand a week," Vinny replied.

"You mean to tell me this mulignan is making a boatload of money in our city and refuses to share it with us? And he's hurting our other establishments in Harlem," said Tony.

"He's a problem, Tony. We sent three guys to talk to him two weeks back, and they never returned."

"What you mean they never returned?"

"They disappeared," Vinny made clear.

"Disappeared? You mean killed?"

Vinny shrugged. "Don't know, but most likely, yeah."

"So, this fuckin' eggplant owning this speakeasy kills three of our men, refuses to pay what is owed, and he spits in our face," Tony griped. "Tonight is gonna become a very uncomfortable night for this eggplant."

"Just be careful with this one," Vinny replied.

Tony removed the cigar from his mouth and scowled. He stared at the storefront location on 145th Street, and there wasn't anything special about it. But they both knew the business was a front. So they marched toward a side entrance with a steel black door and knocked. Right away, a slot opened, revealing eyes.

"Yeah? What y'all want?" said a voice behind the door.

"We're here to speak to the owner. Tell him Tony and Vinny are here. He knows who we are. It's about business," Tony said.

The slot closed, and the two gangsters waited for a moment. Tony grew impatient, chomping on his cigar, fretting. Then, finally, the door opened, and both men were allowed inside. They followed behind the bouncer, a large man named Benny, clad in a black suit. He moved coolly through the dim corridor, Tony and Vinny behind him. They soon entered the place of attraction and saw what the fuss was about. The speakeasy was ritzy and fancy. The joint was crammed and pumping, and it reeked of class. The band was cooking, and the dance floor was packed. Booze, gambling, entertainment, and prostitution abounded.

Tony and Vinny stood out like sore thumbs among the sea of black faces, having a great time at the after-hours spot. They followed Benny through the patrons to another dim hallway leading to a short flight of stairs. Finally, they came to a stop at a black door that was isolated and eerie.

Benny knocked on the door and entered while Tony and Vinny glanced around. Tony was a violent gangster with a hair-trigger temper. And no Black man was going to tell him no or disrespect him. A moment later, Benny emerged from the room and stared at Tony.

"He'll see you both," said Benny.

"I don't like to wait," Tony rudely uttered.

Benny stepped aside and smirked. Both men entered a shadowy room and collided with an aura of blackness. The room was bleak, cold, and strange. It was quiet, gloomy, and utterly different from the vibrant, partying atmosphere above. The obscurity and quiet pressed into their ears, and they felt a chill engulf them.

"Where is this nigger?" Tony uttered impatiently.

"Is there a problem, gentlemen?" a rasping voice asked suddenly from the shadows of the corner.

"Yeah, there's a problem," Tony replied. "You open a business here in Harlem and think it's okay to cut us out. *We* own Harlem. Therefore, we own you."

There was a chuckle that followed Tony's statement.

"Nobody owns me," the figure replied.

"You don't want any problems with us, do you understand me?" Tony countered. "You a nigger, and if you want to survive in this city, know how to stay in a nigger's place."

"You people—your kind will never change. You think you have power, control, and authority. But you have no idea what absolute power is," he replied.

It was then Solomon emerged from the dark corner to reveal himself. He was immaculately dressed in a suit, vest, and tie, appearing to be a gangster. However, he was different and sharp. He looked dangerous and intimidating, making the rumors about him appear authentic.

"Look, nigger, you have two options to appease us: either pay what you owe, which will be a significant amount, or leave Harlem," said Tony. He coolly revealed his holster gun to Solomon to maximize his threat.

Instead, Solomon grinned. "How about a third option?"

"There isn't a third option," Tony replied.

"Yes, there is," Solomon countered chillingly.

Solomon was done toying with them. It was time to reveal his actual appearance. Before they could blink or react by drawing their pistols, Solomon charged at them with great speed, attacking and killing Tony first, then Vinny. Finally, he stood over their bodies and proclaimed, "*I* own Harlem."

Benny stood outside the black door with his arms crossed against his chest. He smirked when he heard the screams of both gangsters. Mobsters being killed was becoming a familiar sound to him, one that he liked hearing.

Meanwhile, the speakeasy was in full throttle with music, dancing, and people. Everyone was entertained. The jazz band was cooking hotter than fish grease on the stage. One of the patrons accidentally bumped into another man standing by the bar, keeping to himself.

The patron apologized. "Excuse me."

The man nodded. "No harm. Enjoy yourself."

Noah was dressed in a button-down shirt with a detachable collar, wool trousers, a black fedora, and sporting eye specs. He looked posh, healthy, and was trained for combat, becoming a vampire hunter. He gripped a fashionable cane that mirrored Kaiser's. It too was a concealed blade. First, Noah's eyes scanned the crowd. Then he focused on the hallway, where he noticed two gangsters had disappeared too long ago.

He grinned and said to himself, "I found you."

To be continued.

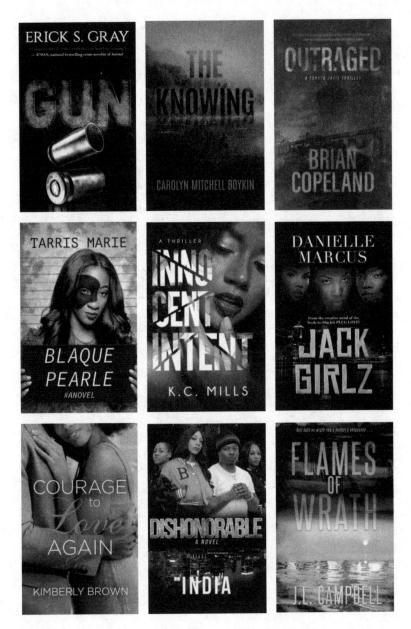